Clever Girl

Clever Girl

Tessa Hadley

JONATHAN CAPE
LONDON

Published by Jonathan Cape 2013

2 4 6 8 10 9 7 5 3 1

First published in Great Britain in 2013 by
Jonathan Cape
Random House, 20 Vauxhall Bridge Road,
London SW1V 2SA

www.vintage-books.co.uk

Addresses for companies within The Random House Group Limited can be
found at: www.randomhouse.co.uk/offices.htm

The Random House Group Limited Reg. No. 954009

A CIP catalogue record for this book is available from the British Library

ISBN 9780224096522

The Random House Group Limited supports the Forest Stewardship
Council® (FSC®), the leading international forest-certification organisation.
Our books carrying the FSC label are printed on FSC®-certified paper. FSC is
the only forest-certification scheme supported by the leading environmental
organisations, including Greenpeace. Our paper procurement policy can be
found at www.randomhouse.co.uk/environment

Typeset in Stempel Garamond by Palimpsest Book Production Limited,
Falkirk, Stirlingshire

Printed and bound in CPI Group (UK) Ltd, Croydon CR0 4YY

To Sam

The word adventures carries in it so free and licentious a sound . . . that it can hardly with propriety be applied to those few and natural incidents which compose the history of a woman of honour.

Charlotte Lennox, *The Female Quixote*, 1752

One

My mother and I lived alone. My father was supposed to be dead, and I only found out years later that he'd left, walked out when I was eighteen months old. I should have guessed this – should have seen the signs, or the absence of them. Why hadn't we kept any of his things to treasure? Why whenever he came up in conversation, which was hardly ever, did my mother's face tighten, not in grief or regret but in disapproval – the same expression she had if she tasted some food or drink she didn't like (she was fussy, we were both fussy, fussy together)? Why did none of our relatives or friends ever mention his name? (Which was Bert, unpoetically.) What had he died of, exactly? ('Lungs,' my mother said shortly. She had hated his smoking.)

But it didn't really matter. We were pretty happy living *à deux* – at least I was.

This was in the 1950s and the early '60s (I was born in 1956), so many things that seem quaint now were current and powerful then: shame, and secrecy, and the fear that other people would worm themselves into your weaknesses, and that their knowledge of how you had lapsed or failed would eat you from the inside. My mother used to wear white gloves to go to the shops in summer. She used to carry a basket on her arm, real willow, shaped like a segment of orange, with a tan leather flap and a fastener like a little brass barrel turning in a brass slot. Later on, when I was a teenager, I thought she was dowdy, in her boxy good coats and silk scarves and low-heeled court shoes. But looking at the photographs now, I see that it's me who was a fright – I'm small, and I was pudgy in those days, with my eyes made up like black pits – and that she was elegant and even sexy, in a cautious, respectable kind of way.

She had to go out to work in an office, to support us. So I spent a lot of time with my nana, my mother's mother, who lived just round the corner from our flat. (That's another thing: didn't I wonder why we never visited any grandparents on my father's side?) Nana was miniature, with a tiny-featured face and black eyes, like a mouse or a shrew; on her cheeks there really was a kind of downy pale fur, if you caught her in a certain light, and when I was very young I liked to stroke it. She bought her clothes from the children's department (cheaper), and went to the hairdresser's every week to have her hair set in skimpy grey-brown rolls pinned to her scalp: not out of vanity, but as if it was her duty to submit to this punishing routine. There was a sticker on the underside of every piece of furniture in Nana's house, saying who should have it in the event of her death: Edna (that was my mother), Uncle Frank, or Uncle Ray. This was when she was still in her early sixties. ('That old junk! No thank you!' Mum said, but only when Nana was out of earshot.) I had already decided what I wanted: a jewellery box that played music when the lid was opened.

Nana was also a widow (a real one). I can't remember my grandpa. Her house was very bare and there wasn't that much furniture in it to inherit. This was because she was poor, but also because she was continually in the process of clearing out, giving things away, as if she were trying to weigh less and less, as if life itself were a mess that she was gradually getting to the bottom of. In the summer, when it wasn't too cold, I used to play upstairs in the bedrooms while Nana in her housecoat cleaned downstairs. (What was there to clean? She survived in that house as neatly as a mouse living on crumbs.) I played with the jewellery box, and with my dolls, and with a vanity set that Uncle Ray had given Nana one Christmas, pots made of soft thick plastic with blue screw tops. You were meant, I suppose, to transfer your assorted creams and unguents into these, to take away travelling with you: but Nana only used Nivea and never went anywhere. I can remember being flooded with happiness once, alone (apart from the dolls) in Nana's bedroom. The floorboards were stained dark brown up to the edges of the rug. I was lying on the floor looking up at the underside of the bed – its springs and the flock mattress with its pompoms, turned each week. The dressing table had its back to the window, blocking the light. Silky mauve curtains were drawn part way across behind it, to keep out prying eyes or save the furniture from fading. The window was open three inches at the top for airing and a breeze was tickling the curtains; my chest swelled with the full awareness of the moment, as if I was breathing in a different medium, thick and heady. Dust motes swam in the air. I turned my hand in them and thought: I'm alive! In this world!

Was this before I went to school?

It must have been. I didn't hate school but it put an end to that rich slow expansive time, when I was free.

Mum and I were close when I was a child. We deluded ourselves that we were alike and would always be the best of friends. We snuggled together with hot-water bottles under the eiderdown on the sofa to watch *Compact* on TV, or *The Man from U.N.C.L.E.* We were both strong-willed, and that was fine as long as we were pulling in tandem: both of us were fastidious and opinionated and ready to disapprove of other people's tastes, though we kept these judgements diplomatically between us. (Later, our tastes diverged and we disapproved of each other.)

Nana said we should move in with her. She couldn't see why we were wasting our money renting a separate place. I took no notice of this – I thought of Nana as harmless, lightweight, easy to brush away. My uncles teased her patiently, they found her comical. But I knew from my mother's face that for her the idea of moving back into her old home was a living danger, the place was a trap that could close on her again at any time. If Mum smoked at Nana's kitchen table (she'd hated my father's smoking then took it up herself), Nana whisked the ashtray away the moment she'd finished, tipping the ash into the bin and rinsing the ashtray under the tap, wiping it first with the dishcloth and then with a tea towel. Without a husband Mum was vulnerably exposed. The only way for her to defend herself against Nana's bleaching, purging world view was to defy it: to wear scent and lipstick every day ('for the office'), not to bother to take up the carpet every time she cleaned. To treat me, for her birthday, at a Berni Inn. (Which was a waste, as Nana had predicted. Overawed and stubborn, I wouldn't eat a thing.)

Mum came into my bedroom as usual one morning in her stockinged feet and petticoat, with the pile of sheets and blankets she had slept in neatly folded. We only had one bedroom, with a double bed in it and no space for any other furniture; I slept in there and Mum had the sofa. I liked to lie in bed listening to her getting ready in the next room, moving about quietly so as not to wake me. I'd close my eyes when she came in, pretending to stretch and yawn.

— Stella? I've had a telephone call, she said.

Telephone calls were a big event. The telephone belonged to the woman in the flat below ours, whose number we only gave out for emergencies. The call must have come very early — or very late the night before.

— Who from? I asked, suspicious.

5

Mum said that my Uncle Frank had called, because Auntie Andy needed somewhere to stay for a while. Andy had rung Frank, trying to get in touch with my mother.

— You'll have to budge up, Mum said. — I'll be in the bed with you tonight. We'll give Andy the sofa.

She stood for too long, hanging on to the pile of bedding, looking down at me, seeing me and not seeing me. There was something in her face that I didn't like, crumbled and damp. Usually the mask of her brightness was securely in place: spirited, capable. My mother was quite tough. She could be brisk about other people's troubles. She couldn't afford to waste much sympathy; she had herself (and me) to look out for. No one else was looking out for us.

I was eight or nine, at the time this happened.

I could hardly remember at first who Auntie Andy was: she was a relative of my father's, married to his cousin, and she was the only one in that family who'd made any effort to keep in touch. We probably saw her once or twice a year. At Christmas she dropped off a selection box of chocolate bars for me. She may have been moved to this kindness because she had a son about my age, Charlie. (Of course then Mum had to buy a selection box for Charlie too.) Andy wasn't really Mum's type. She was too indefinite: small and plump with faded gingery hair scraped back from her face in hairgrips, her skin blotchy, no make-up. She used to wear a little beige beret tilted to one side of her head, inappropriately jaunty. She was shy and never had much to say, sitting with a plate of our Christmas cake balanced on her lap, fat knees spread in her tweedy skirt, her feet crossed at the ankles, where her nylons wrinkled.

Once she'd remarked approvingly, looking round, 'You've got it very nice here, Edna.'

Mum was still looming above my bed, gripping the pile of blankets.

— There's just one thing, she warned. — When Auntie Andy comes, you mustn't mention Charlie.

So something had happened to Charlie.

Charlie had only come in with Andy once: inches smaller than me, ginger like her but bursting unlike her with sly and hostile energy, ready with contempt for girls and women. He'd ignored his mother when she tried to pass him her handkerchief, and wiped his nose on his sleeve instead; in one of his eyes there was a blot as if black ink had spilled across the iris, and his stare was unnervingly off target. His brown lace-up shoes, polished like conkers, had made me think of the boys kicking in the queue for school dinner. I refused to ask my mother what had happened to him. I didn't want to have unpacked for me whatever unseemly thing had made her face pulpy. I liked the scandals we read about in magazines, but they were safely glazed over with false-hood and repetition; glimpses of raw adult complications appalled me in the same way as I was appalled by the sight of an egg splatted in the pan with its yolk broken and leaking. (I hated eggs.)

Mum probably wouldn't have told me anyway. She was inflexible in keeping secrets.

Almost as an afterthought, she added: — And don't mention Uncle Derek, either.

I hadn't even known his name was Derek. I'd never met him.

Andy was there when I got back from Nana's. I always went to Nana's after school. I was allowed to walk home on my own after Nana had given me my tea: Spam sandwiches, lettuce and tomatoes with vinegar shaken over them out of a cut-glass bottle. Nana already knew all about Auntie Andy's coming but she wouldn't say anything to me directly: not saying things was her speciality. She had a horror of any kind of publicity or exposure touching the family, however remotely.

— I only hope Edna knows what she's doing, she fretted.

I was dreading that I would arrive home in the middle of a big fuss. I couldn't bear crisis: the huddles of women, their lowered voices and smouldering glances shutting the children out and yet looping them in – tantalising them – to the dark, sticky, mucky centre. Girls practised huddling in the school playground. Mum didn't like fuss any more than I did: whatever it was that had happened to Andy (and Charlie and Uncle whatshisname) had been bad enough to shock her out of her usual poise.

I had vowed to myself that I would never be looped in.

But when I got there Andy was sitting quietly at the end of the sofa, in the same tweed skirt that she had worn on her last visit. — How are you, Stella? she said kindly. — How was school?

She did look odd in some way – what?

I began gabbling about how well I had done in my mental arithmetic test, and how in our books we had drawn around plastic stencils of the United Kingdom with little holes to put your pencil where the cities were, and how I had to bring in something for the nature table next week, now that it was spring. I knew my mother was frowning at me urgently because by talking about school I was indirectly bringing up the subject of Charlie (although I couldn't imagine Charlie ever shining at mental arithmetic or contributing to the nature table). But I didn't want there to be any silences, out of which raw truths might tumble.

Auntie Andy commented admiringly that I must be very good at my lessons.

Her face was rather white. She reminded me of a girl at school who had been slapped for extreme insolence (they usually only hit the boys): when this girl walked back to her desk she was in a sort of smiling daze, vivid with shock. What was odd about Auntie Andy, I realised, was that her shyness had been blasted out of her by whatever had happened, the way an explosion can leave people deaf afterwards. When she had sat in the same place on our sofa eating cake, a few months earlier, she had been stuck for anything to say, apologetic, glancing round at the walls of our flat for inspiration. Mum had been imperiously, chillingly polite. (I suppose she'd chosen this as the right register for relations with my father's family.) Andy had blushed and stumbled over her words, and I had guessed that her feet were hurting her in her stilettos. The time Charlie came in with her, she had been suffused with maternal pride and surprise ('Can I really have made this?'), touching his hair and his shoulders surreptitiously, making him wriggle away; but she had also suffered, seeing his nose run in front of us.

Now she sat almost serenely, as if nothing ordinary could touch her.

Well, of course it couldn't.

— I wanted to come here, she said to my mother, with no hint of worry that she might be an imposition. — I remembered how nicely you'd done it up. When they asked me if I had anyone to go to, I expect they thought I'd go to my sister's. But to be honest, Edna, I don't want anything to do with the whole lot of them, just now.

That first afternoon she must have been experiencing severe trauma, as we'd call it these days. I don't suppose she knew what she was doing or saying. But her shyness never did come back. It wasn't that she became bold or greedy for attention or anything like that, far from it. Her shyness transformed into something like itself, but different: reserve, or dignity.

The only outward sign of extremity was the fact that they were drinking sherry. Or Mum was drinking it, and smoking with hasty, nervous fingers: Auntie Andy's glass, on the coffee table in front of her, looked untouched.

— Go on, Mum said tenderly. — It'll do you good.

I'd never heard her tender like that before, with any adult; even our mutual appreciation was mostly chaffing and teasing. Obediently, Andy picked up the glass to sip, but something happened to it between the table and her mouth, as if her hand simply wasn't under her control: her arm jerked helplessly and the sherry spilled over the top of the glass, a big gout of it, on to her skirt and our carpet. She wasn't just shaking – it was something more violent, like an avalanche or a volcanic eruption. Andy's old self would have been mortified; but she only put the sherry back carefully on the table and folded her hands in her lap again, while Mum knelt beside her, blinking in the smoke from her cigarette, blotting the mark out of Andy's skirt with a tea towel. I saw that if anything it was Mum who was shy now: not shy of Andy in herself, but of whatever had happened to her, as if it were added on like an annexe to her personality for ever, exacting a kind of homage of respect and service.

I supposed that as I soon as I was sent to bed the two women would talk, and I would hear the dramatic music of their murmured scandalising revelations and commis-erations, penetrating the dividing wall. (I'd heard my mother talk like this with Auntie Jean, Frank's wife, and had felt betrayed because usually we made fun of Jean. It was our joke that she knew the gossip before it even happened: 'jungle telegraph', Mum called it.) However, when Mum told me to get my pyjamas on, Auntie Andy announced that she would go to bed now too.

— The doctor's given me some pills, she said. — So I should be all right. I didn't get much sleep last night.

My mother didn't try to explain about the sofa, and that this meant she too would have to go to bed, hours before her usual time: as a rule she never turned in before eleven or midnight. She made up the sofa for Andy with clean sheets, filled a hot-water bottle for her. Then Mum and I were shut in the bedroom alone together. It was strange to have her undressing in the room with me when I was still wide awake, tussling to take off her underwear under her nylon nightie, pulling out her brassiere through a sleeve, settling down beside me with her book and her glass of water. She couldn't concentrate on what she was reading and her restlessness communicated itself. When she turned out the bedside light (I whined that I couldn't sleep with the light on), I could feel the frustration of the long hours stretching out ahead of her in the dark, when she was so charged up with vitality and energy.

— So what happened to Charlie? I whispered.

— Oh Stella. Not now, for goodness' sake.

Heaving the bedclothes over, she turned her back on me. For a while we both lay awake, listening for signs of whatever unimaginable reverie was unfolding in the next room: but there was nothing to hear. And in the morning when Mum got up, Auntie Andy was already dressed, sitting there on the sofa with her slapped face and vague smile, and all the sheets and blankets neatly folded.

On the way to school, Mum told me that Charlie was dead, flinging the word at me impatiently as if it was somehow my fault and I ought to have guessed by now: as indeed I had guessed, from the beginning. The actual word, spoken between us, worked its ravages nonetheless. I resented Charlie with a pure rage. Why couldn't anyone else have been dead? He seemed a usurper in a realm that gave him a huge advantage of pity and terror: he surely didn't belong there, with his ugly stamping feet. Only his squint (it had made its impression, that inky blot) had been a sign of difference, marking him apart.

— Dead, *how*? I insisted, and she looked down at me – bright and smart in her office outfit – with distaste, I'm sure.

— A nasty accident, she said.

I couldn't ask, for shame: what accident? But the uncertainty squirmed in my imagination, taking on foul forms.

— You're not to repeat a word about it to anyone, is that clear? Not one word, or I'll take my hand to you.

She rarely smacked me, though she quite often threatened it; I was wounded that my mother could think I wanted to pass on our contaminating secret. Becoming the centre of one of those huddles of girls, darkly informed, didn't appeal. I feared I wouldn't carry it off, somehow the tables would be turned and the dirty story would stick to me, making me a pariah. I was too odd – too small and sexless, too good at English comprehension – for those girls to trust. My instinct in those days anyway was to smother any unpleasant truth, push it back into its hole. I was (rather abstractly) enthusiastic about dogs and horses, because the emotions these roused seemed to me clean, unproblematic: I had a dreamy image of myself running through long grass with a collie dog jumping up beside me, trying to lick my face (after long deliberation, I had elected collies as my favourites). This

13

image was my idea of 'nature', and had in my private world a religious resonance.

Determinedly, all that day at school I held Charlie at bay, inventing games to play with my couple of oddball friends. We lived together in an old farmhouse on an island. A portion of the playground was the sea and we couldn't walk on it, only row across it when we needed to get to the shops to buy provisions. Sometimes there were dreadful storms.

— Here boy!

I whistled and clicked my tongue commandingly; fed imaginary sugar lumps to imaginary horses with my hand held out flat.

What had happened to Charlie was worse than anything my fears could dredge up. It all came out in the trial. Needless to say I was never in the court, but my mother got as much time off from the office as she could to sit through it with Auntie Andy. (They were 'very understanding' at the office, even if that meant they didn't pay her for the time she was out.) So she heard almost all of it; and over the years it filtered through to me. Also, Nana kept the newspaper cuttings and I found them when she died – though in those days the coverage wasn't as lurid as it would be now, and not everything that came out in court got into the papers. It was a surprise to me that Nana had kept the cuttings. She had never let Mum talk about the case, and she certainly hadn't manifested any prurient interest in the details. (What else to expect, anyway, from my father's family?)

14

Apparently, for years Uncle Derek had been hitting Auntie Andy (Andrea, she was, in the newspaper reports). His own mother admitted in court that he had a violent temper, though she also said that Andy ought to have known how to 'get round' him. (Perhaps Uncle Derek's father had been a wife-beater too?) The defence tried to make out that Andy had goaded her husband with her 'passivity', her 'unresponsiveness'. The whole topic of men's violence against their families was kept better hidden in those days. People had mixed feelings about it: it was disgusting, but it was also, confusedly, part of the suffering essence of maleness, like the smell of tobacco and the beard-growth. I think that sexuality itself was sometimes understood, by the women in my family, as a kind of violence that must be submitted to, buried deep in the privacy of domestic life. Presumably the implication of the case for the defence was that Auntie Andy had driven her husband to murder out of sexual frustration.

They made a great point of Derek's sobriety ('He never touched a drop,' Auntie Andy loyally testified), and his good reputation at his place of work. He was a salesman in a car showroom, he 'brought home very good money'. Who knows how Uncle Derek would have fared in court if he'd killed Auntie Andy? On the night in question, however, he didn't. He arrived home from work at the usual time and his tea wasn't ready. ('Tea', in this context, meaning meat and two veg, not Earl Grey and triangles of sandwich.) It wasn't ready because Andy had been asked to go in to talk to Charlie's teacher after school.

(She hadn't been planning to tell her husband this, but it came out as their row unravelled.) She had thought that perhaps Charlie was in trouble – he sometimes got into fights in the playground – but it turned out that the teacher was worried about his slowness in learning to read. ('Because I don't have any other children,' Andy said in court, 'I didn't know that he was slow. I wish I'd known.') Derek had had a bad day altogether. He'd been working on a deal to sell a fleet of cars to a driving school, and it had fallen through.

My mother said they made Andy show them on a plan how he chased her around the house, punching and kicking her from room to room. — That's why I ran out in the street, she said, — without my coat or my bag. And I couldn't go back inside, because I didn't have my key. He'd never have let me in. But I didn't want the neighbours watching while I hung about out there in the cold. So I thought I'd better go to my sister's, who only lives round the corner.

She'd waited a couple of hours for him to cool down. She had gone to her sister's before in the middle of one of these rows, and left Charlie with his father.

— When police officers saw you later that evening, the defence objected, — they didn't observe any signs of violence on your person.

She said he never hit her where the marks would show.

— Could you speak up, please?

He'd said he didn't want her flaunting it to everyone.

Charlie's body had been found in the bath (with no water in it). They asked Andy where her son had been when she left the house: as far as she knew he was in the living room, eating beans on toast (because the chops weren't ready) off his lap in front of the television. He might or might not have been aware that his parents were quarrelling. They had both of them always tried to keep him out of it. Andy had been planning to get out his reading book later as the teacher had recommended, although she hadn't been very hopeful that he would agree to work on his spellings with her. — He had a mind of his own, she said. She repeated that Derek had never hurt Charlie before. He wasn't a bad father. He had been worried about his son's problem with his eyes, he had even come with her to see the doctor. But she agreed with the defence: she shouldn't have left Charlie alone with him that night. She would never forgive herself. She didn't know, now, what she had been thinking of. They had arrested Derek in Nottingham. She had no idea why he'd gone there. He had no connection with the place.

I really wished, at the time when Auntie Andy was staying with us, and then later during the trial when we saw a lot of her again, that I hadn't known any of this (and I didn't know all of it then, though I did know about the bath, and it haunted me). I tried not to listen when anyone talked about it (mostly my mother with Auntie Jean), but I couldn't help being curious too, against my better judgement: as if amongst the details there was information that I needed for my own survival. Innocent-seeming fragments would get in past my defences (the reading book, Nottingham, chops for tea), then stick to my imagination like tar.

Inevitably, they got to know at school about my connection with the case. A deputation of older girls came up to me with solemn faces one playtime, and presented me with a posy of flowers – probably picked out of the front gardens on their way to school – tied up in raffia from the craft cupboard. They wanted to say how sorry they were about 'my little cousin'; one of them actually stroked my hair as if I moved her to spontaneous pity. I wanted to tell them that I'd hardly known Charlie, that he was a snotty-nosed kid and I'd hated him, and that he would have hated me back if he'd even deigned to notice my existence. But I didn't dare; I knew they wouldn't be able to forgive me if I cheated them of their syrupy pleasurable sorrowing. So I thanked them and said that I would give the flowers to my auntie. On my way home I buried them in a dustbin. For a couple of weeks I was accorded a kind of sepulchral respect at school, and then they forgot about me.

From time to time when I was alone in a room I would suddenly have full chilling consciousness that Charlie had been alive inside his own head once, as I was at that moment inside mine. And also that this person which he really was had undergone those things I knew were factually true, in a present moment as real as this one, and continuous with mine because it had baked beans in it and a bathroom with a familiar boring sink and towels and a toilet. My mind expanded to take in new possibilities. This open-air recognition was what lay in wait behind all the gloating, smothering words ('poor little chappie').

A blast of wind blowing through space, icy clean.

Most of the time, naturally, when Auntie Andy wasn't around I hardly thought about Charlie. I got on with my life.

My mother used to say, in one of her set pieces, that she had never known what courage was until she saw how Andrea stood up to the lawyers in court. — She was so perfectly polite and patient, but she never let them get under her skin. I couldn't have kept my composure the way she did.

But once the trial was over the two of them didn't see much of each other. Their lives took them in different directions, and they had never really had much in common. Andy didn't become a new person after Charlie was killed, she never became one of the bright, quick, funny women Mum chose for her best friends. Andy was always rather sweet and blank and – what's the word? Not conventional, because Mum was every bit as conventional. Andy was *receptive*, like a deep vessel into which life was poured. If this terrible particular thing hadn't been poured into her, she would have been happier – it goes without saying – but less of a person. She was filled out by her fate. I actually think this is quite rare, this capacity to become the whole shape of the accidents that happen to you.

And it wasn't just a passive thing. I remember when Auntie Jean first came round while Andy was staying with us. Jean had a big forthright bust and piled-up black hair, she wore dangling earrings that were vaguely gypsyish. When Andy came out of the bedroom where she'd been lying down, Jean knelt on the floor in front of her, wrapping her arms around Andy's knees, sobbing extravagantly.

— I don't know how you can bear it, she said. — I know I couldn't.

(Jean had three boys.)

The murder had cleared a social space around Andy. People didn't know how to address her; probably Jean was just trying to broach that space in her overblown way. You can't deny that her gesture matched the extremity of what had happened. But Andy wasn't either touched or embarrassed. She stood very still and unresponsive until Jean let go.

— I'm sorry, I don't like scenes, she coolly said.

I'm sure that Uncle Derek was less interesting than his wife; he wasn't interesting just because he had killed someone. As an adult I lived for a while in a house that had brick steps leading down into a narrow coal cellar like a passage to a dead end, where we kept the brooms and buckets and broken things we hadn't got around to fixing. It used to flood with filthy water at certain times of year, and I imagine Uncle Derek's inner life like that: cramped and musty-smelling, shut away from daylight, subject to the drag of tides of violence. The little despotism he installed inside the four walls of his home mattered only because it derived its authority from the whole towering, mahogany-coloured, tobacco-smelling, reasonable edifice of male superiority in the world outside.

And mattered, of course, because of its consequences in other lives.

My mother reported that in court he said he 'got the worst of a bad bargain' in his wife. They did let him out of jail eventually, I believe, after he had served fifteen years of his sentence. He went to settle in some part of the country where he wasn't known.

During the time Auntie Andy was staying with us, Mum left me alone in the flat with her on Saturdays while she went out shopping. Sometimes Andy played dolls with me. This was a new experience; the adults I knew didn't play with children, unless it was something organised like cricket. But Andy didn't put on a childish voice, and she entered into the reality of the different dolls' characters and sensitivities with what seemed like an authentic interest, almost naive – I checked her face to make sure she wasn't teasing me. We undressed and dressed them in their tiny clothes, flipping them over to do up the poppers, skewering plastic boots on to hard pointing feet. (After the trial was over Andy made a dress for my teenage doll with layered skirts in orange nylon trimmed with minute roses made of satin ribbon: unbelievably pretty, though it was a bit tight and wouldn't do up down the back.)

Sometimes when she and I were alone in the flat, Auntie Andy went into the other room to lie down and I heard her crying, although Mum had told Jean that she never did. It didn't occur to me to try to comfort her. I would pretend to carry on with my play, feeling miserably guilty. I was only a child, there was nothing I could offer, and I must have been a living reproach because I wasn't Charlie: though Andy never made me feel this, by any word or sign.

Auntie Andy had to find a job, she had to get a divorce and a place to live by herself. She couldn't go back to that house, obviously.

All of this worked out well for her.

I think she must have come to our flat in the first place, not only out of a revulsion against everything to do with her old life, but also because my mother's solitary cheerful style – frilly aprons and nail polish and lemon-yellow guest towels – had signalled to her, even before the disaster, a vision of possibilities different to the ones she knew. And Mum was honoured by Auntie Andy's choosing us; it seemed a consecration of Mum's situation as a single woman, managing bravely by herself. (Though Andy's staying was an inconvenience and a strain too; my mother acquitted herself with exemplary generosity, she really did.) And then, within a couple of years, they both found themselves a man, as if that had been the whole point of the enterprise.

Andy went to work on the factory floor of the chocolate manufacturers where Uncle Ray was in dispatch. She made a little face of apology when she told us about the job, as if she knew it was beneath her. But in fact she enjoyed the company of the women there, though she kept aloof from the roughest of their bantering and raucous kidding

(I saw this because Ray got me a summer job at the factory when I was sixteen). She brought us paper bags of half-priced, imperfect chocolates whenever she visited: violet creams and Crunchies and Turkish delight, my favourite – I picked off flakes of the chocolate with my teeth and then ate the jelly. Even after she married, Andy went on working there.

— Carrying on for the moment, she said suggestively.

Her new husband, Phil, was lugubrious with faded good looks, stick-thin. Not long after their wedding Andy began hinting with proud smiles that she might be pregnant; she must have been forty-ish by then, she was a lot older than my mother. Some of this I picked up at the time from conversations between Mum and Auntie Jean: their twilight tones alerted me to the fact that they were talking about bodies. Apparently she suffered from real morning sickness, her stomach swelled, her breasts were sore. (They hardly ever used that word, 'breasts'. It was reserved for medical matters, only uttered in lowered voices.) But in the end nothing came of it, it was a false alarm.

— Doesn't it just break your heart? Jean said.

Andy never did have another baby, although that pattern of phantom pregnancy repeated itself over and over well into her fifties, by which time it had become a bit of a joke among the people who knew her, though not an unkind one. To Uncle Phil's credit he never gave the least sign of scepticism about her symptoms; he was punctilious in his attentions, urging her to put her feet up, bringing the barley water with soda that she'd 'suddenly taken a fancy to'. Andy talked about her 'disappointments' as if they were miscarriages, but Jean didn't believe she ever really conceived in her second marriage. My mother said she didn't know, it wasn't any of her business. However painfully these disappointments were felt in private, nothing altered Andy's queenly kindness and distance. And as far as I know, these phantoms were the only outward sign of continuing trauma from what had happened. I can't help feeling, thinking about it now, that there was an element of histrionic performance in them, contrasting with Andy's usual reserve. Exacting our sympathetic goodwill, under false pretences, she claimed some latitude, some indulgence: in return for the magnitude of what she had undergone, and what she had lost, which could never be restored.

Two

I was staying over at my nana's. I was ten. I woke miraculously early, which was unusual for me. The blankets at Nana's were meagre, ex-army, in prickly grey wool with an oily smell. They would only stay tucked in if you kept unnaturally still, which I never could – in my sleep I had shifted and burrowed, the blankets had come untucked, and a little slit of freezing air was probing my warm body like a knife. Then I rolled over on to the inflexible hand of my plastic doll. Sometimes if I woke up I turned the bedding around and put the pillow at the foot, and to Nana's dismay went back to sleep upside down – which was a revelation of a different room, another world order. But the doll's hand that morning seemed to poke me with a message: 'Arise!' (I was reading a lot of books set in the past, which was grander and better.)

It was Saturday. It was spring – yellow squares of light transformed the unlined curtains at the window, their pattern of purple bars wound with a clinging vine.

Usually by the time I came to consciousness Nana was already busy downstairs with her mouse-activity, sweeping and wiping and soaking, smoothing out brown paper bags and saving them, un-knotting scraps of string and winding them into balls. But today I couldn't hear a sound in the house. I was the first to break the skin of the day, stepping out on to the lino which struck its frozen cold up through the warm soles of my feet. When I parted the curtains and looked out, the familiar scrappy back landscape – trellis and dustbins and old bikes and crazy-paving stepping stones – was glazed in sunshine, gleaming from its dip into the night. Cats were dotted around the vantage points like sentinels; glass windows black with dirt were a shed's eye pits. Nana's lilies of the valley set out on a forced march down the cracks between the pavings.

If I got dressed, I thought, I could walk out into this – what could stop me? Because no one had ever thought of it, I'd never been forbidden to go out before anyone else was up. My latchkeys were warm on their ribbon against my chest, under my vest – though I wasn't supposed to sleep in them in case I strangled myself. I could go home by myself without telling Nana, and surprise my mother. Gleefully I imagined the reversal of our roles: Mum's tousled head raised, blinking and sleepy and astonished, from the pillow at the end of her sofa pulled into its night-position; my own bright wakefulness, airy and full of implications from its journey through the outdoors. For once, I would have the advantage of her. Pulling on my knickers and socks and slacks, buttoning my check shirt, diving into the V-neck of the jumper Nana had knitted in rust-brown stocking stitch, I was light-headed with sensations of freedom and power. All the time I was listening out for mouse-noises from Nana. Now I had started, I couldn't bear to be prevented. I had worried sometimes about making the transition into being grown-up – how did you know when to begin? Now I understood that you stepped out into it, as simply as into a day.

People forget that in 1966 there were still bomb sites: it took a long time to stitch back together that fabric of our cities ripped open by the war – or rather, not to stitch it back at all, but to tear the fabric out and throw it away and put something different in its place. Every time I made my way home from Nana's I walked across an open area where bombs had fallen: you could still make out different wallpapers on the high standing walls, distinguishing the squares of vanished rooms, washed by the rain to faint ghosts of their former patterns. Traces of staircases climbed in zigzag patterns; doors opened on to nothing. Whatever desolation there must once have been was softened and naturalised after two decades; overgrown with buddleia and fireweed, the sites were as consoling as gardens. We played out there and boys rode their bikes round on the grass in the evenings.

Our flat was on the first floor of a spindly Georgian terrace in Kingsdown, Bristol; because it was on a high bluff, from our back windows we surveyed the plain of Broadmead sprawling below, punctuated then by the spires of churches, ruined and otherwise, and only just beginning to be drowned under a tide of office blocks and shopping centres, a new world. These Georgian houses were five storeys tall if you counted the basements which were at garden level at the back; they were mostly raddled and neglected, broken up into flats and bedsits, showing up on their exterior – like intricate dirty embroidery – the layers of complex arrangements for living inside. There was broken glass in some of the windows; at others filthy torn lace curtains, or bedspreads hooked up to keep out the light. A frightening old woman next door wore a long black dress like a Victorian. Mrs Walsh – kindly but with a goitrous bulge on her neck I couldn't bear to look at – lived in our basement with her elderly son (she used to say, 'Can you believe it, he was my little boy?). Beneath that basement was a windowless cellar, its mineral cold air as dense as water, where stalactites grew down from the vaulted ceiling (I knew what they were because we'd been on a school trip to Wookey Hole caves). They used to say there were iron rings where they chained the slaves in some of the Bristol cellars – and secret tunnels leading to the docks. In Bristol stories there were always slaves and sugar and tobacco.

You should see our old road these days. I shouldn't think those houses change hands for much less than a million. Everyone now covets the 'original features', the spindly height, the long walled gardens, the view. Those places sing with money and improvement. Nana's little Victorian box around the corner, which we used to think was so much 'better', can't compare. Sometimes I'm nostalgic now for that old intricate decay, as if it was a vanished subtler style, overlaid by the banality of making over and smartening up that came later. My mother never was nostalgic. She got out the minute she had the chance.

I pulled Nana's front door shut behind me. From somewhere far off came the ruminative stop–start of the milkman's electric float, but still I had the morning more or less to myself. I could hear the crêpe-soled creak of my sandals on the pavement and the jangled clang of the gate as it closed with finality after me, as if these sounds bounced off the silent houses opposite. I could almost see my surprising self, setting out about my own business in the streets, my windcheater zipped up and my hands in its pockets; I fancied I walked with a masculine casual bravado, brown hair chopped off in a clean line at shoulder length. I wasn't interested at that point of my life in being girlish – what I admired were horses and the boyish girls who hung around horses.

Turning the corner at the end of Nana's street, I started along the path across the bomb site. When I saw a man sitting facing away from me on one of the broken low walls, it was too late to go back, but my heart beat with shy anxiety: I hated the idea of any strange adult speaking to me, perhaps telling me off. Wearing a dark overcoat, the man was bent over with his head in his hands. The path ran close behind where he sat, and hurrying past I could make out the black cloth of his coat worn to gingery brown across the shoulders, freckled with scurf from his greasy hair. I thought it was strange that an adult man came out to sit alone on a pile of stones: I couldn't imagine either of my uncles doing it. I didn't know much about men but in my experience they were always purposefully on their way somewhere. Then I realised that the man was Mrs Walsh's son Clive. I hadn't recognised him because it was the first time I'd ever seen him beyond the end of our street. He lifted his head and peered over his shoulder at me: doleful long face, unshaven cheeks and chin, the beard-growth specked with silver. The inner rim of his lower eyelids was lined in sore, wet red.

— Come and look at this, he said.

Clive was strange. One of his boots was made up with a special thick sole because of his sloping, dragging walk; he had had meningitis when he was three and his twin sister had died of it. We had lived in the same house since I could remember, but he and I had an unspoken agreement not to acknowledge each other, except when our connection was mediated by our mothers. — Can you believe he had yellow curls once? Mrs Walsh would sigh. — Say hello to Stella, Clive.

— Say hello to Clive, my mother would order, shoving me sharply in the small of the back. She was full of ostentatious pity for the 'poor thing', but also thought it might be better for everyone if he was 'put away', whatever that meant. — It's not much of a life, she said.

I'm not sure whether Clive really recognised me that morning; we never spoke about it afterwards. I might just have been any passing little girl.

— Look what I've found, he said.

Warily I stepped over the wall into the interior of the vanished house. Swallows were flitting and shrieking inside the space, they nested there. Against the wall where Clive was sitting, fallen into the cracks in the stones and rolled into the grass, was an improbable slew of buttons of all sorts – thousands of buttons, much more than a handful or even a tinful. I crouched down to them, wondering, not touching yet.

— Who do they belong to? How did they get here?

Clive said he had known the woman who once lived here and they must be hers. I'd played here often and I'd never seen the buttons before, but I began to believe him because he was so certain. Did he mean a woman who'd lived in this house before it was bombed? Some of these buttons were old: carved jet ones, brass ones with military insignia, cream cloth-covered ones for shirts. Others looked modern: coloured plastic ones, like the ones my Nana put on my cardigans, were still sewn on to the cards they'd been bought on. Some were fastened into sets – miniature mother-of-pearl buttons for baby clothes, pink glass drops – but most of them were loose, jumbled chaotically together: ordinary black and brown and white ones, a coral rose, wooden toggles, a diamanté buckle, big yellow bone squares, toggles made of bamboo.

Something about the sheer multiplicity of the buttons – the fact that you couldn't get to the bottom of them – started an ache of desire in my chest. I thought that Clive was feeling the same thing. He breathed through his mouth noisily. His cheeks under their strong beard-growth were dramatic, hollow as if they'd been carved out with something clumsy like an axe; the raw mask of a man's face was overlaid on his life which was more like the life of a child. Every afternoon Clive was allowed to wander out along our road. He always stopped at one particular lamp post, as if it was a limit his mother had set him; he would be standing there when the children came home from school, hunched over, smoking and watching us, wearing his overcoat in winter, a short grey mac in summer. We squealed and ran past him – even I did, pretending I didn't know him. Every teatime Mrs Walsh came out to bring him back, pulling him coaxingly by the hand; a small, bent, fat old woman tugging at a tall, scowling, resisting man, showing her patient smile around to anyone who might see them.

   – We could take them home for your mother, I suggested.

   But I wanted the coral rose for myself, or the buckle. I put my hand out to pick them up; angrily Clive pushed it away, scuffing some of the buttons into the dirt with his normal boot.

   – Don't touch them. Leave them, he scolded.

   Close up, I could smell his familiar smell, the same as in their flat: stale like damp feather cushions or mouldy bread, mixed with something perfumed he put on his hair (or his mother did). Reasonably, I pointed out that if anyone wanted them they shouldn't have thrown them away but he didn't listen, he was preoccupied, sorting through the buttons with clumsy yellow-stained fingers as if he was searching for one in particular. Clear snot glistened on the curves of his upper lip. I watched jealously, crouched on my haunches, balancing on the balls of my feet with my hands on my knees. Really, where could so many buttons have come from? Someone might have had a button shop and given it up: but then, why pour out the cornucopia here? I was frustrated that Clive was not a real adult who could offer answers – though often they only dismissed my questions. (— Oh Stella. Don't be silly. Whatever for?) Clive held a big button up to the light: it was pearly white, so translucent it was almost green, carved with a leggy bird with a long beak, perhaps a heron. I had never thought with any interest about clothes before, but I had a heady vision in that instant of a black velvet cape, full-length, dragging behind me along the smooth floor of a place I'd never been. — Behold, I thought to myself, out of the books I was reading. — She cometh.

I couldn't help reaching out to take the bird-button. Clive smacked at my hand.

— They're not yours, I said indignantly. — They're anybody's.

Then he pushed me hard on the knee so that I overbalanced and fell backwards. Standing up, he towered over me; it was a surprise to be reminded of how wholly he filled out his big man's body. Because of the child's life he led, traipsing everywhere after his mother, it was easy to discount his grown-up shape as if he'd only borrowed it, the way girls dressed up in their mothers' shoes and lipstick. Now I saw that Clive's size fitted as inevitably around him as mine did around me, and

33

that he was at home in it. In fact, because he walked sloppily and mumbled to himself, he was more deeply burrowed away inside his body than other grown-ups were. Other grown-ups, especially women, had learned somehow to live on the surfaces of their bodies, controlling them and presenting a prepared version of them to the world.

Sometimes when Clive stood under the lamp post and watched the children coming home from school you could see he was rubbing himself with his hand down in his trousers – not in any kind of sinful frenzy, more as if he was only half aware of doing it, comforting and reassuring himself. There was an old man who did something like this at the swimming baths too, sitting on the edge of the pool, staring at the girls squealing and splashing, rocking himself in a rolling movement back and forwards against the pool's rim, taking his weight on his hands. If you caught the pool-man's eye he was jeering and slippery whereas if Clive ever looked at you he was contemptuous, as if you had nothing for him. I knew it comforted men to touch themselves. I had seen Uncle Ray and Uncle Frank putting their hands down there, adjusting themselves inside their underwear, sniffing their fingers afterwards. My mother would make a little face of distaste at it, clicking her tongue. Auntie Jean would dig her elbow in Frank's ribs, reminding him he was in company.

— Don't look, my mother snapped if she saw Clive busy in his trousers; she would close her expression tight shut as if it was my fault for shaming her. — Cross the road, Stella!

I ought to have been afraid of him that morning but I wasn't. I had been relieved all along that it was Clive I met on the bomb site and not a stranger; in relation to Clive I was still powerful and not obliterated. When he stood looming over me I felt more outrage than fear, and rolled over, scrambling to my feet, dusting off my knees, which were not grazed but lightly stuck with bits of gravel and grass. I wasn't hurt in the least, only shocked and humiliated.

— You're not supposed to push me!

He took a step towards me, making a threatening gesture with his hand in the air like the one my mother made to me sometimes. I stepped backwards, deliberately insouciant. Then I turned and skipped away. How I used to love that skipping – two bounces on the one foot, then two on the other – which carried you as fast as seven-league boots, buoyant and flinging forwards, rebounding off the ground each time with double strength. What a loss when one day I wasn't able to fly along like that any longer, ever again. I can't remember what stopped me. Was it inhibition, because I grew older and reached the point where I wanted to be like the grown women who presented themselves with such poise? After I had a child, in any case (and I was very young when I had my first) something was physically unbound in me, so that if I jumped or ran for a bus my insides seemed to churn in a new disorder.

Clive came lumbering after me but I knew he couldn't

catch me. The smack of his heavy boots when he reached the pavement was loud as gunshots in the empty street. I stopped and waited for him by the grocer's shop, where the beige sun-blinds, cracked and torn, were still drawn down inside the windows: between the glass and the blinds was stacked a pyramid of tins of peas, their labels faded almost to illegibility. I had looked at those peas a thousand times.

— Here, grunted Clive when he caught up with me, stopping at a respectful distance, holding out his big greeny-white fist.

I held out my open hand to him.

He gave me the coral rose and the diamanté buckle.

I still have them.

Before I turned the corner into our road I had put the encounter with Clive out of my mind – though not my new treasures, which I kept clenched tight in my hand. The only thought I spent on him was that I would tell my mother I had 'found them'. Standing facing our front door – I had two keys, one for this and one for the door to our flat inside – I was daunted for the first time by my adventure. I had used my keys many times before; but then I had always been expected. Now, because I was not supposed to be there, the street seemed bleached and flattened by its unaccustomed emptiness – though the milkman's float was working its way by now from the other end. The grandeur of our door was suddenly forbidding: elevated from the street up its flight of worn steps, with an iron boot scraper set into the stone and an ancient heavy iron knocker (no one needed to use the knocker because of the cracked row of plastic bell pushes to one side, where names were written in ink on slips of card). Inside the hall, its air sour with forgotten coats and shoes, the foggy light was freckled with ruby from the coloured glass in the back door, where steps led down into the garden.

There were two rooms on each floor, and for the whole house one bathroom, two toilets. Beside the front door lived old Tom with a cleft palate who was in the Salvation Army; behind him, the woman who worked in the fish and chip shop. On tiptoe I started up the staircase which wound around the deep well at the house's core: the handrail was polished wood and the banister rods were shaky in their sockets, some of them missing (I had bad dreams in which they gave way and I fell down towards the bottom). There were still brass brackets for gas lamps on the wall; light sifted down through the dirty skylight set into the roof, which leaked when it rained. In the flat above us lived a couple with a baby I had knitted bootees for, and in the attic above them was reticent Geoffrey, who fed me spoonfuls of condensed milk from an opened tin in his cupboard, and painted huge abstracts in cream and brown and black (he left them behind when he flitted without paying his rent). From Geoffrey's casement windows you could climb out into the lead-lined channel that ran the length of the terrace, eighteen inches deep, with a stone parapet between it and the street so far below. I had sat out there on the parapet more than once, with my back to the street and my feet in the gutter.

I was startled as I let myself into our flat – staggering slightly because the key was still on its ribbon round my neck, and the keyhole was rather high up on the door – to see the sofa untouched, pristine in its daytime identity. Mum couldn't be up already, could she? But there was no sign of her – and we only had two rooms. Always, if she was up, she was busy: vacuuming, dusting, rinsing our clothes through in the sink – she called it 'rinsing' as though that made it a lighter and smarter job than washing, less like drudgery. And she couldn't be out. Her handbag was on the table, her bright silk scarf flopped, plumy and exotic, between its handles. Beside the sink in the kitchen-end of our living room (the kitchenette, Mum called it determinedly), were two teacups and two glasses, filled with water to soak. I closed the door quietly behind me and stood taking in whatever extraordinary thing had happened. I knew I'd found my mother out in something, although I didn't know what. Who had been here with her while I was away? Was it Auntie Jean? The glasses came out for Jean sometimes. I wanted to go stamping around the room, to assert my right to do it, but I kept stony still. Mum's coat was on its hanger. Her high heels were kicked off beside the sofa; I knew how she eased her feet out of them, grimacing in relief. I could smell her perfume and the faint stale-biscuit smell of her nylons, which I liked, as if it was a secret weakness I kept safe for her.

She must be asleep in my bedroom, next door. I hadn't made much noise, unlocking and stumbling in on the end of my ribbon, but I imagined the effect of it rolling out from me like waves towards the bedroom door and pressing through it; the bed – my bed – creaked and sighed in its intimately known voice. Someone stirred, rolled over – the style was alien in our home, uninhibited and loose and large. Then a growling, deep-throated rumble, one of those satisfied private noises from the borders of sleep, was unmistakably a man's. I was appalled, invaded. I might have thought he'd murdered my mother and taken her place if I hadn't heard afterwards her own neat little squeak, sleepy and humorously protesting. He was in there with her; they were drifting together into wakefulness. But what life did my mother share with an unknown man? Who knew her this well, apart from me – to share her sleep with her? I had never thought of bed before as anything but an innocent place.

In a daze of rage I stepped over to the table, felt in Mum's handbag for her purse, slipped the worn clasp, and helped myself to her change – not all of it, two half-crowns and a sixpence and a few pennies and halfpence. I had never done such a thing before, or even dreamed of it. I couldn't remember why my right hand was clenched awkwardly shut; when I unlocked my fingers my palm was grooved with the impress of the sharp edges of the buckle. I put back Mum's purse, tipped the coral button and the buckle on to the table and left them there. Disgust made me deft and bold; I exited as soundlessly as if I'd never been inside the room.

My hands tasted of hot copper from the pennies. I knew where to wait, five minutes' walk along the road from our house, because I caught this bus with Mum every Saturday afternoon, to go to the stables where I had my riding lesson. Only the number 83 called at this stop outside the high wall, topped with broken glass stuck into cement, of a red-brick factory which made brake linings (I pictured these as brilliant coloured, silky). The bus company's yellow tin sign on its concrete post seemed for a long while a forlorn flag announcing nothing, and I felt conspicuous though no one passed except the milkman, his bottles jostling and chiming.

But an 83 did come. I paid the conductor and he didn't question me, dropping the money in his leather bag and winding my ticket from the machine slung across his shoulder. I had to change in the city centre to go to Keynsham; for a long time this second bus sat without a driver while I waited inside, the only passenger, too agonised with shyness to get out and ask when it would leave. I was hungry by this time for my breakfast. We began our slow progress eventually, through the suburbs to the outskirts of the city. Everything I saw from my window at the front on the upper deck, where my mother never wanted to sit – boys setting out a cricket game on a recreation ground, the bombed-out shell of a church with the grass neatly mown around it, car showrooms with plate-glass windows – looked more real, dense with itself, because I saw it alone. When I stepped down at last at my destination from the platform of the bus, I snuffed up triumphantly the perfumes of manure and of clogged, rotten ditches overgrown with brambles, rejoicing at the crunch under my sandals of dried mud grown with sparse grass, set in its deep ruts and tyre tracks, whose forms I broke as I trod.

What I'm thinking now is that it was a long way for my mother to bring me on the bus every Saturday, just for me to have the riding lessons I yearned and pleaded for. No doubt there was an element of snobbery and aspiration in her determination to get me to the lessons, and to pay for them – just as there was in her wanting me to go to the High School. (We fought about these aspirations, later.) For all I know she was imagining Elizabeth Taylor and *National Velvet*. But it was still a long way to Keynsham and back on her only free day of the week (on Sundays we went for dinner to one of my uncles' houses). She had to get all her shopping done on Saturday mornings. What did she do while I lumbered around the paddock on the backs of the fat little ponies, Dozey and Boy and Melba and Star and Chutney? I think she brought her library book with her (Erle Stanley Gardner or Georgette Heyer or Harold Robbins). I think she boiled the stable girls' electric kettle and made herself instant coffee, and that in fine weather she sat reading and smoking on one of those folding wooden chairs on the collapsing verandah that ran along the end of the pavilion (as we grandly called it – it was really more like an overgrown garden shed). Mostly it wasn't fine weather, and she must have stayed inside where it stank of leather tack and pony nuts and where in winter they lit a fumy paraffin heater. She took no interest in the horses and wouldn't go near them.

She waited after the lesson when I was allowed to

groom Star, going at him with the body brush, lifting his mane to work underneath, releasing the potent musk smell of his sweat, dusty and greasy. Kissing his nose I made contact, through the hot pelt grown close like stubbly chenille on the hard bone of his skull, with that urgent wordless horse life which moved me so inexpressibly. And then we set out home again on the two buses.

The stables were at the back of a grand half-ruined old house where nobody lived; the couple who ran them had a ramshackle bungalow in the grounds. Jilly was fierce, lean and sun-dried; Budge (their surname was Budgen) tubby and uneasily jovial. They were both perpetually distracted in an aura of money-anxiety and failure; even though the place must have run itself, pretty much. They had to buy the feed and equipment but most of the work was done for free by a clique of girls fanatical about horses. The great prize was to be allowed to ride the ponies bareback to the field after the lessons were over. These girls were older than I was, thirteen or fourteen, and I was in awe of their swagger and their loud talk about feed supplements and gymkhanas (a lot of this was wishful thinking – we didn't go to many gymkhanas). Their ringleader was Karen, decisive and devoid of humour, with a stubby neat figure, startling light blue eyes, and a stiff mass of curls the non-colour of straw. She lived locally and seemed to spend all her time at the stables, although I suppose she must have gone to school. It was impossible to imagine Karen compliant in a classroom – her independent competence seemed so sealed and completed.

Karen was in charge by herself that Saturday morning when I arrived; she had taken the ponies down to the field and was in the middle of mucking out. Wiping sweat from her forehead on to her sleeve, she peered at me, frowning: I wasn't supposed to arrive until hours later. And she must have registered that I came for the first time without my mother, though she didn't comment. I babbled something about wanting to come up early, to help out; she swept me with her focused, narrow glance, summing me up.

— You can help with this lot.

She handed me one of the stiff brooms we used to clear out the filthy straw from the stalls. I didn't have my stable clothes on but in the abandonment of today it didn't matter. With Mum's money I had bought chocolate and an orange drink at the shop across the road from where the bus stopped, so I wasn't hungry any longer and I set to work energetically. Soon I stripped off my jumper. Karen and I settled into a companionable unspeaking rhythm of labour and procedure. I loved the noise of the bristles hissing against the cobbles in the wet from the hose. The forbidden nursery stench of horse shit and piss was gagging, overwhelming; there was a triumph in getting so deep into muck, then resurfacing into an order where all the stalls were spread with clean straw and all the hay-nets full. I suppose as little girls we were excited by the ponies' shamelessness, which was also innocent; and by the matter-of-fact way we were thrust up against

43

their gargantuan bodily functions, cheerfully chaffing and scolding them for it. We couldn't help seeing the male ponies' penises, sometimes extended in arousal – the older girls joked about their 'willies', but joking couldn't encompass the naked enormity, appalling, stretching imagination and inhibition. Sometimes as you led the ponies back into a stall where you'd just put out clean bedding, they pissed into it voluptuously.

When we'd worked for a good hour Karen made us instant coffee and I shared the rest of my chocolate with her. I'd never actually drunk coffee before but I didn't say so, I told her I took three sugars; I was excited and happy to see her stirring for me, there in the pavilion whose light was always heavy with dust motes, the inner sanctum of the stable-cult. From time to time I was visited by the knowledge that trouble waited for me at the end of this interlude of escape. No one knew where I was. I had begun something catastrophic when I slipped out of the routines of our life, to act by myself. I knew without thinking about it that what seemed plain to me – my dereliction's existing in counterbalance with my mother's – would never for one moment be admitted or discussed by her. But I wasn't sorry. I was exulting – even though in my chest I felt a pain of postponed anxiety like a held breath.

Karen began to open up to me, complaining about Jilly and Budge. Jilly had been supposed to help with the mucking out but there was still no sign of her. — Sleeping it off, Karen said contemptuously. We went together to fetch the ponies up to the paddock, ready for the morning's classes to begin; as we strolled she ripped off bits of wild clematis and sticky burs, lashing with them at the hedge in her indignation, rousing flurries of dust and papery moths. The air was warm and stuffy. The field was at the back of a new housing development; I had some inkling even then that this was not the real, deep countryside but something scruffy and indeterminate, washed up like a residue around the edge of the city.

I didn't mistake Karen's confidences for friendship – she would have unburdened herself to whoever was there. She was also the sort of talker who didn't bother to fill you in on the background to what she was discussing, so that in order to follow I had to make great leaps of comprehension through a dense web of detail: dates and times, things done and words spoken, disputed interpretations of what had been promised. Her grudges were obscure and passionate. Budge she seemed to tolerate ('He knows what's going on and doesn't like it'), but Jilly was 'two-faced' and 'could be a right cow'. She dramatised their conversations, ventriloquising Jilly's words in an exaggeratedly posh accent. 'I'm not very happy with your attitude, Karen.' In these duologues Karen had all the clinching and flattening ripostes, Jilly was lost for words. I gathered that Jilly was leaving more and more of the work at the stables up to Karen, paying her sometimes, but not on any agreed or regular basis. Sometimes she didn't even turn up for the classes and Karen had to take them. I had imagined the world of the stables as a happy cohesion. Karen's revelations were wrenching for me, but they also seemed an inevitable part of the initiations of this morning; I braced myself and grew into them.

— They've got me in a cleft stick, Karen said.
— Because I love the horses, I won't leave them.

When we opened the gate to the field the ponies lifted their heads from where they were cropping grass; I felt a pang at our intrusion but I knew better than to say so. Karen would think that was soppy. You wouldn't have known that horses were her life unless you watched her carefully. She wasn't tentative or tender as I was and she spoke about them as if they were comical, exasperating, a trial to be got through. But in the field they tolerated her approach when she came coaxingly towards them at an angle, holding the bridle out of sight behind her, making encouraging chirruping noises; whereas they wouldn't let me get anywhere near them. She told me to ride Dozey up to the paddock; she would ride Chutney, leading Star, and we would go back for the others.

We mounted at the stile. I had never ridden without a saddle before, but as with the coffee I didn't say anything. Dozey was the smallest of the ponies, only about ten hands. I pivoted awkwardly over the slippery broad barrel of her back, swinging my leg across, copying Karen's movements; struggling not to slither immediately down the other side, I was hot in the face, knowing her assessing eye was on me. Because of her closed, blinkered perspective it was easy to think that she wasn't noticing you, but in fact nothing escaped her.

46

— Grip harder with your knees, she advised offhandedly as if my incompetence were only a thing of the passing moment. — Sit up straight. Relax. You can do it.

Tears stung in my eyes, wrung out by the great kindness of her condescension. (When Karen taught the beginners' classes she was merciless.) And I relaxed, I found my equilibrium. I felt the pony's muscle and sinew moving under mine, I breathed her smell as if we were one hot flesh.

So it was that I came riding into the yard at the very moment my mother made her appearance at the stables (she probably didn't even notice I was bareback). I think that I must have first turned up there at about nine – she arrived just before eleven, when morning lessons started. I saw her climb out of the passenger seat of a maroon-coloured car parked beyond the yard gate; she was wearing her heels, unsuitable in the mud, and her coat was hanging open with the silk scarf loose inside around her neck. She made an impression subtly different to the usual one, when she had toiled up with me on two buses: today she looked womanly, commanding and perfumed. At the same moment Jilly appeared out of the pavilion in wrinkled slacks and polo neck, sour-faced, dishevelled, hair scrunched in an elastic band, cigarette dangling off her lip. She raised an eyebrow in mild surprise at the sight of me on Dozey (her eyebrows were plucked to nothingness and had to be drawn back in brown pencil), but didn't comment.

— Take the ponies through into the paddock, Karen,

she drawled around her cigarette, as if she'd been in charge of the whole operation from the beginning.

I half expected Karen to break out angrily with her grievances, but she only clicked her tongue at Chutney and rode on, her face surly and suffering like a boy's. Jilly unplugged the cigarette in a way she had, with a light popping noise, extending her free hand to my mother and putting on the caramel baritone charm she kept for parents. She obviously couldn't remember my mother's name. (I expect she thought Mum was a prole and a bore, beneath consideration. But she needed her money. And Mum would have been thinking that Jilly looked 'a fright'.) Mum spoke politely in her most stand-offish, stilted public manner. Of course she didn't make a scene about my being there, she never would. She saved the scene for later, in private.

— Come on, Stella, she said briskly, as if her collecting me had been planned all along. Awkwardly I slithered down from Dozey, landing somehow on my bottom on the cobbles. — Look at the state of you. I'm going to have to find something for you to sit on.

And we made our way to the maroon-coloured car.

Where in the driving seat a man was waiting.

Mum had called round at Nana's at about half nine and no one had answered the door. Nana was inside (Mum had a key) but she had suffered a stroke. 'A slight stroke,' Mum said decisively, tidying it away. Uncle Frank had taken Nana to hospital. (So that was why I hadn't heard Nana when I woke up. Unless – this troubled me for a while – she'd had the stroke because she found me missing. Nana recovered but she was never her old indefatigably busy self, she meandered into troughs of bewildered absence. She died when I was fourteen.)

Mum had guessed immediately where I might have gone. We never once spoke of the possibility that I had come home first and been inside the flat where she was sleeping, not alone. She never asked about the money I had taken, although she must have noticed it was missing, in that time when she had to count every penny. (I hid what was left of it at the bottom of my treasure box, spending it gradually on sweets.) Not long afterwards, when I was reading one evening on my bed, she came in and opened her hand, showing me the coral button and diamanté buckle.

— Are these yours?

I had forgotten about them. There had been too many other things to think about.

— Yes, I said. — I found them on my way home. On the bomb site.

— Pretty, she said. And gave them to me.

That was all.

Three

My stepfather wasn't a big man, not much taller than my mother. He was lithe and light on his feet, handsome, with velvety black brows, a sensual mouth and jet-black hair in a crewcut as thick and soft as the pelt of an animal (not that I ever touched it, though sometimes out of curiosity I wanted to). His face was one of those where the features seem compacted as if under pressure inside a frame. He was energetic, intelligent, diligent, faithful – a stroke of luck for my mother, a lightning bolt of luck, illuminating her grinding, narrow future and transforming it. They'd met at work, at the Board Mill where the packets for Wills cigarettes were made; he was the manager of cost accounting. It was a real love match, much more than she could have hoped for, past her first youth and with a half-grown daughter tagged on as part of the package.

If I knew him now as he was then, what would I think of him? I can imagine watching him, restless in a group of his friends, jumping up to buy them drinks, fetching extra chairs: he is a charming man, they like him. He is eagerly indignant, as they are, over money, hierarchy, immigration, discipline. He doesn't like the dirty jokes but only shakes his head, disapproving, smiling. No doubt one or two of his older colleagues are in the Masons, which he views with wary amusement until he's invited to join himself, a few years later. All the time, it's as if he's preoccupied with some inward effort which he thinks no one else sees – an effort of decency, of fitting in. There is a little flame burning in him, in spite of himself, lighting up his expression and his movements. His judgement – not of abstractions like immigration and taxes, but knowing how to hold himself, when to be still – is unexpectedly delicate and true. I can see it now, from this distance.

We moved from Kingsdown into Stoke Bishop: respect-able, sleepy, leafy. Our house was in a new cul-de-sac called Beech Grove, carved out by a developer where there had once been a little wood among the rows of houses from the 1930s. Mum had promised me a bedroom of my own and I was looking forward to something pretty and pink. I had thought that perhaps this good luck of possessions was what you could get in exchange for the other changes you didn't want. I calculated that I might get a horse, too, and jodhpurs and a hard hat of my own – I had only ever rented my hat from the stables. (I did get the jodhpurs and the hat, eventually.)

But when we drew up outside the new house in Gerry's car, minutes before the removal van arrived, it wasn't

51

what I had bargained for. The house was so new it was raw. There were still labels stuck across the glass in the windows, so that it seemed to stare with lifeless eyes at a ruined landscape of red clay. The paving and the wood of the fence palings were stained red and filthy. Although there were people already living in the finished houses to one side up the Grove, in the other direction there were only half-built shells in the mud; monstrous machines snoozed among piles of breeze blocks and timber, bags of cement. We sat on in the car for a few moments after the engine died, and I thought Mum and Gerry must be thinking what I was thinking: that it was too bleak and ugly to bear, that we would have to give up and go home.

But they weren't.

Mum must have been drinking in the newness in deep draughts.

How could she not want to get away from Mrs Walsh and Clive, and the old woman in the Victorian dress, and the broken windows? (And Nana, and her childhood past, and her failed marriage?) She tied her hair in a scarf and Gerry rolled up his sleeves; unpacking, directing the removal men, they made a team. Mum boiled water and unpacked a bucket and a tub of Vim, then she began washing out the red mud. Gerry helped carry things in and made sure every item went into the room it was labelled for. Though he wasn't big, he was strong, and he always got on well with men who worked for him. Mum and I hadn't brought much with us from the flat, most of the furniture in the van was Gerry's. (He had been married before – until his first wife 'ran off', I found out later – so I suppose that these were things he'd bought with her.) — It'll do for the time being, my mother said about this furniture warningly, as if she had plans. Her plans were a flirtation between them, abrasive and teasing – her female conspiracy (shopping) against his male suspicion and resignation.

— Don't get under our feet, she said to me. — Why don't you go out and play?

— Couldn't you find her something useful to do? said Gerry.

— You don't know Stella.

This was the first time I'd heard that I wasn't useful. She'd never asked me to be useful, had she? Anyway I was glad, I didn't want to help. My new bedroom was an empty cell smelling coldly of cement, not adapted to my shape or anyone's. I wanted my old window back, surveying the familiar intricate wilderness – gardens overgrown with brambles, tottering garages, the tracery of fire escapes on the backs of houses, an old Wolseley up on bricks. Our new garden, which my new window overlooked in blind indifference, was only a rectangle of red clay, marked off with fence posts and wire from the clay rectangles belonging to the other houses.

I wandered out into it, taking my doll. (— Aren't you too old for dolls? Gerry had asked already.) At the far end of our rectangle were the stumps of two huge trees cut down to make way for the new development. I gravitated towards these stumps as the only feature breaking up the new-made symmetry. Under my sandals the ridges and troughs of hardened clay were unforgiving. From the base of the tree stump little feelers of new growth were pushing up in doomed hope, waving their flags of leaves; sticky resin oozed from crevices on the cut surface. Even the sky out here – thinly clouded and tinged with lemon where the sun strained to break through – seemed blanched and excessively empty. Once, I supposed, its emptiness would have been full of tree. Carefully I sat on the stump, not wanting to get resin on my shorts; I put my doll beside me. Because she was jointed at the pelvis but not at the knee, she had to have her legs stretched out in front of her in a wide V. She was wearing a blue and white ski suit I had knitted, with Nana's help. (Even when things went dark after her stroke, Nana knitted expertly as ever, and still won at cards.)

A girl came out from the back of the house next door, picking her way easily across the red clay. For a while she and I were intensely mutually aware without seeming to notice each other, behind the convenient fiction of the fence wire. When we outgrew that pretence she stepped across it and approached my stump.

— Hello, she said. — Have you moved in next door?

— It's you who's next door to us, I said logically. — Counting from here.

She didn't notice that I'd corrected her perspective.

— Oh good. We can be friends. I hoped there'd be a girl.

Her threshold for friendship wasn't exacting, then. I didn't have high hopes of her: she seemed unsubtle and

54

I was a wary, reluctant friend. At least because she was eager, it was easy for me to withhold my approval. She was pretty: breathy and bouncing, with round eyes like a puppy's, a mass of fuzzy, fair hair, and a tummy that strained against her tight stretch-nylon dress. I liked her name, which was Madeleine. She picked up my doll and began to walk her in silly, jouncing steps around the stump, see-sawing her legs; I snatched her back. My belief in my dolls at that point was in a delicate balance. I knew that they were inert plastic and could be tumbled without consequences upside-down and half naked in the toy-box. At the same time, I seemed to feel the complex sensibility of each one as if it existed both in my mind and quite outside me. This doll – her name was Teenager – was stiffly humourless; my teddy bear on the other hand was capable of a tolerant irony. Teenager was outraged by Madeleine's travesty of real play.

— I suppose these were the beeches, I said, to distract Madeleine's attention.

She was blank. — What were what?

— These trees. The road is called Beech Grove. A beech is a kind of tree.

— What trees?

She was looking around as if she might have missed them. I explained that I meant the stump I was sitting on and the one next to it. I pointed out that there was a stump too at the end of her garden, and others all along behind the row of houses. — There must have been a little wood. A grove. That's what a grove is.

My relationship to her began to take on an instructional form that was not unsatisfying. Madeleine looked down at the stump with dawning comprehension. — Oh, is that a tree? she said.

— What did you think it was?

— I didn't think about it really. I s'pose I just thought they were part of the ground. Like rocks or something.

Her oblivion seemed so extreme that it might be disingenuous. This was Madeleine's performance – eyes so wide open that she seemed to be finding her own obliviousness as amusing as you ever could. You never got to the bottom of what she actually knew, or didn't know.

— They shouldn't have chopped down a grove of beech trees, I said sternly, improvising. — It's unlucky.

— Why?

— Because they were sacred. In the olden days, people worshipped them.

She thought about this. — What d'you mean, worshipped?

— Prayed to them. Believed that they were sacred – you know, like God.

— God?

Perhaps she'd never noticed who she was praying to at school. I stood up carefully, respectfully from the stump. — I hope the gods aren't angry.

— Is it alive now? Madeleine asked warily.

— Kind of, in a way.

I showed her where the tree was feebly sprouting. — It's still trying to grow.

— Ooh, I don't like it, she squealed, backing off in a pantomime of shuddering.

She looked like the kind of girl who would join in when there was squealing over anything: blood, wasps, veins in school-dinner liver – although she wouldn't quite mean it, would just be enjoying the noise and distraction. She was too robust to be properly squeamish.

— You'd better not say you don't like them, I said. — They might hear.

A gleam of inspiration pierced her vagueness. Taking me by surprise, she dropped to her knees on the clay, squeezing her eyes shut and clasping her hands together. — For what we are about to receive, may the Lord make us truly thankful, she gabbled in the prescribed drone. — In the name of the ferrership of the spirit. (She meant fellowship.) Oh holy tree. Who art very nice; and we're sorry that they've cut you down.

I knew that this was mostly for my benefit. Nonetheless, I glanced involuntarily upward. A few fat drops of rain fell without warning or follow-through, darkening spots on the dried clay.

— See? said Madeleine. — It doesn't mind.

That evening my mother boiled eggs and warmed beans on a primus; our gas stove wasn't connected yet. We buttered sliced bread straight from the bag and had the milk bottle on the table.

— Isn't this an adventure? she said excitedly.

I was suspicious of something new in her face: not romance, exactly (she was never soft), but as if a force had filled her out, carrying her forward in exhilaration. She must have been just waiting to be married, I realised. I tried intently to imagine my father (missing, presumed dead) taking up the space that Gerry was filling now; but my picture of my father was too vague, Gerry was too assertive. He was sweaty, naturally, after the work he'd done; his hair was wet because he'd doused his head under the tap in the bathroom. His bodily presence intruded every way I turned, making the new house seem crowded when I ought to have felt its succession of spaces flowering ahead of me, after the two rooms that Mum and I had shared since I could remember. As twilight thickened outside, the house's shell seemed too pervious, swelling with the electric light as if it were as insubstantial as the canvas tents at school camp.

Mum and Gerry discussed with deep interest the economics of using the immersion heater. After he'd dried each cup and plate he held it up to the light to inspect it. He complained that when I washed up I splashed water on the floor and used too much squeegee. Already I didn't like living with him, and it had only been a matter of hours. I retreated to my cell-bedroom where at least now a bed was installed – though it wasn't the old double bed that I'd slept in since I outgrew my cot. That bed had never been ours, apparently; it had belonged to the old flat. On this new narrow one was a pile of ironed candy-stripe sheets. With a martyred consciousness – where did they think I was? why didn't they wonder? – I tucked them inexpertly over the mattress, then climbed between them in my knickers and vest. I heard my mother and Gerry talking downstairs. Though I couldn't make out their words, I knew that they were deciding with wholehearted adult seriousness where to put each piece of furniture. The rumble of their dialogue was lulling, melancholy, remote. Then someone was running a bath; unfamiliar pipes groaned and eased too near at hand. There were no curtains at my window yet. In the dark I missed the view from my old room intensely, and I didn't want to think about the non-trees I had conjured into being.

We moved just before the beginning of the summer holidays. (I had one year left of junior school.) Madeleine and I were bound to become friends over that summer – we had nothing else to do. During the holidays in the past, when Mum went to work I was left at Nana's or at Auntie Jean's. Now (Nana wasn't capable any longer and Gerry didn't like Jean) I stayed at home, under the supervision of Madeleine's mother Pam, who offered because it meant that Madeleine had someone to play with. Pam was cheerfully casual and didn't bother us; she sometimes took us swimming. I think she felt sorry for me, left all alone, but actually I was relieved to have the house to myself. Mum left paste sandwiches and crisps and Penguins in the fridge. Madeleine watched me eat, sliding her feet under the kitchen table and hanging from its edge like a monkey: for a tubby girl she was unexpectedly flexible, turning cartwheels easily and walking on her hands. There was no one to stop me

beginning with chocolate and finishing with my sandwiches stuffed with crisps. I gulped milk from the bottle,
wiping its creamy moustache on to my sleeve; I cooked
up messes of butter and sugar in a pan.

I moved around the new house in the adults' absence
as if I were taking soundings. Sometimes Madeleine and
I were experimentally raucous, clattering and screaming,
flying down the stairs two or three at a time. The house's
air, one moment after we'd shattered it, was blandly
restored. I picked up ornaments, poked in the miscellany
of small things that had been put inside them for safe
keeping, opened drawers. I had no criteria of taste by
which to judge what was there (wood veneer, streamlined
forms, tapering peg-legs, fitted carpets, a television inside
a cabinet with doors, curtains with a print of autumn
leaves); and so I felt the impact of the rooms purely, their
bright brisk statement, their light and order which aspired
to weightlessness and dustlessness.

Gerry's desk drawers were boring, full of papers having
to do with dull mysteries: mortgages and insurance. With
a kitchen knife I made a tiny nick in the wood at the
back of the kneehole in the desk, near the floor. I was
filled with trepidation next time he sat down to do the
accounts and pay the bills, but he never noticed – nor
when I added new nicks in the years afterwards, every
time I was most incandescently angry with him. He did
notice that I had been through his drawers, and also that
we had bounced on the sofa, rucking the covers and
denting the cushions. And although I had washed up
after my sugar-messes, like forensic scientists he and

Mum somehow discovered traces of my cooking stuck around the bottom of the pan.

— She's got to learn, Gerry said. — She's not a baby any longer.

I was clumsy, easily distracted, I was 'always in a dream'. Gerry dug out the form of this hapless personality for me; out of perversity, defiantly, I felt myself pouring into it and setting hard. I wasn't pretty or charming or malleable. I went around with a suffering face. I read my book with my fingers in my ears. I wouldn't laugh at Gerry's jokes. I lost my door key or I went out with Madeleine leaving the back door unlocked. I left the hot tap running in the bathroom, then I forgot my cardigan at the swimming pool. Gerry rarely lost his temper with me; not in that early time. He never, ever hit me.

And of course days passed, even weeks sometimes, when he and I weren't in any sort of outright conflict. Sometimes we were even all right together. Once, when he and Mum both had time off work, we went out for the day to Brean Down and Gerry and I climbed the dunes in our flip-flops, sliding back one step for every two we took on the shifting sand; he held out his hand to me and pulled me up after him. His hands were brown and strong with neat-trimmed nails as thick as horn. He always wore a watch with one of those expanding metal bands (I worried that it must catch in the curling black hairs on his arm), and a wedding ring, which men didn't often do in those days. Mum stood below with her hair escaping from her headscarf, whipping across her face in the wind, calling out to us to be careful, that the dunes were treacherous, we could be buried alive. And Gerry and I laughed together.

When I was in trouble, however, he sat opposite me in the lounge, leaning forward with his elbows on his knees and his forehead wrinkled: I felt the whole force of his personality bent upon me – thwarted, concentrated, blinkered. (— You'll find nothing's handed to you on a plate, he said. — It's no good thinking you can stay wrapped up in your own little world. Do you have any idea how hard your mother has to work, to earn the money to buy you food and clothes?) In a reasonable voice he communicated his warnings about the meanness at the heart of things, which he understood and I, in my childishness, was refusing to acknowledge.

No doubt he really thought it was his duty, in my father's place, to teach me to adapt to the way things were. The trouble was, I hardly knew him. I didn't exactly argue with him. I sometimes said, 'I didn't mean to' in a flippant voice, or denied things it was obvious I had done. If he asked me why I'd done them I said I didn't know. I put my hands under my thighs on the chair, swung my legs and looked off into the corners of the room; my expression was a slippery mask clamped on my face. All my effort was used to keep my mouth curved upward in a grimacing smile, which I knew was my best weapon because it made Gerry squeeze his fists and raise his voice.

Then Mum would appear from the kitchen. — That's

enough, she would say, tactfully as if she was saying it to me. — Go up to your room, Stella.

Tugging me backward and forward between them, she and Gerry expressed the tension in their new life together. He wanted his new wife to himself; he hadn't reckoned on finding me his rival for her attentions. Mum, with her quick scepticism, must have seen how he deceived himself, dissimulating his resentment, pretending to be impartial. She must have remonstrated with him over how relentlessly he came in pursuit of me, though it was part of their code that she would never openly take my side against him. (And although I was wounded by his taking her away from me, I also dreaded catching sight of any rift between them.)

Let's be clear — our fight was mutual. I was set against Gerry just as he was against me. Only I was a child, so he had power over me. That's all tyranny is: it's not in a personality, it's in a set of circumstances. It's being trapped with your enemy in a limited space — a country, or a family — where the balance of power between you is unequal, and the weaker one has no recourse.

Because the tree cult began in the shapeless days of summer, there was no drudging sanity of school at first to counteract its power. I came up with the idea of kissing the stumps and leaving offerings among the roots or pressed into the cracks — salt, currants, sherbet. We smeared the resin on our foreheads. (— You're filthy, my mother said when she got home. — Go and wash your face.) The three stumps in our gardens grew distinctive personalities and we named them (Iskarion, Vedar, Mori). They were jealous, capricious, closely informed about our daily lives. More awesome and less easy to propitiate were the nameless stumps we had no access to, in other gardens. Madeleine used to dab the resin on her tongue and then groan and double up, clutching her stomach, making a great fuss over how it had poisoned her. It was her idea that we should cut ourselves and rub our blood into the bark.

The ritual half slaked a thirst I hadn't known I had. I'd never been touched by religion at school, though we'd traced St Paul's journeys in our scripture books and coloured in donkeys for Palm Sunday. Mum and Nana had only ever referred to the church suspiciously; it was good for children but also a conspiracy of certain social types, thinking themselves superior. I pushed myself, trying to receive intimations of the sacred trees' living existence; occasionally, alone, I could fall into an ecstasy of belief. At other times I watched myself, sceptical of the authenticity of my transports. Sometimes, after the sessions with Madeleine, I was visited by a kind of Protestant disgust at our excesses; the more we thrilled and overdid it, the more it was only a game. For a couple of days I wouldn't play, no matter how much Madeleine pouted and sulked. Then – once on a Sunday evening in my bath when late sunlight, reflected off the bathwater, made restless patterns on the ceiling – I'd be visited by the balm of a vision of great trees, at the very moment when I least thought of asking for it.

At the end of the summer, when Madeleine and I went

back to our different schools, the cult cooled down but didn't die. Out of superstitious habit we still left offerings at the stumps for good luck, and carried bits of bark around in our pockets, fingering them out of the teachers' sight.

Gerry insisted I should sit the entrance exam for the direct-grant secondary schools. I got good marks in class and always had my head stuck in a book. Anyway, not many children in Stoke Bishop went to the local comprehensive. Madeleine was taking the exam, too – though she didn't have to do so well in it, because her parents could pay. I needed a scholarship place. I sat the exam. I didn't care how I did, I wasn't frightened of it: school up to that point had left me unscathed. I didn't make the connection that Gerry did between the power of what I read in books and the outward husk of learning, perfectly functional but not involving, that went on in the classroom.

Consulting no one, I had promoted myself at our local library to adult books – which meant climbing three steps, covered in yellow lino, into the upper portion of the brick building with its sensuous hush and beamed Arts and Crafts ceiling. I didn't know where to begin; I was drawn to complete works in uniform bindings because I thought they would be series like the ones I had loved in the children's section: *Anne of Green Gables* and *The Naughtiest Girl in the School*. Often I hardly knew what was happening in the novels I fell upon by chance (Compton Mackenzie, Faulkner, Hugh Walpole,

Elizabeth Bowen), but I read absorbedly nonetheless, half disappointed, half revelling in the texture of these worlds jumbling in my ignorance: servants, telegrams, cavalry, race, guilt, dressing for dinner (what time was dinner? and were they still in their pyjamas?) – and elliptical conversations unlike any I'd ever heard, signifying things I could only guess at. I gave up on some, but the books were an initiation. I began piecing their worlds together in my comprehension.

I got a scholarship for the Girls' High School (and Madeleine got in too, without the scholarship). Mum took me out to buy me a briefcase and we had lunch in British Home Stores. She was proud that I had proved myself at least good for something. Gerry said, — She'll have a lot more to live up to, now.

I can't remember how I found out that Gerry was brought up in the Homes – I suppose Mum must have told me. He didn't speak to me about it until long afterwards. (At the time he only said, — Not everyone has your opportunities.) The Homes was an orphanage, a vast neoclassical grey stone building set back from a main road, its front implacable as a hospital or a prison. We said at junior school that the children who came from there smelled of wee and wore one another's clothes. They didn't have real mothers, only aunties.

This knowledge I had of Gerry lodged in me like a stone. It didn't make me like him any better. It seemed an extra twist to how arbitrarily he and I were fastened together: I had to bear the burden of his childhood

66

sorrows too. He had done heroically well, working his way up at the Board Mill, overcoming the handicap of his beginnings (his mother hadn't been 'able to look after him'). I was determined not to care. My own selfishness seemed to eat me up; I worked at being oblivious of all my advantages. I ran away from home and went to Nana's. ('Your mother's been out of her mind with worry.') Out at the stumps with Madeleine, I smoked cigarettes and threw up. I told my mother I was only happy at the stables. Madeleine came riding with me, bouncing unconvincingly on Boy, her smile uneasy, double chin squeezed in the too-tight strap of the brand-new hard hat Pam had bought her. She held her nose and pretended to retch when the ponies dropped their dung.

I hated the High School. Madeleine and I hated it together, though differently. Her face, wiped clear of guile, goaded one or two of the more savage teachers who mistook her blankness for insolence. At first it seemed that I had the gift of invisibility. I sank back into the middle of the range of achievement. I kept my mouth shut in class and out of it. I absorbed obsessively the intricate system of their prohibitions, so as not to attract attention by transgressing – no fewer than five lace-holes in our outdoor shoes, no green ink, all textbooks to be covered in brown paper, girls not to use the toilet in twos (in junior school we had often crowded three or four into the little cubicles, to gossip). By the end of the first week I knew that I'd found my way, through some terrible error, into enemy territory where I must as a matter of life or death keep my true self concealed. The school was a mill whose purpose was to grind you into its product. Every subject shrank to fit inside its exam questions; even – especially – the books we read in English lessons. We were supposed to be grateful, having been selected for this grinding; and most of the girls were grateful. Madeleine and I didn't fit in. Our tree cult revived and garnered new passionate power through being driven into opposition – with our bark fragments in our pockets we were like Catholic recusants fingering hidden rosaries, and we had a code of words and signs to communicate our refusal and our mockery.

Meanwhile my mother began wearing looser dresses. It wasn't the fashion for parents to explain themselves to their children. Mum never told me she was pregnant; only hinted at a significant change coming. I was slow to the point of stupidity in picking up her suggestions. Why was she putting her feet up every evening after supper, while Gerry and I did the dishes in competitive silence? Some conspiracy surrounded her, which I recoiled from as if I guessed it had humiliation in it for me. One Saturday morning, watching from my bedroom window while she hung out washing on the metal clothes tree in the garden (turfed at least by this time, if not yet the little paradise of planting it later became under Gerry's green-fingered stewardship), I saw what I had not allowed myself to see: the wet sheets billowed like fat sails filled with the wind, and she billowed too. Ducking out of sight behind my window, so that she wouldn't know I knew, I crouched around my discovery in the tight space between the bed leg and the dolls' cot, with my back to the pink-sprigged wallpaper I had chosen and Gerry had cut and pasted and put up. (I picked at the edges of this paper sometimes, where he wouldn't notice it, when I was in bed at night; sometimes I spat into the gap beside the bed and let my saliva trickle down the wall.)

My mother had betrayed herself, pretending to be complete and then letting this invasion inside her body as if she was not herself but any other woman. I'd never considered any relationship between my own mother and the not-quite-interesting mystery of prams and bibs and bottles. She was too sensible, too old, I had always thought. She had never even seemed to like babies, or made any fuss over them. Except me. Once upon a time she must have changed nappies and heated bottles of milk for me, fussed over me. But that was a lifetime ago.

My mother had to go into hospital for the last weeks of her pregnancy, because her blood pressure was too high. Gerry and I were left in a tense proximity at home. He made my tea when he came in from work, a procedure we both found painful. He tied Mum's apron over his shirt and suit trousers, then with an air of weary duty set about producing fish fingers, baked beans, bacon, sausages, pork chops, chips. For a man of that era he really wasn't bad at it. In fact, he may have been a better cook than my mother was – she was pretty awful. Only he didn't know the little foibles of my likes and dislikes the way she did. I ate everything he put in front of me. I think I was afraid of him, alone in the house without her – afraid at least of his contempt. But I didn't eat it enthusiastically. I cut every piece of toast, or potato, or sausage laboriously into minute pieces before I even tasted them. Then one by one I swallowed these pieces, trying not to chew, washing them down with mouthfuls from my glass of water, asking for more water frequently. Though he couldn't have known it, I was doing my best.

I saw that I put him off his own dinner (which he ate with the apron still on).

– Just eat it, for goodness' sake, he said. – Chew it up.

He sat at an angle, hunched around his plate, so that he didn't have to watch me. After tea, he made me do my homework on the dining-room table. We never used the dining room to eat in except at Christmas or on the rare occasions that we had guests, so it was chilly and transitional: papered olive-green, with doors at either end and a serving hatch, African violets on the windowsill, a memory of stale gravy in the air. Letters and paperwork and Mum's sewing washed up on the repro rosewood dining table, among the place mats with scenes from old-world English villages. Miserably I cleared myself a space. I had to spread newspaper in case I made marks on the polished surface.

After long days of lessons, we were given two or three hours of homework every night. For most of that first year at the High School I aimed for average marks that would not draw anyone's attention. I wasn't consciously holding back – it hadn't yet occurred to me to desire praise, prizes, distinctions. In science and maths I struggled anyway. The physics teacher was merciless. Handsome, tall, unmarried, with a rope of white hair twisted round her temples, she belonged to the generation of women who had sacrificed everything for their education. We were supposed to learn the principles of physics not by rote but through problem-solving. One evening I was wrestling with a question about acceleration: the hare catching up with the tortoise in a race. Actual tears splashed on to the page, blotting the blue ink of my workings; my mind ached with the effort. At junior school I had been good at problems: 'If Harry and Dick together weigh nine stone four pounds, Dick and Tom together weigh eight stone twelve pounds . . .', and so on – but those problems had been for beginners, I saw now. I urged my mind to take the intuitive leap into comprehension, but again and again it baulked. Gerry looked in on me, bringing the cup of milky, sugary, instant coffee my mother usually brought. He really was trying hard.

– What's the matter? Are you stuck?

Our voices startled us, alone in the house without Mum – they seemed to break a silence locked like rusting machinery. I knew how I must look to him, slumped in defeat at the table, pasty-faced with worry. The teacher's scorn made no distinction between those who tried and failed and those who didn't try. I had no pride where my school work was concerned – it occurred to me that Gerry might be able to help me. He worked with numbers all day in the office; I took it for granted he would understand the problem.

— So long as it isn't French, he said cheerfully enough, and pulled up a chair beside me, striped shirtsleeves rolled businesslike up to the elbow. He always radiated a clean heat, from those strenuous sessions in the bathroom which left the walls dripping and the mirrors cloudy. I explained that the hare was sleeping at a location twelve hundred metres from the finish line; the tortoise passed him at a steady speed of five centimetres per second. Six and a half hours later, the hare woke up. All of these elements by now had attained a hallucinatory meaninglessness in my head.

Gerry read the problem over to himself, biting my pen, frowning down at the worn-soft, scrambled page of my homework book. What minimum acceleration (assumed constant) must the hare have in order to cross the finish line first? He worked out easily in his head how long it would take for the tortoise to get there; then went over and over the other elements, sketching a little diagram for himself, the hare's trajectory cutting across the tortoise's just before the finish line. I saw that he wanted it to be like one of the Dick and Harry problems, giving way to common sense or to a trick of thought.

— How do we calculate acceleration? he asked. — Haven't they taught you how? Have you done other problems like this one?

I found in the back of my book a formula that the teacher had given us, expressing D in terms of O, V, T and A, but I didn't even know what those letters stood for. Gerry thought that perhaps D was distance, but we already knew the distance. His hand began to leave sweat marks on the page as mine had. He wondered just when the hare needed to pass the tortoise in order to get to the finish line ahead of it; how tiny might the difference between them be? His efforts snagged on this doubt, building up behind it. — You have to concentrate better in class, he said. — She must have shown you how to do this. Can't you remember?

I shrugged, recoiling. I should have known that I would be to blame.

— Physics is boring.

He tried again, stating the elements of the problem over in a reasonable, steadying voice. All the time, he must have been consumed with his real worries about my mother's condition and what lay ahead for them; about his responsibility for me.

— Write me a note, I said. — Tell the teacher I was ill.

— Don't be silly. All you need to do is to ask her to explain it to you.

— You don't understand what she's like! I wailed.

And then somehow we upset my coffee cup. It really wasn't clear to me which one of us did it: I may have thrown out my hand rhetorically; he may have reached for a pencil without looking. Hot, milky, sugary coffee flooded everywhere, soaking instantly through the layers of newspaper, slewing into our laps, pooling on the precious polished surface of the table. We both threw ourselves backwards. I snatched up my homework book – though not before a few splashes dashed across the page, elegant illustrations of the physics of liquid form. (The teacher, the following week, would ring these splashes in red biro, writing 'Disgusting & slovenly presentation' – but by then I didn't care.) Gerry grabbed at a heap of bills, and Mum's sewing – she was making things for the new baby. Too late; coffee stains had seeped already into the cut-out pieces of the little gingham romper suit.

— Stella! You idiot! he yelled, shoving me roughly out of the way of the coffee dripping on to the carpet, and on to my fawn socks.

I stumbled backwards, genuinely confused. — Was it my fault?

Gerry ran to fetch tea towels from the kitchen to soak up the coffee, then filled a bucket with soapy water and disinfectant. He set to work systematically, mopping and rubbing and wiping just as my mother would have done, changing the water every so often. Spilt milk was one of the things Mum and Gerry dreaded above all else; if you failed to eradicate every trace, the smell as it soured came back to haunt you. While he wiped, I stood frowning at my homework.

— What are we going to do with that skirt? Gerry said, his voice embittered, doomsday-flat. — You'd better take it off. If I wash it out, it'll never be dry for tomorrow. I'll try to leach the worst of the coffee out of it without soaking it. At least you've got a clean shirt I can iron.

I unbuttoned the skirt and stepped out of it, still staring at the book. Something had happened; I could see all the elements of the problem differently now, as if they had arranged themselves naked under a bright light. — Look, I said, exulting. — D is distance. A must be acceleration. We need to rearrange the equation so that A is by itself on one side of the equals sign. OV must be original velocity, which is nought – the hare's asleep – so that cancels out. Times both sides by two, divide by time squared. Acceleration equals two times distance over time squared.

He didn't even answer; naturally enough, at that moment he didn't much care about my physics home-work. He was too busy trying to sop spilt coffee from the carpet while his sulky stepdaughter stood in her knickers, not lifting a finger to help him.

Or he hated his failure to know more than I did, be cleverer than I was.

That was how I got to know that I was clever. When I cleaned my teeth that night in the bathroom, my face was different in the mirror: as if a light had gone on behind my eyes, or an inner eye had been strained open. Every inch of my skin, every pore, every fixture in the bathroom was accessible to my vision pressing remorse-lessly onward, devouring the world's substance, seeing through it. I could see my own face as if it wasn't mine. I pressed my nose to the mirror, baring my teeth at myself, misting the glass with breath. At first this clever-ness was like a sensation of divinity; then after a while it ate itself and I couldn't turn the mind-light off, couldn't stop thinking through everything, couldn't sleep. I saw Gerry – and my mother, and my school – all as if they were tiny, in the remote distance. I believed that if I wanted to I could solve all the problems in the physics teacher's book. When eventually sleep came, I seemed to hear the soughing of trees outside in the empty air. I understood all about those trees, I grasped what they were: how they existed and did not exist, how both contradictory realities were possible at once.

Four

Madeleine and I are waiting at the bus stop at the bottom of Beech Grove in our summer school uniform: green print dresses, short white socks and sandals, blazer. In the summer we are allowed to leave off our hated green felt hats. Summer is thick everywhere, a sleepy, viscous, sensuous emanation; hot blasts of air, opaque with pollen from the overblown suburban gardens, ripe with wafts from bins and dog mess. We are mad with summer, chafing and irritable with sex. We're in the fourth year, studying for our O levels; we have breasts (small in my case – luscious in Madeleine's) and pubic hair and periods. A breeze, stirring the dust in the gutter sluggishly, tickles up round our thighs, floats our dresses – we can hardly bear it.

Our talk is rococo with insincerity, drawling, lascivious. We sound at that age huskier from smoking than we ever do later when we smoke much more. We say that the pods in the gardens are bursting with seeds, and that we like to eat ripe melons, and that the cars are covered with sticky stuff dropped off the trees – everything seems obscene with double significance, even though it's only quarter past eight in the morning and behind us in our homes our mothers are clearing the breakfast tables, scraping soggy Rice Krispies and burnt toast crusts into the bin, wiping the plastic tablecloths. My mother is bending over Philip in his high chair, playing pat-a-cake to trick him into letting her wipe his face and hands, making his mouth spill open in delighted laughter, his eyes roll up. She lifts up his little shirt and kisses his belly; I might be jealous except that I haven't got time to crane that way, backwards towards home and the cramped circle of old loves. My attention is all thrusting forward, onward, out of there. I've burned my boats, I can't go back – or rather, I do go back, dutifully, every evening after school, and do my homework still at the same table in the same stale olive-green dining room, and still get the best marks in the class for every-thing, nearly everything (I even manage not to fail in physics). But it's provisional, while I wait for my real life to begin. I feel like an overgrown giant in that house, bumping up against the ceiling like Alice in Wonderland after she's found the cake labelled 'Eat Me': head swollen with knowledge and imagination, body swollen with sensation and longing.

Madeleine and I have never even kissed boys: at fifteen we don't have any actual sexual experience whatever except a few things we've done with each other, experi-mentally, and out of desperation. (Not shamefaced after-wards – flaunting and wicked; it is the 1970s, after all.

But it's boys we want.) At an all-girls school we don't get many chances to meet boys, although there are usually some on the bus, going in to the Grammar School. This is a part of our excitement, at quarter past eight. There are certain boys we are expecting to see, and we may even pluck up the crazy courage to speak to them, a word or two; any exchange will be dissected afterwards between Madeleine and myself in an analysis more nuanced and determined than anything we ever do to poems in English lessons. ('What do you think he really meant when he said that his friend had said yesterday that you weren't bad?')

Anything can happen in the bus in the next half an hour; even something with the power to obliterate and reduce to dust the double maths, scripture, double Latin and (worst) games which lie in wait at the end of the journey – a doom of tedium, infinitely long, impossible to bear. After games, the nasty underground shower room with its concentrated citrus-rot stink of female sweat, its fleshly angsts, tinpot team spirit, gloom of girls passed over, games teacher's ogling, trodden soaking towels.

Something has to happen.

Into our heat that morning came Valentine.

He walked down to join us at the bus stop. We'd never seen him before: into the torpor of the suburb his foot-steps broke like a signal for adventure on a jaunty trumpet. I loved his swaggering walk immediately without reserve (and never stopped loving it). His glancing, eagerly amused look around him – drinking everything in, shaking the long hair back from around his face – was like a symbol for morning itself. (His energy was no doubt partly the effect of the Dodos – caffeine pills – he'd have swallowed in the bathroom as soon as his mother got him out of bed. Soon we were all taking them.) A Grammar School blazer, hooked by its loop around one nicotine-stained finger, was slung over his shoulder, his cigarette cocked up cheekily between lips curved as improbably, generously wide as a faun's. The pointed chin was like a faun's too, and the flaunting Caravaggio cheekbones, pushing up the thick flesh under his eyes, making them slanted and mischievous. He was tall, but not too tall; his school trousers slid down his impossibly narrow waist and hips, he tucked his shirt half in with a careless hand. The school tie others wore resentfully as a strangled knot became under his touch somehow cravat-like, flowing. The top two buttons of his shirt were undone. He was sixteen (a year older than we were).

He grinned at Madeleine and me.

At me first, then at Madeleine, which was not usual. Madeleine in her lazy indifference had bloomed, she was willowy and languorous, sex had dusted a glitter into her long curls and kitten-face, her pink cheeks. I was too small, too plump and shapeless, and my eyes, I knew, were blackly expressive pits in a too-white face. Madeleine, trying kindly to advise me on my sex appeal (I asked her), had said I might be 'too intense' – but I didn't know how to disguise that. Valentine stopped at the bus stop and offered us his cigarette, me first. It was not any ordinary cigarette, oh no! (we went to school stoned for the first time, but not the last).

— Hello girls, he said, beaming. — Does this bus go into town? Do you catch it every day? That's good. I like the look of you.

We looked at each other and giggled and asked him what he liked about us. Thinking about it, surveying us up and down, he said we looked sceptical.

What did he mean, sceptical?

Thank God we weren't wearing our hats.

I longed for the bus not to come. Proximity to his body – a glimpse via his half-untucked shirt of hollowed, golden, masculine stomach, its line of dark hairs draining down from the belly button – licked at me like a flame while we waited. His family, he explained, had just moved into one of the posher streets behind Beech Grove. When the bus did come he sat on the back seat and took Beckett out of his rucksack: *End Game*. The very title, even the look of the title – its stark indiscreet white capitals on a jazzy orange cover – was a door swinging suddenly open into a new world. I'd never heard of Beckett; I think I was ploughing then through *The Forsyte Saga*. None of the other boys on the bus read books. Val smiled at us encouragingly, extravagantly, over the top of his.

— He was gorgeous, I liked him, Madeleine conceded as we trudged in a tide of other green-gowned inmates up the purgatorial hill from our stop to where school loomed, the old house frowning in the sunlight as a prison. — But I couldn't actually fancy him, could you? There was something weird.

81

I was disappointed in her; I was already wondering if I'd find Beckett in the local library. (The librarian, warmly supportive of my forays into Edwardian belles-lettres, would startle and flinch at my betrayal.) And my heart raced at the idea that Valentine might not be at the bus stop the next day. (But he was – and was there most days, right through to the middle of the upper sixth.) Madeleine didn't insist on her doubt, she never insisted – and I closed a door on an early intimation of danger. I wanted Val because he was different – as I was different. What I felt at my first sight of him that summer morning was more than ordinary love: more like recognition. When I read later in Plato about whole souls divided at birth into two separated halves, which move around in the world ever afterwards mourning one another and longing for a lost completion, I thought I was reading about myself and Valentine.

And it was the same for Val. He recognised me too.

I truly do believe that, even now, even after everything that happened. We found each other out, we were kindred spirits, it was mutual.

— What a scarecrow, Gerry said after he came to my house for the first time. — I can't believe the Grammar School let him get away with that hair.

— He looks like a girl, my mother said. — I'm not that keen, Stella.

Following up the stairs behind Val, I was faint from the movement of his slim haunches in his tight white jeans. How could she think that he looked like a girl?

Yet all we did in my bedroom was cosy up knee to knee, cross-legged on the bed to talk. We swapped our childhood stories. He was born in Malaya, he had had an ayah.

— What were your family doing in Malaya?

— You don't want to know.

— I want to know everything.

— My father worked for the government, he's an awful tax expert. Now he's retired, he's just awful and old. What does yours do?

— He's not my real dad. My real dad's dead.

Mum brought in a pile of ironed clothes to put away in my chest of drawers. Then she called to ask if we wanted coffee. Philip came knocking at the door, asking us to play with him. Afterwards Mum spoke to me awkwardly, about self-respect. The familiar solidity of the house and its furniture melted away around Val; after he'd left I couldn't believe I really lived there. I couldn't hold in the same focus my two worlds brought into conjunction. Yet I wanted Val to be brilliant for my parents and he wouldn't, or couldn't. He never made any concessions to them, or small talk. If they asked him questions he sometimes didn't even seem to hear them; his eyes were blank. He seemed to simply pause the flow of his life in the presence of anyone unsympathetic.

He was stoned a lot of the time.

Yet among our friends he was magnetic, commanding, funny. He was a clever mimic. In the evenings we started getting together at Madeleine's – a whole gang of six or seven of us from the streets round about. Madeleine's father was often away; her mother Pam was bored and liked flirting with teenagers. She brought home-made brownies and cheese straws and jugs of weak sangria up to Madeleine's room and we cadged her cigarettes. Madeleine fancied a boy who played the guitar and wrote his own songs; we tried to talk a shy, blonde girl out of her faith. Madeleine bought a red bulb to put in one of the lamps, we draped the others with Indian silk scarves. When my stepfather was sent across to fetch me home, he never stepped across the low fence between our front gardens but went punctiliously via both front paths and gates. He said if Pam wanted teenagers carrying on under her own roof it was her business.

— What's this? he joked, when I brought Beckett back from the library.

— He's a play writer. Haven't you heard of him?

— Playwright. (Gerry did crosswords, he had a good vocabulary.) — Aren't they all waiting for some chap who never turns up?

Gerry had been so keen for me to go to the High School; yet he was hostile to the power my education brought me. He thought I was putting on airs – and I expect I was, I was probably pretty insufferable with my quotations from Shakespeare and Gerard Manley Hopkins, my good French accent (I corrected his: *ça ne fait rien*, not san fairy ann). He could still usually trip me up, though, in geography or history – my sense of things fitting together was treacherously vague. Gerry knew an awful lot, he was always reading. He subscribed by post to a long series of magazines about the Second

World War, which he kept in purpose-made plastic folders on a shelf. Already, invidiously, however, I had an inkling that the books he read were somehow not the *real* books.

He was amused and patient, correcting my mistakes. He did it to my mother too: so long as we were wrong, then he was kind. If I could have given in gracefully to that shape of relations between us – his lecturing me and my submitting to it – then we might have been able to live happily together. My mother didn't care about knowing things, she just laughed at him. ('Oh, for goodness' sake, Gerry – as if it mattered!') But I couldn't give in. It was a struggle between our different logics. Everything I learned, I wanted to be an opening into the unknown; whereas Gerry's sums added up in a closed circle, bringing him safely back to where he began, confirming him.

I took Beckett up to my bedroom.

It wasn't the kind of writing I was used to. I'd taught myself to stir in response to the captured textures of passing moments – the subtle essence of unspoken exchange, the sensation of air in a room against the skin. Now, I learned to read Beckett (and then, under Val's influence, Ginsberg, Burroughs, Ferlinghetti) like a convert embracing revolutionary discipline, cutting all links with my bourgeois-realist past.

— Is he your boyfriend then? Madeleine wanted clarification.

I was disdainful. — We don't care about those kinds of labels.

— But is he?

— What does it look like?

Val and I were inseparable. We saw each other almost every day – not only on the bus going to school and coming back, but in the evenings, as often as my parents allowed me out or said he could come round. They claimed they worried about my school work but I didn't believe them, I saw in my mother's face her recoil from what she dreaded – the dirty flare of sex and exposure; my making a fool of myself. (They were so innocent, I don't think they guessed about the drugs until much later.) Sometimes I went out anyway when they'd forbidden me, and then there was trouble. When I got home Gerry took me into the lounge for one of his old lectures, screwing up his forehead, leaning towards me, pretending to be impartial justice. From my dizzy vantage point (high as a kite), I believed I could see right through him to his vindictiveness, his desire to shoot me down where I was flying.

— They hate me, I said to Val. — Under his pretence of being concerned for my future, he really he hates me. And she doesn't care.

— Don't mind them, Val said, his eyes smiling. He blew out smoke, he was serene, bare feet tucked up on his knees in the lotus position. — They're just frightened. They're sweet really, your parents.

We were talking in his bedroom, so unlike my little pink cell: a draughty attic where his books and clothes lay around in chaos on a Turkey carpet grey with cigarette ash. (When I asked if his mother never cleaned in

86

there he said she didn't clean anywhere, they had a woman in.) His attitude towards his own parents was coolly disengaged. I was afraid of them, I tried to avoid meeting them on my passages through the rambling big house (built when Stoke Bishop was still the country-side). They were both tall and big-boned: his father was stooped, with brown-blotched skin, long earlobes, thinning white hair; his mother had a ruined face and watery huge eyes, she wore pearls and Chinese jade earrings at the dining table in the evenings (unlike us, they actually ate in their dining room). The arrangement of their furniture – elegant, shabby, mixed with exotica from the East – seemed provisional; they had only just moved in, and might move on. They were polite with me, and their conversation was as dully transactional as anything in my house – yet in their clipped, swallowed voices they seemed to talk in code above my head.

Val had older sisters and brothers who had left home but often came visiting, or taking refuge from some drama in their complicated lives: all good-looking and daunt-ingly confident, even if they seemed conventional beside Val. They called their parents Mummy and Daddy (Val didn't call them anything, in my hearing). His sister Diana – next to him in age, excitable, with dark hair cut in a thick fringe and very white teeth – chatted to me about horses and somehow I knew not to give away too much detail about Budge's ramshackle stables. When I asked if Diana had been to university, she laughed at me. — Darling, I can hardly read. I've never passed an exam in my life, I'm virtually an idiot.

When he was bantering with his sister, petulant, I got a glimpse for a moment of a different Valentine: less sublimely solitary, more a type – their type, mannered and competitive. Valentine was the baby of the family; conceived at an age when his parents ought to have known better, he said disgustedly. — I'm the painful reminder of lost virility.

— Don't take any notice of him, Diana said. — He's Mummy's little pet.

He chucked a cushion at her head. — Di's a dirty slut, he said. — She thinks through her yoni.

— My what? she giggled. — Yogi Bear?

— Ignoramus.

Apart from Diana, Val's family never came up to his attic room (nor did the cleaner). Sometimes his mother shouted up the stairs, if a meal was ready or Val was wanted on the telephone. We were private up there. I loved the evening shadows in the complex angles of the sloping ceiling. In summer the heat under the roof was dense; in winter we cuddled up for warmth under the blankets on his bed. Our bodies fitted perfectly together – my knees curved into the backs of his, my breath in the nape of his neck, his fingers knotted into mine against his chest, under his shirt; we lay talking about everything, or listening to Velvet Underground, Janis Joplin, Dylan. The shape of the long, empty room seemed the shape of our shared imagination, spacious and open to everything. I couldn't believe the long strides he'd made in his mind, all by himself. Sometimes, depending on the pills, he would talk and talk without stopping.

— How do you know that I really exist, outside you? he asked me urgently. — I might be a figment of your imagination.

Our heads were side by side then on his pillow. How lucky I was to lie like that, so intimate with his lovely looks that I couldn't see them whole: teasing green eyes, down on his upper lip, curving high hollows in his cheeks. I longed for him to begin kissing me, as he sometimes did – but I had learned that I must not try to initiate this. — But I just know! I insisted, stroking his face as if the feeling in my fingers was proof. — And I'm not a figment of yours either. I'm really here, I promise.

— I believe in you. I'm not so sure about me. You're solid. You're fierce.

I wasn't as solid as I had been. Since I met Val, I'd stopped bothering to eat. I couldn't bear my mother's gluey gravy any longer, I drank black (instant) coffee and gave up sugar; the weight had flown off me. Although I was small and Val was taller, we nonetheless came to look like a matching pair: skinny and striking. By this time we were on the fringes of a set who gathered at weekends in a sleazy bar behind a cinema in town. Val had a good instinct for the people worth getting to know – a man with freckled hands and a mane of red hair who sold him speed and other things; a clever art student, half-Greek, who played in a band (they sounded like art-punk before punk had really happened). These men were older and powerful and a lot of people were eager to be their friends, but Val was able to impress them. He was good company, with his quick wit and the cultural know-how he carried off gracefully.

I knew it mattered to Val that I looked right. I wore his shirts and his sleeveless vests and his Indian silk scarves, over the tight jeans he helped me to buy. I put kohl round my eyes, and so did he sometimes. We both dyed our hair the same dark liquorice colour (my mother was aghast, another scene – 'whatever are they going to say at school?'). I paraded up and down the attic in different outfits for his approval, getting the effect just right – and yet when we went out we looked as if we didn't care what anyone thought. Val's idea of me was that I was single-minded, fiery, uncomplicated, without middle-class falsity (– But aren't I middle-class? I asked, surprised). And I performed as his idea, became something like it.

We made plans to live abroad together – Paris or New York. He'd been to both these places, I hadn't been anywhere except Torquay and Salcombe. He described walking around the streets in those cities, buying French bread and coffee, and how we'd earn money and rent an apartment. I believed he could really make these dreamed-of things come about in real life: he had the imagination, the bravado, there was a rare blend in him of earnestness and recklessness. And he seemed to know instinctively what to read, where to go, what music to listen to. He was easily bored, and indifferent to anything he didn't like, as if it didn't exist. Psychological novels were dreary, he said. The Beatles were consumer culture. I didn't talk to him about the old-fashioned books I used to love before I met him.

— In New York I'll work as a waitress, I said, — and you can write.

— Sometimes I think I could do something with my life, he said. — But sometimes in the middle of the night, something awful happens.

— What kind of awful?

— I feel as if I've already done it, this important thing – writing a book, or whatever it is. I feel as if it was a mountain to climb, and I've toiled up the mountain and achieved the thing and then I'm coming down the other side and it's behind me, and it's nothing, it doesn't alter anything in the world by one feather's weight. And then when I wake up I panic that because I've dreamed the end of the work like that, now I'll never be able to begin.

More often Val's mood was buoyant and exhilarated, he was impatient to get started. Everyone supposed he would take the Oxbridge entrance exam, go to university. For the moment he went along with them. — My English teacher at school, he said, — he's invested a lot of hopes in me. He's giving me special tuition. I don't know how to tell him I'm leaving, not yet. Soon I will.

— Wherever you go, I said, — I'll follow you.

It was often this English teacher who phoned him up.

We ran into him once – the English teacher, Mr Harper. Val and I were arm in arm, walking down Park Street on a Saturday in the crowds of people milling and looking in the shops – jeans boutiques, bookshops, places selling Indian and Chinese knick-knacks and silver jewellery. A stubby middle-aged man was staring in at a shop window;

he veered away from it as we passed, almost walking right into us and then recognising Val, putting on a show of surprise which seemed contrived, as if he'd actually seen us coming from miles off and prepared for this scene. I thought at the time that he must be socially inept because he was such an intellectual. I knew what respect Val had for him, and that it was he who had put Val on to reading Pound and Beckett and Burroughs. But I could see that Val wished we hadn't met him – he looked shocked by this collision of the two worlds of school and home.

— Hello Valentine, Mr Harper said. He was staring leeringly at me. — What a good way to spend your Saturdays. Aren't you supposed to be revising?

— We're on our way to the reference library, Val said sulkily, blushing.

— Oh – then, I mustn't get in the way of virtue! God forbid. But I will see you Tuesday, after school?

— Is it Tuesday? Val was vague. — I'm not sure.

— You must come on Tuesday. We're broaching the divine Marianne.

I was disappointed. Val had talked about Fred Harper (the boys doing Oxbridge Entrance called him Fred) as if he was a portal to higher things – and here he was chaffing and prodding about work like any other teacher. Also, he was rumpled and pear-shaped, with pleading eyes, and a bald patch in his hair which was dark and soft like cat fur. He had a drawling posh voice. I knew there was a Mrs Harper and also children; and that Mrs Harper got bored if her husband and Val talked for hours about poetry. Sometimes she went to bed, leaving them to it.

— Who's the divine Marianne? I said jealously when we'd walked on.

Valentine shrugged, irritated. — A poet in the A-level anthology.

Mum and Gerry were afraid I was bringing contamination into their house. When I bought junk shop dresses Mum made me hang them outside in case of fleas. Val found an old homburg and wore it pulled down over his eyes.

— What does he think he looks like? Gerry said.

— What's the matter with that boy? asked Mum. — What's he hiding from?

He stood in our neat kitchen with its blue Formica surfaces, improbable – in his collarless shirt, suit waistcoat, broken canvas shoes, scrap of vermilion scarf at his neck – as an exotic bird blown off course: immobile, silent, quivering, a smile playing along his lips that was not for their benefit. Even in those days when he was fresh and boyish the drugs did leave some kind of mark on him – not damage exactly, and not unattractive, more like a patina that darkened his skin to old gold, refining its texture so that minute wrinkles came at the corner of his lids when he frowned. His eyes were veiled and smoky. He smelled, if you got up close: an intricate musk, salty, faintly fishy, sun-warmed even in winter – delicious to me.

— Hello? Anybody home behind that hair? my mother said.

Val looked at me quickly, blissfully. He would imitate her for our friends, later. While he was with me everything was funny. Without him I was exposed, on a lonely pinnacle – afraid of tumbling. They were still strong, my parents, my enemies. Their judgement of what I loved (Val, books, freedom) I couldn't, wouldn't yield to – but it weighed on me nonetheless, monumental as a stone. If I tried to carelessly condescend to them then they found me out. I was clever, I was still doing well at school, but Gerry was clever too.

— What's so wrong with communism? I'd lightly say, trying to be amused at their naïve politics. I really was amused, I knew about so much – poets and visionaries – beyond their blinkered perspective. I'd read *The Communist Manifesto.* — Doesn't it seem fairer, that everyone should start out equally, owning a share of the means of production?

— It's a nice idea, Stella, Gerry said. — Unfortunately it doesn't work out in practice. People in those countries wouldn't thank you for your high ideals; they'd rather be able to buy decent food in the shops. The trouble is, a command economy just isn't efficient, wherever it's been tried. Breaks down because of human nature in the end. Every man naturally wants to do better than his neighbour.

Because he knew those words – 'command economy' – and I didn't, how could I answer him? His knowledge was flawed, but substantial – an impregnable fortress. My attacks on it – so effective when we were apart and Gerry dwindled in imagination to a comic miniature – melted in his actual presence, so that I battered at the fortress with weak fists. In those days, even in the seventies, the establishment was not very much changed from the old order. Young people wore their hair long and had Afghan coats and went to music festivals – some young people did those things. But at the top, bearing down on everyone, there were still those ranks of sombre-suited men (and the occasional woman) – politicians, professors, policemen; inflexible, imperturbable in their confidence about what was to be taken seriously and what was not. You could jeer at them, but their influence was a fog you breathed every day, coiling into your home through their voices on radio and television and in newspapers. Gerry said that Africans suffering in a famine should know better than to have so many children, or that feminists did women no favours when they went around like tramps, or that there was no point in giving to charities because it was well known that they spent all the money on themselves.

As for my mother, cleverness could never beat her.

In my mind, I couldn't bear her limited and conventional life: housework and childcare. But in my body, I was susceptible to her impatient brisk delivery, her capable hands fixing and straightening – sometimes straightening me, brusquely, even then, when I was half grown away from her: a collar crooked or a smudge on my cheek which she scrubbed at with spit on her handkerchief. No doubt she was very attractive then, in her late thirties, if I could have seen it – compact good figure, thick hair in a bouffant short cut, definite features like

95

strokes of charcoal in a drawing. Probably she was sexy, which didn't occur to me. Being married to Gerry – and Stoke Bishop, and the baby – had given a high gloss to her demeanour, wiping away the hesitations I might have shared in once when there were just the two of us. And in her withholding and dismissive manner she seemed to communicate how women knew something prosaic and gritty and fundamental, underlying all the noise of men's talk and opinion. Something I ought to know too, or would have to come to know sooner or later.

I wanted to resist knowing it with all my force.

The summer I got my O-level results (all As apart from Cs in physics and chemistry), Uncle Ray got me a job at the chocolate factory. I wept to Val, about how the women there hated me and put me on to the worst tasks (I had to take the moulds off the hot puddings – at the end of the first day my fingers were blistered) because I was only a student worker and because I took in a book to read in my breaks. I wanted him to tell me to give it up but he didn't – I think that actually he liked the romance of my working there and having relatives who worked there – it was not 'middle class'. He said he loved my Bristol accent. Really? Did I have one? I didn't think so, my mother had always so strictly policed the way I spoke at home ('I wasn't doing anything', Stella, not 'I weren't doing nothing'). Apparently, however, I said 'reely' for really, and 'strawl' for stroll.

— Your mother has an accent too, he said. — Broader

than yours. Can't you hear it? But I prefer it to the way my parents speak.

Valentine and I were bored one night with the flirting in Madeleine's bedroom. He rolled a joint – quickly in the fingers of one hand, as only he could – and we went outside to smoke. It was summer and a moon, watery-white, sailed in and out behind dark rags of cloud blown by the wind; we lay spreadeagled on our backs on Pam's lawn. Only our finger-ends were touching – through them we communicated electrically, wordlessly, as if we emptied ourselves into each other. As the dope went to my head I thought I felt the movement of the world turning.

Then I was sure someone was spying on us from our garden next door. Madeleine's garden was perfunctory, compared to ours: there was a patio swing with chintz cushions, a birdbath on the scrappy lawn, a few plants in the flower beds. Ours was densely secretive behind fences top heavy with clematis and rose and honeysuckle; it had a trellised arbour and young fruit trees and a rockery which Gerry built to make a feature of the old tree stumps left behind by the developers. I despised his prideful ownership, the ceaseless rounds of pruning and spraying and deadheading. And I thought now that he was hidden in there, aware of Val and me. He did walk out in the garden in the dark sometimes; 'to cool off', he said. He must be skewered with irritation, snooping involuntarily.

— I don't think that my real dad's really dead, I said

aloud to Val, the words spilling unexpectedly, making the thought actual for the first time although it felt at once as if I'd been preparing it for years. I didn't know if Gerry could hear what I was saying from next door. — I think he just left my mum when I was a baby, before I had time to have any memories of him. The way people talk about him – or don't – is all wrong, for a dead person: not polite enough. Not as if he's finished. Perhaps she had to divorce him, before she married Gerry. Only they didn't bother to tell me anything about it.

Val turned his head in the grass towards where he couldn't see me clearly. — That makes sense. I wondered why there weren't photographs of him. Why don't you ask her? Do you care?

— Not really. Not if he didn't ever care, to come and find me.

— If he's alive, he's a cunt.

I agreed. — Why exchange one cunt for another?

Consoling me, Val began to stroke my hand, rubbing his thumb around my palm, then pushing it between my fingers, one by one, over and over, until I was sick with love for him, but knew better than to make any move towards him from where I lay dissolving. Val didn't like me all over him. There was a rustling from among the shrubs next door; a head like a pale moon-blob rose above the top of the clematis mound, looking far-off.

— Stella, come inside, the blob said. — You'll catch your death. That grass is damp.

98

Gerry's voice in the night was sepulchral, ridiculous, tight with disapproval.

Only when I heard it was I aware of myself sprawled so provocatively on my back with my legs spread wide apart, my arms flung open. Let him look, I thought. I didn't move. I pretended I didn't see him.

— Did you hear something? I said to Val, squeezing his hand in mine.

We were going to laugh, I knew we were.

— Come inside, Stella, now, at once, Gerry said, but keeping his voice down as if he didn't want my mother to know what he had to see. — I'm telling you. Get up!

Pointedly he didn't address Valentine, ignoring his existence.

— I think I heard something, Valentine said. — Or was it cats?

Leisurely Val sat up, crouching over the cold end of the joint, hand held up to shield it from the wind and hair falling forward, hiding his face. Then came the scratch and flare of the heavy, shapely silver lighter that had been his mother's until she gave up smoking; fire bloomed momentarily in Valentine's cave, I saw him aflame – devilish, roseate. I scrambled to my feet. I really was stoned, the garden swung in looping arcs around me.

— Oh, I cried, exulting in it. — Oh . . . oh!

We were laughing now. Under my soles, the world rocked, and steadied itself, and rocked again.

— What's the matter with you? Gerry hissed. He must have been balancing on something – a rock? or a box? – on the other side of the fence, because it was too tall ordinarily to see over; his two fists, hanging on, were smaller moon-blobs against the night. — Are you drunk?

(They still didn't get it, about what we were smoking.)

— You'd better come back the front way. Come round by the front door.

— Back the front way, Stella? Valentine imitated softly, looking at me, not at Gerry. — Front the back way? Which way d'you like?

I had always had this gift to see myself as my stepfather saw me – only in this vision I used to be a small and thwarted thing, blocking him. Now in the moonlight I was transfigured: arms outstretched, veering like a yacht tacking, I was crossing the garden, flitting ahead of the wind, like a moth, weightless.

Valentine and I looked so consummately right as a couple: stylish, easily intimate without fuss, his arm dropped casually across my shoulder, our clasped hands swinging together. We looked sexy. I knew that because I saw it in the others' faces. Oh well. The truth was, we hadn't had sex much. (I think Madeleine half guessed this.) All those times we lay down on his bed together (or, occasionally, mine) we hadn't done an awful lot – apart from our talk – for Mum and Gerry to disapprove of.

We did work ourselves up, there was some touching and fumbling. I touched him, mostly; if he touched me he turned it into a joke, put on a funny voice as if my breasts were little animals squeaking and crawling around on my chest. Kissing, he pecked dry kisses all over my face with a satirical, popping noise, smiling at me all the time with his eyes open. Then sometimes if his mother banged the gong for supper, or the phone rang and she called upstairs to say that Val was wanted, he grabbed my hand with sudden aggression, pushed it down inside his jeans, used it to rub himself fiercely and greedily for a moment, before he flung off the bed and ran to the phone, zipping up as he went, cursing, pushing his erection away inside. Remember, I was wholly inexperienced, a virgin. I wasn't disgusted; actually I'd say I was more fascinated, by my transgression into that crowded heat inside his stretched underpants, his smell on my fingers afterwards. But also I was confused – if that was desire, it was unmistakably urgent. So what was the matter?

Who wants to remember the awful details of teenage sex, teenage idiocy?

I loved him because he was my twin, inaccessible to me.

One evening I was supposed to babysit while Mum and Gerry went out to a Masonic Ladies' Night. My little brother Philip was four, I liked him very much (I still do): he was always an enthusiast, entertaining us with jokes and little performances, looking quickly from face to face for our approval. He had to sit on his hands to keep them from waving about and he swung his legs under his chair until it rocked (all of this got him into trouble at school later, where he also struggled with learning to read). When Mum came downstairs, perfumed and startling in her silver Lurex bodice and stiff white skirts, he and I were laughing at *Dad's Army* on the telly. She stood clipping on her earrings by feel, giving us her instructions. This whole process of her transformation, she managed to convey, was only another duty to discharge.

— Stella, I don't want anyone coming round.

— Madeleine said she might.

— I don't want Valentine hanging around Philip if I'm not here.

I wasn't even expecting Val: he was at one of his sessions with Fred Harper. But out of nowhere – everything had been all right, the previous moment – I was dazzled with my rage. — What's the matter with you? I shouted. — Why have you got such a nasty mind?

I knew in that moment she regretted what she'd said – but only because she'd miscalculated and hadn't meant to start an argument. She was afraid it would make them late: she glanced at the wristwatch on a silver bracelet which had been Gerry's wedding present. — Who you choose as your friends is your own business, Stella, she said stiffly. — But I'm not obliged to have them in my house.

— Your house? Why d'you always call it your house? Don't I live here or something?

My stepfather hurried downstairs in his socks, doing up his cufflinks. He'd heard raised voices: I loathed him for the doggy eagerness with which he came sniffing out our fight.

— What's going on, Edna?

He irritated my mother too. — For goodness' sake

get your shoes on, Gerry. We're late already.

— I won't let her get away with talking to you like that.

— I'll talk to her how I like, I shouted. — She's my mother.

Philip went off into a corner, dancing on tiptoe with his head down, shadow-boxing, landing tremendous punches on the air: this was what he did when we were quarrelling, trying to make us laugh. *Dad's Army* wound up, the ordinary evening melted around us; then they were too late for their dinner-dance, their treat was spoiled. Mostly I was shouting and they pretended to stay calm. Soon I couldn't remember how it had all started: I felt myself washed out farther and farther from the safe place where usually we cohabited. I couldn't believe how small and far away they seemed. It was easy to say everything. — You think you're so sensible and fair, I said to Gerry. — But really I know that you want to destroy me.

— Don't be ridiculous, he said.

— Oh, Stella. D'you have to make such a performance out of everything?

Gerry said that I wasn't a very easy girl to like, and that I was arrogant and selfish. He crossed the room to close a window, because he didn't want the neighbours to hear us. At some point Philip went quietly upstairs. I said I would die if my life turned out as boring and narrow as theirs was.

— Just you wait, my mother warned. — Boring or not, you'll have to get on with it like everybody else.

Gerry called my friends dropouts and deadbeats, a waste of space.

— That's what we think you are, I said. — We think you're dead.

— I'd watch out for Valentine if I were you, my mother said. — You might be barking up the wrong tree.

Gerry did lose his temper eventually.

— Get out, Stella, if you can't respect this house. Just get out.

Mum remonstrated with him, half-heartedly.

— Don't worry, I said. — I'm going. I wouldn't stay in this house if you begged me.

They didn't beg me. It was that easy. I let myself out of the front door, into the street.

Freezing without my coat, and weeping, I went to Val's. His mother let me in and I waited for him in his attic, getting under the blankets to keep warm. When he came home from Fred Harper's I heard her expostulating downstairs, saying I couldn't stay, she wouldn't put up with it. So she didn't like me either. And I heard Val's voice raised too, shouting awful things. ('You silly bitch. Don't touch me!') Some contamination of rage was flashing round between us all that night, carried from one through another like electricity.

— I can't go back, I said, when he erupted into the room.

And I saw he understood that it was true. Anyway, he'd had a row, too – with Fred Harper. He was leaving school. We'd both leave school. What did we want with school any longer? We'd leave home too. I felt this was the beginning of my real life, which I had only been waiting for. My real life, in my imagination afterwards, always had that attic shape, high and empty and airy, cigarette smoke drifting in the light from a forty watt bulb. Val said he knew someone who had a flat where we could stay. Tomorrow he'd sort it out. For tonight I could stay here. He didn't care what his mother thought.

– Poor little Stella, he said. – Poor little you. I'm so sorry.

He was stroking my arms and nuzzling between my shoulder blades, trying to warm me up where I was rigid with cold. And there you are: that night he made love to me, properly – or more or less properly. Anyway, we managed penetration. And we did it another time too, in the early morning a few days later, in a zipped-up sleeping bag in the front room of a fantastically disgusting ground floor flat belonging to the freckled red-haired man, Ian, who sold Valentine his drugs. We lay in the dawn light, crushed together on our narrow divan in the blessed peace of the aftermath, Val's head fallen on my breast: proudly I felt the trickling on my thighs. I suppose we must have heard the milkman's float passing – or perhaps by that time we had dozed off.

Then someone threw a full milk bottle through the closed window. Though I didn't understand at first what had happened: it was just an explosion in the room, appalling and incomprehensible, the crashing glass loud as a bomb, milk splashed violently everywhere. (It seems improbable that a drug dealer had a daily delivery – the bottle must have been picked up from someone else's doorstep.)

— What the fuck? Val leapt up from the divan, naked.

Ian came running in, pulling jeans on. — What the fuck?

He cut his feet on the glass.

I knew from Val's face that he knew what the explosion was, and who.

Some other girl, I thought. Some old love. Someone he loves, or who loves him and is desperate for him the way I am.

Of course it wasn't any girl. It was his English teacher.

I thought – when the whole truth came out, when at last I'd understood about the sex, and Ian was so fucked off with Val about the window and the milk and was looking for him everywhere, and Val got the money from his sister and went to the States, and it was all such a collapse of my hopes – I thought I could still go back, defeated, to my old life. Back home and back to school, and pick up where I left off, and be a clever girl again, and get to university. Even if I could never ever again, in my whole life, be happy.

But I wasn't that clever, was I?

Had I forgotten everything they'd taught us at school? That you only had to do it once, just once, to get into trouble. We had even done it twice.

Five

Mrs Tapper saved me. I ought to be grateful to her. We met when I was sitting on a park bench on Brandon Hill and Lukie was asleep in his pram: I was eighteen and he was twelve weeks old. I'd been sitting there too long. It was late afternoon on an autumn day in 1974 and the wind was blowing dead leaves and black bits of twig down from the trees and into drifts on the wet grass littered with worm casts; the bench's wooden slats were cold as metal against the underside of my thighs, my feet were numb in thin plimsolls, I was trying to keep my hands warm in my pockets. From time to time I reached out to push the pram back and forward if I thought I heard Lukie waking up. The chrome pram handle too was freezing cold – but he was snug inside in his cocoon of nappy and babygro suit and bonnet and bootees and blankets. I'd tested to make sure he was warm enough, pushing my own hand in there between the sheets, down beside his hot little body, damp and urgent in sleep. I wished that I could sleep, and be tucked up in a cocoon of blankets and rocked to and fro, and not have to think about anything except myself.

I did love him.

I'd loved him from the moment he arrived in that awful chaos in the foyer of the maternity hospital – they had to cut my knickers off, he came so quickly. Apparently this happens with young mothers. I still had my shoes on when they handed him to me to hold; the maternity dress my Auntie Andy had bought me, when I couldn't fit into my jeans any longer, was a bloody rag wrapped up somewhere around my waist, it had to be thrown out (not that I cared – I didn't need maternity dresses, I was never, *ever*, going to go through that again). Lukie gazed into my eyes when they gave him to me with such a searching, surmising, reasonable, open look: surprised but not dismayed to find himself in existence. Now that I know my son Luke as an adult I can say that the whole of him was there in that first look, everything he's ever done and been began from that. (My other son's so different, so complicated.)

— My God, my mother had said as soon as she leaned over Lukie (not that soon – she didn't come to see him for weeks after he was born, we were by no means reconciled by then). — He's the spit of your father.

Now why did she say that? When for so many years we'd never mentioned my father. She was pushing the baby away, I knew it – she didn't want it connected to her. Needless to say she hadn't wanted me to have a baby. Never mind all the other stuff, about shame, and

108

loss of face, and people asking 'How's Stella getting on at school?' and my tripping up on my merry road to being so superior: not only that, but it was only a few years since my mother had her own second baby, she was bored with the whole fuss and the puking and crying, no cute little grandson was going to win her round. She had wanted me to triumph and prove something to my stepfather, and I had made a fool of myself instead. Her look at me was hard and flattened and lustreless, it had been for months: as if she'd let go of something. Let go of me, I suppose. But she did bring me some tiny vests, and a matinee jacket she'd knitted herself (she was hopeless at knitting, too impatient, it was full of dropped stitches). And money, most of which I gave to Jean.

I was living with my Auntie Jean and I didn't know what to do.

Rock the pram, rock the pram. Mix up the baby's bottles of formula, sterilise the bottles. Change his nappy, mix up the soaking solution in a plastic bucket, rinse the dirty nappies then soak them and then put them in Jean's twin tub, heaving the scalding nappies in clouds of urine-smelling steam in wooden tongs between the washer and the spin dryer. Wash his clothes, wash mine. Help Jean make tea. (Jean worked in the afternoons, sewing for a Jewish tailor in Stokes Croft. She was a skilled tailoress, she could cut out and make a winter coat, a man's suit jacket and trousers.) Feed the baby, rock him. (Jean loved to give him his bottle and nurse him. She was a natural. He slept content against the handsome mountain of her bosom.) Watch telly with my cousins in the evenings.

Pick the baby up from his cot when he cried in the night and rock him.

Was that it, then?

We had a back room. It was my cousin Richard's room, he was a trainee motor mechanic and he'd had to move in to sleep with his two brothers. At first he didn't mind. They were that kind of family: generous and spontaneous, always giving shelter to refugees from some crisis or other among their friends or relations. But after a while, naturally, Richard would have liked his room back. Also, I wasn't quite grateful enough: this was just a flaw in my character at that time in my life, I couldn't help seeing things bitterly, looking at everything – even kindness – with irony. Where I should have had a heart, there was a dry husk. I loved my good-looking boy cousins, how they teased their mother, and their touchy loyalty and dignity as if they were a tribe set apart; but I couldn't quite belong to the tribe. I should have talked more and made more effort – but I suppose I was making all the efforts I had in me, just to get through every day. There were pieces of motorbike lying around on the floor of Richard's room and sometimes in the dark when I was walking up and down with Lukie because he wouldn't sleep I stumbled over them in my bare feet, and cut my toes and bruised my shins. That back room seemed like the end of the world, some nights.

But where else could I go? I wouldn't, I couldn't, go home.

Anyway, at home they did not want me.

Some nights, if Lukie had been fretting on and off for

hours my Auntie Jean came in, voluminous in her nightie. — Give him to me, Stella love, she said. — I'll have him. You get some sleep. And I was too weak to refuse her: I handed my baby over. She knew just how to hold him, to comfort him; right away I heard him calming down in her arms out of his frenzy. I longed for my bed, I crept into it and embraced my pillow like an addict, sinking down and down into oblivion. I knew that Jean would take my baby permanently if I wanted her to. I could go away and possess myself again; Luke would grow up to be part of the tribe. Not that it would be easy for her (what about her job, sewing?). She had a thing about babies, though, and she loved Lukie. I knew that he'd have a good life with her – I didn't know what kind of life he'd have with me. (I didn't think about Valentine. I never even mentioned his name, after the moment I learned he'd left for the US. My mother never even asked me if he was the baby's father; if anyone did ask me I wouldn't answer them, nobody told his parents, he never knew.)

Some nights I stood in my pyjamas in the dark at the back window, my baby son dozing against my shoulder, breathing him in: yeasty, milky, eggy, sweet. Whatever my mind was busy with in those moments, my body calmed to be in tune with his; there was still an animal match between the smell of his sweat and mine. My aunt and uncle lived in Totterdown, on a terraced house on a precipitous hill: I could see all the lights of the city spread out below me on the river plain. I'm not dead yet, I thought in the middle of the night. This is my life.

111

It's not nothing. And my imagination was too passionately imprinted with Luke's miniature features, it was already too late to leave him: the pearly globes of his closed eyelids, a swathe of shiny milk-rash spots across his cheek, the wrinkling frowns that passed over his face with wind, the dark blood-colour of his lips pressed so precisely together, his tiny decisively hooked nose (making me think of the ribs of an umbrella waiting to be unfurled later).

And then Mrs Tapper found me in the park. Brandon Hill wasn't anywhere near my cousins', it was in a much smarter part of the city. I'd pushed the pram on and on through the afternoon, not knowing where I was heading, until my feet were sore – and Lukie had slept all that time. I first spotted Mrs Tapper walking fast along the paths beside the frost-stricken flower beds, the heels of her shoes scraping assertively. She was dressed in a beautifully cut camel-hair coat, the collar turned up round her ears and her hands pushed deep into the pockets. Her face was lifted in that remote, sardonic way she had, avoiding meeting anyone's eye; the colour of the coat didn't suit her because her hair and her complexion were too close to the same yellowish fawn. She was fairly tall and very thin and middle-aged (older than my mother, I guessed); powder was stuck in the shallow wrinkles on her forehead and her hair was cut to shoulder length, pulled back in a tortoiseshell clip. When I thought about it afterwards, once I knew her better – Vivien, she told me to call her Vivien and sometimes I remembered – I wondered if she'd come out to walk there that day after she'd had a row with her husband. They didn't get on very well. She wasn't the sort of woman who found the time for walks in the park by herself – her life was packed efficiently tight with important errands and busy-ness. It may have been an exceptional afternoon for her – if I was feeling desperate, then perhaps she was too.

All the benches along the path were empty but she sat down beside me. — Do you mind? she said. She asked me sympathetically all about Lukie, she said she had two children of her own, a girl and a boy, eight and fourteen.

— It's such a shock, isn't it? she said. — The responsibility, descending like that all at once out of the blue. I was much older than you are but I wasn't prepared in the least. I know I thought I'd go under with it. But you don't go under, you know.

I opened up to Mrs Tapper as I hadn't opened up to anyone. Perhaps I had an instinct that in her dryness and measured analysis she was a more useful model to me just then than Jean with her instinctive mothering. I told her about my mother and stepfather, and giving up school. I told her about the back bedroom at Auntie Jean's and the motorbike parts. I even told her that the baby's father didn't know about him. I could tell her anything, I thought, it wouldn't matter – I'd never see her again afterwards.

— So you're stuck, Mrs Tapper said. — I know how that feels.

It reassured me that she wasn't the motherly type and

yet she had children: so perhaps I might manage it after all. Her long legs in sheer nylons were crossed under her coat and she was swinging one foot restlessly, the shoe dangling, as if she wanted to jump up and take off somewhere.

— Actually I'm looking for a girl, she said abruptly. — I don't suppose it's a job that would interest you. But I want someone to come and live in, to help with the chores and the children. I've got my own business, selling antiques: it takes up more and more of my time. We live in the school where my husband works. (I thought at first she must mean he was some kind of caretaker, but of course he wasn't, he was housemaster at an expensive private school.) — You could have your own room. And I'd pay you on top of that: say, thirty pounds a week. But probably the job isn't what you want.

Her impulsive gesture wasn't like her; mostly she was solitary and wary of commitment. She must have felt a momentary kinship with me, with my plight. She really had been looking for a girl – but she didn't have to take one with a baby. Afterwards, I think she partly disliked me because of the rash gesture I had drawn her into; which was a shame, because we had genuinely opened up to one another for that twenty minutes in the park. After I worked for her we never spoke like that again, intimately as equals. But that was all right too. We had each needed the other for something, which wasn't kindness or love.

I said that I was interested. I yearned at the thought of a room of my own.

114

— You're not a smoker, are you? Can you clean a house? And can you make cake? If you're a housemaster's wife the boys expect you to feed them ghastly cake, day in day out.

I said I could make cake and it was true, I could produce a passable Victoria sponge. And my mother used to pay me pocket money for cleaning; she'd been a hard taskmaster. Mrs Tapper was frowning into the pram. She was probably already half regretting her offer.
— Does he sleep through the night yet?

I lied. I said he did.

She said she would need references. I got references from one of my old teachers and from my Uncle Ray, because of the summer job in the chocolate factory.

So Mrs Tapper saved me. And I did the right thing, going to work for the Tappers: but that doesn't mean I was happy there. At that point I had given up on happiness. I used to think back sometimes on the plans that Valentine and I had made – living together in Paris on French bread and coffee and writing – and I didn't feel nostalgic or regretful, I only felt contempt for my deluded previous self. What a fake he was! I thought. And what a fake I was! I knew now how things really were. And I was better off at Dean's House than at Auntie Jean's because I didn't have to feel grateful or guilty, and my cousin Richard could have his room back. At least this was my own life now, not anybody else's. At the end of each week Vivien Tapper gave me six five-pound notes in a buff envelope. She handed them over in a funny way with her face averted, not saying anything, as if it was vaguely shaming that this was what kept me installed in the centre of their lives; and yet she was tough when it came to her own money. I heard her on the telephone to her partner in the antiques business, quibbling over small sums, sticking to her guns.

Mr Tapper was handsome, younger than his wife, with rosy skin, tight-curling charcoal-black hair and gold-rimmed glasses; he was always joking, nothing he said was what he really meant. I saw him holding up a dessert spoon once at the dinner table, making satirical remarks to that. He taught mathematics and bowed his head from the neck without moving his shoulders as if he was wearing some kind of inhibiting corset; if he spoke to me it was in an awkward innuendo, commenting on my legs or teasing me about imaginary boyfriends. I don't think he was flirting; he simply had no other register for communicating with girls. Mrs Tapper got him to fetch up from the cellar the highchair and cot and playpen they had used years ago for their own children. Hugo – pale and plump, acting the clown to make his friends laugh – was a pupil at the school, belonging half to the institution, half to his family. Juliet went to a nearby girls' prep school; she was subdued and sceptical with a flat, freckled face. I never told the Tappers where I'd gone to school, they never asked; I suppose they presumed I was a failed product of one of the comprehensives. They never asked much about anything – to ask would have been prying. This suited me.

Their family quarters were the tall cold rooms on the

ground floor of Dean's, a solid Edwardian house across the road from the main school buildings and the chapel and playing fields and statue of Field Marshal Haig. Upstairs in the same house were dorms for the younger boys. Rich parents in those days paid for their sons to sleep in long rooms with bare floorboards, on narrow iron bedsteads made up with the same kind of coarse blankets I'd slept under once at my nana's. I didn't have to tidy the boys' beds, they tidied their own.

I was a good worker. Mrs Tapper said so. There is a bleak kind of satisfaction to be had from working till your hands are sore, till your calves and shoulders ache and you're heavy with exhaustion. In the mornings when I tied on my apron I felt as if I was girding myself in armour. I was consumed in the discipline of housework and I thought of my mother often – not affectionately; more in a spirit of emulation. I thought of how she cracked the sheets in the air when she was folding them off the line, how she wielded her brush with the dustpan into every recalcitrant corner, how she scrubbed the kitchen lino on her knees and bleached the cloths and shook out the dusters and washed all her delicates by hand, rinsing in three changes of clean water. Of course I couldn't be good at everything all at once. I wasn't much of a cook – I could make cake all right (jam sponge, chocolate sponge, coffee and walnut sponge) but at first I didn't know how to cook chops or make a stew. It was awful when Juliet pushed what I'd dished up to the side of her plate. (Hugo ate school meals with the other boys.)

And I made stupid mistakes. For instance, I used a

vacuum cleaner when the back of the plug was broken, with all the contacts exposed, and then after I'd finished vacuuming I left it plugged in at the wall where anyone could have electrocuted themselves by poking a finger in – Juliet or Hugo or any of the boys. Or even Lukie, maybe, if he'd rolled over and reached out. Mrs Tapper gave me a little lecture when she found the broken plug in its socket, smiling, her pale plucked eyebrows raised incredulously. I squirmed in shame though I didn't let her see it, my face was stony. I apologised. I could have killed someone. It would never happen again. Another time, I put a pale wash on in the machine, not noticing Mr Tapper's black sock left inside the drum; all Vivien's white blouses and underwear turned grey and she was furious. But mostly she was too grateful to be a hard taskmaster, exiting out of the front door every morning, snatching her bag and car keys in a show of hurry, sometimes hanging on to her breakfast triangle of toast between her teeth while she pulled on her coat.

At least I had my own room in Dean's to retreat to, with its own lock and key. It was on the first floor, with windows all along two sides and lozenges of green and yellow glass set in around the clear panes; very light, but very cold in winter. I think in the past this room must have been used for laundering the boys' clothes, because there were two huge enamel Belfast sinks in there – one of which I used for bathing Lukie in the evenings – and racks for drying washing, hoisted by ropes and a pulley up to the ceiling. I kept the place neat and clean. Mum gave me a bedspread Nana had knitted of coloured squares of wool sewn together, and an oil-filled electric heater. Our room was at the opposite end of the house to the kitchen, so that when I put Lukie to sleep in his cot in the day I couldn't hear him if he cried; but the boys listened out for him, and he slept reliably for three hours in the morning, when I got most of the heavy work done, and all evening. It was only in the middle of the night that Lukie was inconsolable. In the evenings I watched television with Juliet or read to her before she went to sleep. In all the time that we were at Dean's House, the only books I ever read – apart from recipe books – were the ones I read to her (P. L. Travers, Noel Streatfeild). I had once thought I couldn't get through a day without reading. Well, now I had woken up out of that dream.

I did a funny thing one morning while I was tidying: I looked up my real father's name in the telephone directory. I'd never done it before – because my parents had married in London and I was born there, I'd assumed he stayed on after they separated. But if my mother had moved back to Bristol then why not my father too? Anyway, I found someone who had his name, living in Bedminster. The someone was a driving instructor.

Mrs Tapper paid me extra to cook and wash up for her dinner parties. I was getting better at cooking, using the recipes I found in her cordon bleu books. I served at the table and took away the plates; Mrs Tapper carried in the food as if she'd made it herself. At these parties she tried to mix up the school staff with her own friends.

119

The antiques women were very made-up and assured, with tanned, heavy-breasted cleavage, helping themselves to refills from the gin bottle; the men smoked between courses and put out their cigarettes in the remains of the food. Her friends weren't ever hungry, while the teachers wolfed everything down. You could see the schoolteacher lot despising the antiques lot but also frightened of them, pretending to find them amusing, exchanging looks. Sometimes a political argument would flare up, because Vivien's friends were all pretty rabid Tories; sometimes the teachers' wives conspired with the outsiders against their husbands.

They gave a party to welcome a new English teacher to the staff. He was small and portly, vaguely familiar as if I'd seen him around, with longish hair and dandruff on the shoulders of his shiny jacket. I'd made chicken-liver pâté, pork cooked with prunes and Vouvray, and profiteroles (which didn't swell up enough). The kitchen had been piled high with dirty dishes; it was difficult managing all that cooking alongside looking after Lukie. Now Lukie was in his cot, and by the time the guests were at the coffee stage I had broken the back of the washing-up. I sat resting in the quiet of the kitchen, listening to the tick as the minute hand on the wall-clock pushed round, aware of the rise and fall of voices in the dining room, shut away from me behind two closed doors. A row of soaking tea towels hung along the radiator like trophies, the room was limp from the assault of mess and heat. I was still tied into my dirty apron. It didn't occur to me to mind that Mrs Tapper didn't invite me to sit with her guests. I was burning up with scorn for all of them – and I dreaded them too, because their lives were achieved and full beside my thwarted unfinished one. My embrace of my solitude (my solitude with Lukie) was fierce during all that period. I didn't want to see any of my old friends – though Madeleine did call round when she was home from university. She thought Lukie was adorable and she tried very hard to be kind to me; I asked flat, dutiful questions about her course, not commenting on her answers. I wouldn't tell her what my life was like when she asked me. — I'm all right, I said. — No, I'm not lonely.

Sometimes I was all right.

I was drinking my own black coffee out of one of Mrs Tapper's set of weightless tiny porcelain cups, blue and gold, with a slug of brandy added from the bottle kept for cooking. The wood of the kitchen table where I sat was three inches thick, bleached and scrubbed into soft hollows (I bleached and scrubbed it), the grain of the wood sticking up in ridges. Mrs Tapper had told me that the table was as old as the house. It was handed down to each housemaster's wife, as it was too big to ever move out of the kitchen; the only way you could get it out was to saw it up. (She sounded as if she would quite like to do that.) There were huge built-in wooden dressers too, with sliding doors, all along one wall. I heard one of the guests come out from the dining room and cross the hall. Thinking they might be looking for the toilet, I braced myself for the intrusion, scowling, willing whoever it was not to try to make conversation with me out of condescension, or because they were bored with the scene next door. It was the new English teacher who looked around the door, balancing his coffee cup. He was plump and mournful; he might have been Italian with his hooded, prominent eyes.

— I know you, he said, closing the kitchen door behind him.

Occasionally a man at those parties (once an antiques man, once a games teacher) had come to try to pick me up in the kitchen; this might be a chat-up line. I fended him off, saying that I didn't think so.

— You're Valentine's girlfriend. We did meet once.

Oh. I recognised him then: Valentine's teacher, Mr Harper.

I knew his first name was Fred: that was what Val had always called him. But I couldn't think of him as Fred now, in Dean's House; even though, out of frustrated love for Val, he had thrown that milk bottle through our window. He sat down with his coffee at my table. — I'm thinking I've made a mistake leaving the Grammar School, he went on conversationally. — My marriage has broken up, naturally enough, and everything's rather in ruins, and I thought it might help if I changed jobs. But this evening hasn't been fun. What ghastly types. Do you work for them, in this pantomime kitchen? Do you hear from Val in the US – how he's getting on? I never do. What a shock, when I caught sight of you carrying in the mashed potato. What are you doing with your young life, since Valentine left?

What was I going to tell him?

I remember sitting there frozen because this man from my past had found me out in the place where I was secret – and behind my silence there was building up a great clamour of complaint and rage which might come bursting out at him if I didn't keep watch over it scrupulously. I made up my mind that I wouldn't speak a word, I would glare at him and wait until he gave up and took himself away. I didn't want Fred Harper, of all people, knowing one single thing about me. Just then the kitchen door opened and Mrs Tapper poked her head in; reluctantly, as if she preferred keeping her body out in the hall passage. Her voice was frigid, finding her guest and her servant shut up together. She told me that the baby was crying. She said she wished I'd remember to listen out for it; one of the boys had had to come down from the dorm because it was keeping them awake. She hoped none of them would go running to their parents with this story.

— It turns out Stella and I knew each other, in another existence, Fred explained.

Vivien didn't like that, she pretended she wasn't interested. She enticed him in her bored, bright hostess tone. — Come back and tell us more about Oxford. Dougie says he wants to take his class to see a play actually performed in Latin. What do you think – wouldn't that be too awful to inflict on the poor boys? I'd rather die, wouldn't you?

I hurried to fill the kettle for warming a bottle of formula, apologising that it was earlier than Lukie's usual waking time. In Vivien's assessing glance around the

123

room, I saw her take in that I was using one of her precious old coffee cups. That had never been forbidden – after all, she trusted me to wash them up. Nonetheless, her powdery pale forehead creased in a quick frown, as if she was used to bearing up every day under other people's carelessness. Or perhaps she could smell the brandy. I could hear Lukie's wailing then, a desperate thread drawn thin across the cold distances of the house.

— Whose baby? Fred Harper asked, smiling from one of us to the other.

Working it all out.

The next week I had my first driving lesson. I had saved up to pay for these out of my wages – I didn't have much else to spend money on, apart from the formula and nappy cream and so on for Lukie. (My mother sent him clothes, in brown paper parcels addressed in her crisp round writing: 'Dean's House' fenced off inside a suspicious bristle of inverted commas. She never came there, though I did invite her.) It was my afternoon off; Auntie Jean was looking after Lukie. I hadn't told anyone what I was doing. In my head I was perfectly calm about meeting this man who might turn out to be my father – but just before he turned up, while I was waiting round the corner from Jean's house, I began to shake. All the time I was thinking coolly that I didn't care if it was him or not, or what he was like. (Luckily the surname on my provisional licence was my stepfather's.) When the car drew up and the instructor leaned over, calling to me, pushing open the passenger door, I could hardly cross the pavement to get in beside him. Of course he just put it down to nerves about the lesson.

I was better as soon as I was sitting in the car. Driving with deft, deliberate movements, demonstrating his technique, he explained that he was taking me to an industrial estate where we could practise basic manoeuvres safely. I kept my eyes on his hands, which could have been like mine – small, for a man, with rather shapeless fingers, freckles on the back. He introduced himself as Al; I knew my father's name was Albert, but on the rare occasions she mentioned him my mother had always called him Bert. It was a good thing for me that he had to look out at the road ahead; every so often while he talked he turned to smile at me, to put me at ease. I'd been expecting him to be stolidly respectable, like my stepfather. But this man was skinny and rakish and teasing, with a thin, lined face and curving, dramatic nose, long hair curling on the collar of his striped shirt. He was the right age; but I couldn't imagine my mother choosing him. We went to an industrial estate and he taught me all the elementary stuff, checking the mirrors and ignition and putting the car into gear; I hardly had time then to study him for clues because I had to concentrate on remembering the sequence of moves, releasing the clutch so that the car slid smoothly forward instead of kangaroo-jumping, steering slowly round a corner. I forgot what I had come for, lost myself in the driving. Before I could make up my mind about anything, my time was up.

Al offered me a cigarette before he drove me back. I didn't often smoke but I took one: I thought maybe this was a sign, the way our two hands matched when he reached his lighter over for me and held the flame steady. I wondered what he made of me. I hardly cared in those days what I looked like: I always wore the same jeans or cord skirt, with a black jumper and no make-up, my hair pulled back. He might be disappointed – he would have looked forward to teaching a young girl, thinking she'd be flirty or sexy. We were parked at the back of a builder's merchant's; pavings and ceramic drainpipes were stacked behind high wire fencing overgrown with ivy.

— Was that so bad? he said gallantly. — Really your first time behind the wheel? You're a natural.

It was true, the driving had come easily, I'd liked it. I'd only ever meant to have one lesson. I had imagined that at the end of it I'd either reveal to Al I was his long-lost daughter, or say I hadn't liked the driving and didn't want to take it any further. Instead I found myself arranging another lesson, for the week after.

I don't think Mr Tapper had wanted me to come to Dean's. Probably he and Vivien had quarrelled over it: they quarrelled often about all sorts of things. Once I heard him call her an 'idiot' and once I think she threw something at him; at any rate, when I came in the room a few moments after the crash, she was stooped, pink in the face, picking up the pieces of a china ornament. Anyway, Mr Tapper had given in and Vivien got me. I suppose he was anxious because I had a baby and no husband; I might be promiscuous and a danger to the boys. On the day I arrived she had announced smoothly,

126

as if it wasn't up for discussion, that I must call myself 'Mrs' and pretend I was married. I hadn't objected, I was used to this already from the maternity hospital.

But he needn't have worried. There wasn't much chance of anything happening, ever, between me and any of those boys. The younger ones were nice to Lukie and sometimes they even came to me for comforting, not because I was particularly kind but just because I was a mother. The sixth-formers lived in an annexe next door to Dean's, and I went in to clean their studies once a week. I used to forget that these were boys of my own age. I wasn't jealous of them with their posters of Bob Marley, their piles of textbooks and their smelly socks, the braggadocio of their empty vodka bottles stuck with flags and peacock feathers – even though they were going to university and I wasn't. I exulted in my hard new knowledge that made theirs innocent. I believed I had become an adult all at once in the passage of that hour of pain in the maternity hospital.

I was supposed to clean their rooms while they were away in lessons but sometimes one of them came back while I was still wiping round the sink or vacuuming the carpet. I must have looked to them like a witch in a fairy tale: hair scraped back in a plait out of the way, no make-up, very thin, eyes burning up in my pale face. Or they might meet me coming out of the toilets or washing the floor in the corridor – I would stand holding my mop beside my bucket of filthy water, and stare down at my shoes, and they'd push past as if they didn't see me, treading dirt across the wet floor. Perhaps they just saw a cleaner, made sexless and ancient by her function. Or perhaps they took in that I was young and female, but felt my ferocity; presuming I must be an enemy of their type and privilege, they were afraid of me. At any rate, I never exchanged more than a couple of words with a single one of them, the whole time I was there.

Though it wasn't because I was a nun, or made of stone.

Mostly, I told myself I was glad I had cut through all the shams of love-dreaming and passion, to some bedrock where only Lukie mattered. Against my will, however, every so often while I was working a haze of need would come over me like a fit – so bewildering that I didn't know where I was. One of the sixth-formers came in once while I was standing with my face pressed in his dressing gown, drinking in his smell, keening to myself; he was so shocked he walked straight out of the room again, and he always avoided me afterwards. He must have thought I had a crush on him; but the truth was I hardly even knew whose room it was. I had only wanted to breathe in his male teenage smell: I suppose it reminded me of Valentine. I still dreamed of Valentine sometimes, though I hadn't forgiven him. The smell wasn't good (not like Lukie's sweet one): stale sweat and cigarettes and dirty hair. But it made me drunk, it made my knees sag, made all my intelligence drain down out of my mind until I thought I would fall on the floor with longing.

The driving lessons went well, I began to look forward to them. Because the rest of my life was so weighed down with responsibility and routine, in charge of the car I felt as if I was flying, I loved its power under my control. Soon I was out on busy roads, keeping up with the flow of traffic, turning left, turning right. — Good girl, Al said. — You've got a feeling for it. He had to touch the steering wheel sometimes, correcting my line, but he never needed to use his dual control. My wits – sluggish from housework and baby-minding – were strained taut, mastering new difficulties: holding the car in traffic in first gear, reversing round a corner.

I still couldn't make my mind up about Al. It seemed incredible that this stranger and I, our relationship shaped so casually in the shared space of the car, might be connected by blood; the idea embarrassed me on Al's behalf. On the other hand, our movements did seem fluidly alike sometimes, as if we were attuned. He told me he hated getting up in the mornings; well, so did I (and every morning Lukie woke me about half past five). There was something familiar – from my mirror, from inside my own skin? – in the way Al squeezed his eyes up when he smiled. But none of this was enough. I couldn't be sure. I liked him, in spite of his dated lazy cowboy style (he got lazier, the more he saw that I was good): his slouchy walk, his missing tooth, his smell of beer and fags and man-talk about fast cars. I guessed that he fancied himself as a bit of a charmer, though with me he was steadily courteous, almost fraternal. He played electric bass in a blues band.

I put off saying anything to him. I didn't want to spoil my own pleasure in our lessons, or Al's pride in how well I did. I told him a few things about Lukie, pretending I was married.

— Do you have children? I did ask him once.

What if he replied that he'd had a little girl but he'd lost touch with her, and it was what he most regretted in his life?

— No, I've missed out on that, he said, cautiously, blandly.

Fred Harper took to calling at Dean's in the afternoons whenever he had a free period, hoping the grown-up Tappers would be out. I wondered at first if he was coming because he was afraid of me, thinking I would tell his story to the school; but it seemed more likely he was just bereft and bored. And perhaps I was touched with glamour for him, because of our shared association with Valentine. I think he found my situation poignant, like something in a book.

Anyway, for a long time I wouldn't speak to him. It began because of the milk bottle and the past; then my refusal became a thing in itself, almost a game. I would be playing with Lukie and working in the kitchen, tidying up, starting preparations for the evening meal; I'd make Fred cups of tea and set them in front of him at the table without a word. If I needed to get on with cooking, I'd shove Lukie down on Fred's lap – he was good with babies, he had children of his own, a girl and a boy; he told me how he missed them, how depressed he was now that he only saw them every other weekend.

Fred was never deterred by my lack of response; he talked on and on, either about the school (which he claimed he hated) or about things I had no interest in any more – books and ideas and poetry. He had opinions about everything. Even under normal circumstances he was one of those men who hog more than their fair share of any conversation. Tactfully, though, he didn't mention Valentine again for a long time. He spoke as if he and I were old friends and had always known each other, though we'd never actually exchanged a word before the Tappers' dinner party. I'd heard him shouting and weeping to Valentine in the street, that awful night, but I hadn't gone out to join them.

If Mrs Tapper came home and found Fred in the kitchen, she couldn't repress her irritation – she was the opposite type to Fred with his operatic range of feeling. She liked to banter quickly backwards and forwards with her friends, she couldn't bear Fred's drawl and his air of being in for the long haul, conversationally. She said he had doggy eyes; he called her 'the walking antique'. But Fred and Juliet had the same quirky humour; they entertained Lukie together or played baby games at the kitchen table, tiddlywinks or snakes and ladders, which they pretended to take deadly seriously (though Juliet wouldn't let her father teach her chess). Fred made a joke to Juliet out of my silence, explaining to her that I wouldn't forgive him for something he'd once done.

— What something?

— Ask her. Fred gave a doleful look.

It was unimportant, I said. It wasn't worth mentioning.

While I was still living with the Tappers, I went home sometimes to spend a weekend with my mother and stepfather. I still quarrelled with Gerry: once, terribly, about independence for Angola of all things, concerning which I had heart-warming expectations though only a vague idea of where it was. But mostly it was OK. I liked my brother Philip, and Philip loved Lukie, he played with him for hours on end; at eleven months Lukie took his first steps towards Philip, who was holding out his hands, chirruping and coaxing. I was snoozing on the sofa, watching telly. I think my mum was sorry for me because of my hard life at Dean's, though she wouldn't say so. She pampered me in little ways that reminded me of long ago when I was a child and there had only been the two of us. She slipped money into my jeans pocket when Gerry wasn't looking and made my favourite things for tea (cheese and potato pie with bacon on top, apple fritters). Gerry sulked, jealous. I asked her once, when we were alone, whether she had any photographs of my real father. (I didn't say I'd guessed he wasn't really dead; and I hadn't mentioned the driving lessons to anyone.)

— Oh Stella, she complained. — Why d'you have to bring up that old story?

She swore she didn't have any photographs, and I commented that this was a bit strange, for a widow. If I'd been married and my husband had died, I said, I wouldn't have thrown away all his photographs. The next morning with an odd, ashamed face she pushed something at me wordlessly: an old manila envelope fuzzy at the corners. I locked myself in the bathroom to investigate, tipping out a few pictures on to my lap as I sat on the side of the avocado-coloured bath: they were black and white, and tiny as if they had shrunk as that old time receded. My mother, whose gaze at the camera was already forceful, had her thick hair chopped short; she wore big-skirted summer frocks and her figure was poignant with that post-war extreme thinness (there were none of her pregnant). My father in all of them was blurry, lean, attentive. There was one picture of him holding up in both hands, at arm's length, a baby stolid and unsmiling – me, I suppose. He was more like a boy than a young man – hungry hollow cheeks, raw jawline, dark hair flopping forwards over his eyes. That boy just might have grown up into Al, but I couldn't see for sure. When I tried to give the envelope back to my mother, she told me to keep it.

I took Lukie out in the afternoons sometimes, if the weather was nice. One day we met Fred Harper on our way to Brandon Hill, where I'd first met Mrs Tapper. Fred insisted on coming with us. I strode along beside him pretending not to see him, sealing my face up and pressing my lips tight shut, levering the heavy pram (which had been Jean's) up and down the kerbs with my foot on the crossbar underneath; or chatting away with Lukie, cutting out Fred. The further I got from the school, the lighter I felt; I thought my young body was so strong I could walk for ever.

— I suppose he's Valentine's baby, Fred said: breathless, because he was out of condition, at the speed I was going. I suppose he felt he could broach this subject because we were outside the school's orbit. — And that Valentine doesn't know.

I wouldn't answer.

— Dear girl, he said. — Dear Stella. It wouldn't have worked out, you do realise, even if I'd never had anything to do with Valentine.

I knew that this was true.

— Why are you punishing yourself, slaving in that mausoleum? Come and live with me, you can keep the flat clean for me instead of paying rent. Come live with me, don't be my love. There won't be any problems on that score. I'm lonely. I'll read to you, I'll heal you. I'll keep your secret.

The sky was blue and cloudless; we were passing in and out of the hot light, which was muffled under the thick-leaved trees and the striped shop awnings. The streets were ripe with the baked smells of dirt. Safely strapped in, sitting up and hanging on to the pram sides, Lukie beamed between us, trying to connect us up. The beauty of the day broke over me in a sensory wave, stronger than my will. — Maybe, I said suddenly, startling Fred: who'd probably forgotten I could actually hear him making his rash offers, getting carried away.

— I'll think about it. I might take you up on that.

Well, serves him right, I thought. That'll shut him up.

I didn't mean it seriously that first time Fred suggested it, I was only teasing him. I had to get to know him first, before I could begin to unpick some of the tension and resentment that keyed me up for working at Dean's

House. I had to come slowly to believe that a better life was possible. I stayed on with the Tappers for a year altogether, more or less. A year and a day: like someone in a story under an enchantment. But however crazy it sounds, I did go to live with Fred Harper eventually. Fred's dead now. But for a long time he was one of my good friends. And when I moved into his flat I cooked and cleaned for him instead of paying rent and bills, and on Saturdays he looked after Lukie, and Auntie Jean had Lukie three afternoons a week, and I took a part-time job working in a nice café where I liked the owners and they liked me. There was a bit of trouble with Fred's wife, who got the wrong end of the stick (again); but we sorted that out, it didn't mean anything. It was a happy time.

I passed my test first try, in August 1975. I hadn't expected my driving lessons ever to get this far; perhaps that was why I was so calm. Smoothly I changed gear, went through the pantomime of ostentatiously checking in my mirror as Al had taught me, slowed down going into a curve and accelerated out of it, reversed around a corner in a tidy arc – all as if I was observing someone else doing it, some dummy automated so she couldn't be caught out. Al was waiting for me outside the Test Centre when we got back – I caught one private glimpse of him before he saw us: abstracted, bored. Then he returned inside his smiling professional self, ground out his cigarette under his shoe, stepped forward while I got out of the car (my knees trembling belatedly), and embraced me. For a moment I was clasped (perhaps) against my father's chest, smelling his smoke and aftershave.

— Now is that a good feeling, he said, — or is that a good feeling?

I expect he did this to all the women who passed: on a sliding scale, exacting a kiss within the bounds of propriety from the younger or good-looking ones, conferring it as a favour on the plain ones and the ones who were too old. But he did always imply that I was his special comrade, because I was a natural driver like him. He couldn't get over my passing after only nine lessons, he said that he'd told everyone about me. He insisted on driving me back after the test; passing went to people's heads, apparently, they got too careless. I didn't know when I was ever going to drive a car again, anyway. I had no prospect of being able to afford one. I asked him to drop me off outside the school; I had a few hours free before I had to pick up Lukie from Jean's house.

— Goodbye then, I said. — Thank you.

— Good luck, he said. — Good driving.

And this time we shook hands.

The school was a strange place in the summer holidays. Deserted, its Victorian Gothic spaces seemed more eloquent: as if the missing boys had all grown up or died – which of course generations of them had. It was only when the school was empty that I ever felt the power of that ideal of gilded, privileged youth, set apart for a different destiny, which the school and staff were always trying to put over. When the place was full of real boys, the ideal seemed a sham. I meant to lie down on my bed after my driving test, in my room that was all windows, and sleep in the afternoon sun. I hungered for my bed and dreamed of sinking down into that vacant time alone, with no responsibility. But every time I closed my eyes I seemed to be driving again – only this time it was a huge effort, fraught with dread and difficulty, gears grinding and smashing, swerving to avoid oncoming traffic and looming obstacles. My heart thudded so painfully that it forced my eyes open; then I was astonished, looking round me at the quiet room. Lights from the small yellow lozenge-shaped panes around the windows were spotted across the bare floorboards like honey; nothing moved.

Lukie started sleeping through the night, thanks to Mrs Tapper. Those night-time sessions with Lukie had been so awful. The trouble usually started around midnight when he woke up and I gave him a bottle; after that, he never really went off again into deep sleep. I loved him better than anyone, than my own life; but in those hours he was also my enemy. I felt I was defending the last spaces of myself, because he wanted them. Lukie at night was unlike his clear daytime self, he was fretful and spiteful; if I took him into bed with me he chattered extravagantly, with an edge of hysteria, as if he were drunk. If he fell asleep in my arms and I managed to lower him into the cot without waking him, all too soon he would begin surfacing again, twitching and grumbling, rubbing his fists into his eyes. Then he would scramble to his feet, reaching out his arms through the bars of the cot for me, babbling a low-level moaning complaint, 'Mamamama . . .', which I knew would crescendo into loud crying if I tried to ignore it. And I couldn't let that happen, couldn't risk waking the whole house. I had promised Vivien that he would sleep. I had to pick him up. I could be walking up and down that room with him for hours: stumbling, vindictive, exhausted.

I wasn't good, in those long nights. Sometimes I was mad. I said some horrible things to Lukie while we were walking up and down together, hissed and whispered them; and afterwards I dreaded that even if he didn't understand the words, the spirit of my madness might have seeped in at his ears and poisoned him for ever. (Although he's never shown any signs of it, I must say. Somehow he's managed to forgive me.) Then one night Vivien Tapper interrupted us. It was two o'clock in the morning. I'd never seen her in her long wool dressing gown before, her face bleached without make-up.

— Come on now, Stella, she said. — This is getting silly.

She reached out for Lukie and I gave him to her; he was too astonished to protest. She was perfectly nice to him as she always was, but held him away from her body as though she was afraid of marks on her dressing gown (all my clothes were stained with baby dribble). Laying him down in his cot, in a firm voice she told him that it was sleep-time now. We left the room, with only the little night light on behind us. I could hear Lukie pulling himself up at once, rattling the cot bars even as we closed the door; then, after one long breath of shocked silence, the beginning of a wail of outrage.

— Won't he wake Mr Tapper up? I said. — And Juliet?

— They'll have to put up with it, Vivien said.

We went down together into the kitchen whose corners at night were cavernous and shadowy; a fluorescent tube-light under a metal shade was suspended on long chains over the table. Vivien switched on the electric fire and tuned the radio to the World Service, not too loud. Behind the radio voices Lukie's desperation was just audible, seizing like a tiny vice on my thoughts and squeezing them.

— You just have to sit it out, she said. — You can go and check him every fifteen minutes, to reassure him you haven't abandoned him. But don't put the light on in there, don't talk to him, just lay him down again, then go. Trust me, it works.

She poured two glasses of whisky and made tea for me, with sugar in; I watched the stuttering hand of the kitchen clock. When I went back after the first fifteen minutes, Lukie was smear-faced, blubbing, frantic, reaching up his arms for me; incredulous when I abandoned him again. In the kitchen, rummaging in one of the drawers of the dresser, under a pile of ironed table-cloths, Vivien brought out cigarettes and a crossword book.

— I have to hide these from Robin, she confessed.

Mr Tapper did the *Times* cryptic more or less easily

every day. The crosswords in her book were of a different species: 'star-crossed lover (5)' was Romeo, and 'replace (10)' was substitute. She lit a cigarette and I smoked one too; we worked through the crosswords one after another, looking up clues at the end of the book if we were ever stuck, as there was no particular honour in victory. I must have gone back in to Lukie five or six times; Vivien refilled our whisky glasses. We sat with our feet tucked up under us out of the way of the cold tiled floor. Then eventually, while we were trying to think of 'something unpleasant to look at (7)', she lifted her head up, listening, and signed to shush me, touching the back of my wrist with her hand.

— There, I think he's gone, she said.

My hearing strained at the absence of what it had grown used to; a blessed silence hung across the house. We gave him a few minutes, to make sure; Vivien said I knew where the whisky was if he woke up again later. But he didn't. It worked as easily as a miracle; and he was always a good sleeper afterwards. (It worked with my second son too, later.) The following night Lukie didn't even wake for his usual feed at midnight. I slipped into bed, expecting to be roused to the struggle at any moment; the next thing I knew it was seven-thirty and Lukie was shouting cheerfully at me from his cot. I think he was as relieved as I was to be rid of the burden of those night-times. I'd given him power over his own sleep – I should have done it months before. I tried to express something like this to Vivien when I thanked her but she brushed it away, it wasn't the kind of thing she liked to discuss. — Someone helped me out with Hugo, she explained dismissively, — at a time when I was going fairly bananas.

I don't think Vivien Tapper and I could ever have been friends. Yet it's surprising how often I've thought about her since those days – not particularly warmly nor resentfully, just aware of her existing somewhere, picking at the knot of her life in her own way. Some people accompany you like this in imagination, long after you've dropped any real connection with them. We used to bump into each other every so often for a while after I left, and she would ask what I was doing; it was always too complicated to tell her. If she's still alive, she's an old lady by now.

I was dusting the books one October morning in the Tappers' study. Mr Tapper did his marking in there, Vivien did her accounts. Neither of them were really readers, not what I'd call readers: not like Valentine, say, or Fred Harper. But there were books on their shelves and once or twice already I'd had to take them down a few at a time, riffle through the pages, blowing the dust off, and then wipe the shelves clean. I was still suspicious of books through all those early years while Lukie was small – I didn't trust them, they had led me too far astray. But my guard must have been down that morning; at any rate, one of the books fell open in my hand while my attention was elsewhere, dreaming – so that my eyes took in almost accidentally what they read. And then it was too late: a message shot directly into my heart, jolting

141

and deflecting me, making me blind to my routines. I didn't even really understand the words I was reading, I couldn't have explained them to anyone: 'lilac blooming perennial and drooping star in the west'. It wasn't their meaning that affected me, it was the words themselves – the solidity of them, their being assembled together in that particular order and rhythm – which stopped my breath. They seemed a signal from another, bigger life than the one I was in, as if a smothering blanket had been torn through. I shut the book quickly and sat back on my heels, wiping my face sticky with sweat and dust, and thought that if I had to spend another winter at the Tappers, I would die. Rain eased and pressed outside against the windowpanes, a frond of dead clematis tapped the glass. Then I thought that I'd die if I had to spend another hour there.

The book was a poetry anthology; I saw that Vivien had won it as a prize at school. I'm sure she never opened it while I was there. Afterwards, when I started reading again, I did find that poem eventually but it never had that same effect on me; I expected too much of it, I'd worn it out before I really knew it (and I had no idea, for years, that it was about Abraham Lincoln). I did grow to love other poems of Whitman's. Anyway, that morning I left the books in their pile on the floor and went upstairs to where Lukie was having his nap. The blinds were drawn down in our bedroom; I tiptoed around the cot in the dulled pink light, gathering our things together and packing them into a rucksack and an old suitcase I'd brought from home. I would have to leave our heavy luggage and pick it up later. Everything we needed for that night – nappies and changing kit, clean clothes for Lukie; money and knickers and a comb and toothbrush for me – I put in a bag I could carry over my shoulder. The sound of the falling rain was so dense in the quiet that my limbs seemed to be pushing against some resistance that made them roused and tingling. 'Lilac blooming perennial and drooping star in the west.'

Then I went downstairs and telephoned Mrs Tapper at the Antiques Market. I wept, I apologised for leaving so suddenly. She was exasperated because she'd have to shut up the stall early, to be home for Juliet. — Fred Harper's? Out of the frying pan into the fire, she warned. (She was wrong about that.) And she made some complaining remark, out of the blue, about the electric radiator my mother had lent me for my room; she said I ought to have consulted her first, didn't they use a lot of electricity? Then I put the phone down on her. There was no point in telephoning Fred yet, he would be teaching. I woke Lukie up and changed him and kissed him, gave him a biscuit and a bottle of juice; I put him in his pushchair (he'd grown too big for the pram) and we went out. It was pouring down – at least I had a plastic cover for the pushchair. It was a kind of madness, really. I had no idea what would happen next. We went into a café – the very one I got a job in later – where, when I'd got over dripping and steaming, I bought us both lunch. I sat proudly with my little son whose instinctive attentive courtesy charmed the waitresses – he sipped so responsibly, carefully from his feeder cup, studied the other customers with such steady curiosity. And as soon as school was over, I telephoned Fred Harper from a call box.

Six

I ought to explain, before I go on, that the father of my second son was killed – and in a horrible, stupid way – just a few weeks before our baby was born. So Rowan never knew his father, Nicky, although he's always known his story and the story of his death. He used to make me tell it to him, over and over, when he was small; and I believed in those days that you should always answer children's questions, tell them everything they want to know. (Well, not everything. There were hidden elements in the story which I held back.) Now, I wonder whether all that openness was healthy for Rowan. Perhaps there was something in the sad story which stuck to him, darkening his spirit and damaging his defences. He isn't at all like Nicky in his personality. Nicky was sweet and happy and good; Rowan is a wonder but he isn't any of those things. He does have Nicky's eyes, though. I had a home birth in the commune, with all the women around me, and that's what I saw as soon as they delivered Rowan up on to my stomach, slippery and bloody, before they'd even cut the cord: Nicky's eyes staring up at me, dark as blueberries, singling me out, accusing me.

What have you done?

(Though Nicky would never have accused anyone, let alone me.)

— I didn't ask to be born, Rowan used to sulk when he was a boy, long after we left the commune, if I asked him to tidy his room or dry the dishes. He was beautiful – strong limbs twisting out of my grasp, silky black curls and skin that burned dark chocolate-brown in the sunshine (Nicky's father was mixed-race Brazilian, though Nicky grew up with his white mother in Glasgow). And I know it sounds foolish, but I took him seriously; his argument seemed a valid one, I was afraid of it. Rowan had never consented to existence: I had cheated him into it. Like a classical philosopher, like Oedipus, he would rather never have lived. What right had I to impose my laws on him?

— You have to play your part, I said. — Everyone has to do their share, and help each other.

(The words fake and tasteless as old gum in my mouth.)

— Why? Why should I? I don't want to.

I met Nicky because students from the art college and the university used to come into the café where I worked. This café was part of a wholefoods shop on Park Row, painted pink and green and yellow. We sold mung beans and mate tea, stodgy slabs of cake flavoured with carob, organic vegetables crusted with earth, and olives from a huge tin on the floor; we made our own coleslaw and hummus and wholemeal bread, and believed we were getting in touch with a more authentic way of life – connected to the past, and vaguely to other cultures abroad. The style of the place – bare sanded boards, an odd assortment of wooden tables and chairs, blue and white striped china – was in itself a political statement. Posters were pinned on a noticeboard, advertising yoga classes or feminist reading groups or political meetings. The girls who worked there wore dungarees over stripy jumpers, or shapeless vintage print dresses and handmade flat leather shoes with straps across the instep like children's sandals. They despised make-up, although they tolerated mine: I painted my eyes heavily with black eyeliner and mascara and brown eye-shadow. I was allowed to get away with it because I was a mother and because of the knocks I had taken.

I liked the art students best because they were less earnest. I didn't single Nicky out at first, though you couldn't help noticing him: he was exuberant and charming, with a Glasgow accent and brown skin and a mop of black curls. I liked him as an element in that whole crowd. In a way I suppose I fell in love with them all collectively, with their excitement as if they were at a perpetual party and their outfits like fancy dress (Nicky wore a miltary jacket with frogging and epaulettes). Jude, who moved into the commune with us later, was from the art college too. And so was Baz, a tall good-looking boy with dyed orange hair. I thought Baz was Jude's boyfriend until Nicky explained to me that Jude was a lesbian and Baz was stalking her: he was obsessed with her and wouldn't let her alone. At the time this just seemed like another part of the drama of that crowd. After my life at Dean's House I couldn't get enough drama. I loved all the little flares and upsets and scandals, but I didn't take them seriously.

Nicky started to pay attention to me. He began by drawing me. I had presumed that all the art students would be able to draw – but it turned out that life drawing wasn't part of their curriculum any longer, they weren't encouraged to make their art look like things or people in real life. Nicky was almost embarrassed by his gift, which seemed to be a trick from an old-fashioned repertoire. He had been able to do these little sketches ever since he was small, and they were what had singled him out as a child and made him special – he had drawn his family and the characters in his neighbourhood, and had won prizes at school. I loved his pictures, which caught and exaggerated some essential quality or gesture in his subject and yet weren't caricatures.

He drew me when I wasn't conscious of him watching: I was making the coffees or collecting the china from the tables or tending to Lukie if he was with me — Lukie would sit happily for hours in the café while the students entertained him. Because Nicky was close to his own mother, he was attracted to an ideal of maternal tenderness (meanwhile I was chafing at the responsibility of motherhood and envying the freedom the other girls had). The drawings seemed to be glimpses into my secret life, which I thought no one else saw – though I couldn't quite connect these glimpses with Nicky's unsubtle outward persona. He was gregarious, noisy, popular: not beautiful, exactly, though plenty of girls found him attractive – his round sweet face, the shadow of silky hair on his upper lip, his nose that was crooked because he had broken it falling off his bike when he was a boy. Everyone liked Nicky, he had no enemies, and he liked everyone. He wasn't suspicious or critical as I was. He was even kind to Baz, whom everyone else avoided because Baz was so dreary in his obsessive pursuit of Jude.

Nicky courted me and I went out with him, we slept together. This was exciting because it drew me deeper inside the set of my new friends. I never let on to them just how lonely my life had been before I met them; because I'd left school at seventeen and was a mother, they imagined I'd tasted more than they had of real life. I hid the self-doubt I felt because I hadn't passed beyond the threshold of education. I don't remember any one moment when I gave my consent to our becoming a couple, Nicky and I; he used to put his arm around me in public and then we began to be asked out together. He looked after Lukie for me and didn't mind playing with him for hours in the park or with his toy cars; Lukie adored him. This made all the practicalities in my life so much easier. I allowed our connection to be established as a certainty – but I always knew that I was keeping something back, a cold stone hidden in my thoughts. I made up for my doubt by being competent and kind and reserved, which was what he liked. And it's surprising how quickly you can get used to being loved. I had been so abandoned and alone – and then all of a sudden this love was available to wrap round me, warm as a blanket. I got used to the warmth and forgot that I'd ever not had it.

Nicky believed that I was good, and innocently natural. Perhaps it was my inexperience that he miscon-strued as innocence; he was the first boy I'd made love to properly, although I never told him this. I was lucky with him, he was a kind and easy lover and undid a lot of the rage from the beginning of my motherhood. He was a good beginning. That's what I used to think, even at the time. Even when I was pregnant with his baby, I couldn't be convinced that Nicky was the end of my story.

And so it turned out.

For a while after he died I actually forgot what he was like in bed, I blanked it. It wasn't something you could ask anyone. No one else could know, and there weren't any photographs or words or mementoes left as traces of those scenes, to act as clues. It used to torment me, trying to recreate the sensations of our intimacy and thinking I'd forfeited them through what I'd done, through my carelessness.

At first our relationship was fitted in around my life at the café and at Fred Harper's. It had worked out well, the arrangement by which Lukie and I lived in Fred's flat rent-free in return for housework. Fred got on well with my new set of friends and they were welcome at the flat, though I held back sometimes from inviting them because I was ashamed of letting them see too much of my daily routines of childcare and cleaning and shopping and cooking; these seemed so unlike the students' improvised, dramatic lives which had no fixed framework apart from the lectures (which they often missed), and their exams and degree shows.

I presumed that the students' freedom was temporary and would end when they graduated. When this time came, however, Nicky's friends seemed to have no idea of moving away from Bristol or changing their lifestyle – it was as if they had embarked on an experiment which wasn't finished yet. For a while it seemed possible that they wouldn't ever return inside the world of grown-up responsibilities; they were inventing a new kind of life, stepping outside the old wrong, repressive patterns which their parents believed in. When some of them decided to live together holding everything in common, Nicky wanted me and Lukie to join them. If he'd wanted us to live in a threesome, as a family, I might have turned him down – the idea of living with a whole crowd of our friends persuaded me. In the end there were six of us: Nicky and me, Jude and her partner Daphne, Neil and Sheila. Seven, counting Lukie. Daphne and Neil had studied literature together at the university; Sheila had done classics.

The house was on a hill in Bishopston, in a red-brick Victorian terrace – the rent was low because it was half falling down and hadn't been decorated in years. It suited us to live with bare boards, uncarpeted stairs, and walls showing their layers of faded wallpaper: we hung up Nicky's paintings and Jude's embroideries. We enjoyed how the spaces of the house were scarred and worn-out from long use, and fancied ourselves communing with the past inhabitants, furnishing it with odds and ends from the junk shops. I bought an old quilt for our bedroom, printed with faded pink roses, and I found a huge Victorian mirror in a gold frame chipped and damaged beyond repair, put out on the street with someone's rubbish. I draped the mirror with my scarves and beads. I wanted the rooms of my life to be blurred and dreamy and suggestive – the opposite effect to the one my mother and Gerry aimed for, where everything was functioning and spotless and sealed against accidents.

Any money we earned, or anything we got on benefits, we pooled for rent and household expenses and bills. If decisions had to be made we sat round the kitchen table and talked them through. Daphne brought a perfectly round white piece of quartz from her parents' holiday home by the sea, and we put it at the centre of the table; you picked it up if you wanted to speak and replaced it when you'd finished. Housework and cooking were supposed to be shared equally, regardless of gender. On summer nights we hung paper lanterns in the old plum and apple trees in the back garden and lay out in the uncut scented grass, drinking cheap wine and smoking dope, confessing our beliefs and our hopes and fears. I had to be careful not to talk too much: Sheila and Neil and Daphne would pounce if they thought something you said was wrong or showed false consciousness. They were tactful about my lack of education but the tact could be worse than the pouncing. Later, another element in the heady pleasure of those nights was the secrets I was holding back, burning me from inside.

The men did try to help with the housework. Neil – plump and softly shapeless, bearded – would do the vacuuming: frowning short-sightedly, cigarette uptilted at the corner of his mouth, poking the nozzle benevolently, vaguely into corners, dropping ash on the carpet behind him. Nicky washed up energetically, breaking things. But in the end Jude and I did most of it – and we didn't mind, it only seemed fair, because the others were out at work all day, bringing in money. Anyway, we weren't obsessed with cleaning like our mothers, victims of the 'privatised family existence of late capitalism'. We discussed all these issues, using the white stone. There was a kind of glamour at first for the ones who found real jobs, joining the working classes. Nicky was working as a labourer, building a bypass; Sheila was in a little factory that made meat pies, Daphne helped on a play scheme for difficult children. Neil was the only one who was still a student, working on his PhD. He was a Marxist, dissecting everything down to its basis in class conflict and economics – cheerfully he saw through everyone's illusions. He always had his working-class background on his side in his arguments against Daphne, because she came from a wealthy, arty family. Daphne was fiercely feminist: she believed that the nuclear family was an invention of capitalism to keep women oppressed, and that all men were conditioned by society to enjoy the idea of violence against women. Even when men thought they were being kind or loving or protecting women, Daphne said, really underneath it was a kind of violence against them because of its context in the wider world, where men had all the power. I was excited by her arguments. Sometimes they seemed triumphant truths which could be superimposed on every aspect of life, revealing its inner nature: they explained my stepfather and my whole history, they vindicated me. I was burning with zeal for a revolutionary breakthrough in my life.

I worked in the café in the mornings because that was when Lukie went to nursery: in the afternoons he fell asleep on our bed and I dozed beside him. When Lukie woke we had tea downstairs in the kitchen with Jude. She and I cooked vegetarian curries and pasta dishes while Lukie played with his cars and Playmobil. Jude was from Bolton, she blushed easily and was freckled and fair with a poised small figure like a child's. Her embroidered pictures had been a great success at the art college; now she had an agent and was selling to London galleries. They were shocking raw scenes of threat and conflict: girls with slashes of red silk for their mouths and vaginas, stiff net sewn on for their skirts, bits of gold braid for their tiaras; stick-men sewn in waxed black thread, in long crude stitches. (These days they fetch astronomical prices. I owned one for a while – but I had

154

to sell it one lean year.) Jude didn't take politics as seriously as Daphne did. She thought everything was funny – her embroideries were funny too, in a zany, extreme sort of way.

She even thought Baz was funny, in his fixation on her. He was a tall skinny guy with a pretty, fine-boned face, startling under the shock of his orange hair. She'd slept with him once, apparently, in her first week at the art college, because she was too shy to tell him she was gay. — Trust me to choose the crazy one, she said. When Daphne called the police once because Baz followed them back to the house and broke a window trying to get in, Baz told the police that Jude was his wife and that she'd been abducted by a cult. You could see that they were half inclined to believe him.

Sheila had got a first in classics at the university, yet it was Neil who was studying for his PhD now, while she worked earning the money to support them both. When she got back from the pie factory in the evenings I could see from her bleached expression how it exhausted and disgusted her; once I found her in tears, scrubbing at her neck and arms in the bathroom, saying she couldn't get rid of the meat smell (it was true, you could smell onions and gravy wherever she was). Because I'd worked that summer in the chocolate factory, I could guess how the other workers might resent her because she was different – but when I commiserated she turned on me. Sheila was tall, austerely judgmental, with white skin that made her face like a marble sculpture, and a mass of red-brown hair which she had to put up in a net for work.

— Other people have to spend their whole lives in these places, she said. — What's so different about us, that we should be exempt? I'd despise myself if I couldn't put up with it for a couple of years.

But I didn't think that the self-sacrifice would last. There was something willed and exaggerated in how she dedicated herself to Neil, serving him as if his work was more important than anything in her own life. Often Neil didn't even get out of bed to go to the university library until lunchtime, and she must know it; it was as if she was giving him as much scope as possible not to live up to her expectations.

Daphne and Sheila were always falling out. Sheila took Neil's side in all the arguments, and she offended people with her blurted, stern remarks, though I didn't mind them; I could see it was difficult for her to speak lightly about ordinary things. She found Daphne exasperating, and scarcely bothered to conceal it. Daphne was voluptuous, with creamy skin and chestnut hair and huge curvaceous calves (she'd played hockey at school). It was true that her assured, loud flow of talk was guilelessly self-centred, muddling together her outrage at patriarchy with her stomach cramps. Yet she was somehow at the commune's heart; without her I'm not sure we'd have hung together. She was bossy and fearless, doggedly principled – it was Daphne who dealt with our landlord when the roof leaked or the immersion heater broke. Her confidence convinced the rest of us. But she couldn't help nagging away at Sheila, wanting to make little scenes and nurse grudges, contrive tearful reconciliations.

Nicky was the peacemaker in our community. He had the gift of attention to other people; he could talk to anyone, and he never forgot what they told him. This wasn't only with his friends: he got to know the men he worked with on the bypass, or locals he met in the pubs who remembered when the city docks were still in use and the dockers unloaded the timber carrying the long planks on their shoulders, or when the bombs fell on Newfoundland Road and destroyed the vinegar works. I marvelled at his practical knowledge of places and histories, which my mind shied away from, indolent. I knew it was admirable that he didn't talk about himself. But something ruthless in me drew back sometimes even from our moments of most tender intimacy. I would think: he's too simple for me. Then I'd be appalled at myself – it was me who was simple: narrow in my selfish, sticky fascination with my own feelings. I made up to him then with my affection and attention.

We gave a party for the summer solstice. There were always extra people at the house anyway, eating with us or staying over in sleeping bags on spare mattresses or on the floor: this sociability spilled over often into a party with music and dancing (it was the era of Patti Smith, Marvin Gaye, Bowie – we didn't pay much attention to the beginnings of punk). The solstice was Daphne's idea. She explained that pagans celebrated it as a fertility festival in honour of the female goddesses. She and Jude made wreaths out of the grasses that grew tall in our garden, woven with the garden flowers which someone had planted in the past and which had pushed up again without our having tended them: giant daisies and Linaria and an old-fashioned pink rose with frail petals which soon dropped. Even Neil wore a wreath. Nicky drew me wearing mine. I cooked a big pan of chilli con carne made with lentils instead of meat, Sheila made cornbread, Nicky made his Brazilian speciality, little cakes with cocoa and condensed milk.

In the folk cultures of Eastern Europe, according to Daphne, they bathed in open water at sunset; we didn't have any open water, but someone got hold of an old inflatable paddling pool. Lukie was blissfully happy in the pool, splashing and pouring from a plastic bucket; he insisted on staying there until his nude little body was white and clammy with cold, though the evening was sultry. The weather had changed after a week of rain; the close heat under the fruit trees and the rank smells of the garden drying out made us all excitable. With uncharacteristic energy, Neil had spent the afternoon chopping down a tumbledown wooden shed in the garden and we burned this, though it spat nails and its layers of ancient paint blistered and fumed nastily. Daphne insisted there had to be fire and water. She wrapped potatoes in tinfoil and buried them in the embers to cook.

I put Lukie to bed eventually, when he had to be fished out from submerging in the pool – he was distraught and sobbing, not from his dousing but at being separated from the party. His cot was in a little cubbyhole separated off from the upstairs landing by a curtain. Nicky had a game he played to get him off to sleep, counting on his fingers and tickling in his palms – but Lukie was too tired and distraught even for that, so we had to leave him to cry. I stayed upstairs in our bedroom, moving around the room in the dusk and tidying it, waiting until Lukie stopped crying and fell asleep, aware of my reflection coming and going in the foggy depths of the mirror. I was breathless and expectant though I didn't know what it was that I expected. By the time I returned downstairs the sun was setting. Daphne had decided that we should throw our wreaths in turn into the paddling pool, then kneel while she poured water over our heads out of her cupped hands. She recited words about the blessing of the goddess, who was 'subtle, deep, and difficult to see' (these were borrowed from something in Buddhism).

Jude submitted to the ritual: in her white cheesecloth dress she looked like a priestess in a play. Some of the other girls joined in but the men were making fun of it. Neil was fairly drunk and his wreath had slipped down across one eye; he had been flirting all evening with a blonde they knew from the university. His flirting wasn't gallant, he was too lazy for flattery; he just directed all his usual conversation and his attention at one chosen person, determined like a pet animal wanting to climb into a lap. Women warmed to Neil's cleverness, even though he was pudgy and flushed pink, with an indefinite beard. Sheila would never admit that she cared about his

159

flirtations, or even when he occasionally slept with these other girls.

— Isn't that bourgeois morality? she said.

Someone new had arrived at the party while I was waiting upstairs. He was sitting cross-legged in the grass beside Sheila: a big-shouldered rangy man in a dirty vest, hunched over his cigarette, long hair hanging forward over his face. He complained that Daphne's ceremony was too decorous. — Like Girl Guides at a camp, he said. — Don't you know those midsummer festivals are all about lust? They swim together, then they go off in the woods together to fuck. The ones wearing the wreaths are signalling that they're available.

— I'm available, said Neil.

— At least you should get right under the water, the stranger said, — and not just wet your heads.

Someone added that it shouldn't be just the girls.

Before the blonde could move from where she was sitting with Neil's head on her shoulder, Sheila stood up and walked across to step into the pool, then lay down in it – you couldn't stretch right out, so she lay with her knees pulled up, and then rolled over. I suppose the water was about a foot deep; in spite of the warm evening the cold must have been a shock. When she stood up the water poured off her dramatically; she was stuck all over with bits of twig and leaves, her hair in streaming rat-tails, her dress clinging to her body. After that, lots of us did it. I did it (and Nicky wrapped me in his jacket afterwards). Even Daphne did it in the end, though she was still sulking because her ceremony had been hijacked.

160

Of course the men couldn't do it solemnly, they had to pretend to be fooling around, falling into the water accidentally or chucking it at each other. Soon the pool was almost empty. I noticed that the stranger didn't join in, the one who'd come up with the idea in the first place.

The stranger was Sheila's brother. They came from a big family of nine children, brought up in a draughty Norfolk vicarage. (— Everything we ever owned was handed down, Sheila said. — It made us horribly materialistic. I prayed in church for patent leather shoes.) We had met some of her brothers and sisters before, but not this one: Andrew. He was older than Sheila, the oldest boy, and she hadn't seen him for five years because he'd had an irrevocable row with his family – she couldn't remember what the row was about. (His hair? His faith?) After the row he had dropped out from York University in his second year, and never contacted them. The family had refused to go after him, though they included him in their prayers. But Sheila and one of her sisters had made great efforts to trace him, writing to all Andrew's old friends and teachers, listing him as a missing person with the police, even travelling by themselves on the coach to York to see if they could find him there.

When Andrew turned up at the party without any warning (he'd got Sheila's address from the other sister), they hadn't embraced or even touched each other. — It's you! was all Sheila had said, when he dropped to sit on the grass beside her. And she had protested, joking, that he could at least have sent her a postcard. Andrew was tall – very tall, six foot four or five – and he looked as marked with damage – eyes extinguished, stale, unshaven grey-white face, lank draggled hair – as if he'd come back from the dead instead of, as it turned out, bumming around southern Europe. His eyes were chinks of blue in his long face: small, indifferent, retreated behind the craggy mass of his cheekbones. He had been playing his saxophone for money or labouring or working on the grape harvest; in jail for a while, waiting to be deported from Spain. When we asked him to play his saxophone, he said he'd sold it.

He stayed with us for a few weeks, in a sleeping bag on his bed-roll on the floor in the front room; then he moved to live in a squat in a filthy spindly old house in a Georgian crescent, where there was more drink and more drugs than at our place and less domesticity. Even after he'd moved out he seemed to spend a lot of time with us. I supposed at first that he came to see Sheila. My heart used to sink when he turned up because his presence had a dampening effect – he was too brooding and dogmatic. He was contemptuous of our commune, the sharing of possessions and decision-making; he said it was only tinkering behind closed doors, not changing anything real. Real revolution, he said, had to happen out on the street. He picked up our white stone one evening, laughing when we explained what we used it for, throwing it indifferently from hand to hand. Only Daphne protested – she was braver at quarrelling with him than anyone else. Andrew never talked much, it was as if you had to drag speech out of him; yet he dominated any conversation he was in. Despite this, people were drawn to him, they wanted his approval.

In the end, I wanted his approval too.

I can't explain the power Andrew had over me, for a while.

That's just what I said to him: — I can't explain the power you have over me. Rashly — but he made me behave as if there was no point in self-preservation. And he said, — It's biological. There's nothing you feminists can do about it. You can tinker around with all the rest but you can't change the shape of fucking, where you need me to overwhelm you. Don't you? Unless you want a man to love you like a baby.

This racked me at the time, because it seemed unanswerably true: that you couldn't reverse the male gesture of possession and penetration which was at the heart of sex. Part of Andrew's attraction certainly was his huge, lean strength – I thought of his size as a force. I supposed it was what made him able to drink so much without losing himself. He drank wine, mostly; he'd picked up the habit abroad. When he was drunk he wasn't garrulous. If he was ever sober, he was silent. His need for the drink and the drugs seemed to come out of a narrow concentration in him that was almost puritanical, some exacting demand he made on life that could not otherwise be met.

Andrew's conscious attention mostly wasn't on women; he only really warmed to the company of men. He described legendary drinkers, scoffers and fighters he'd met on his wanderings, in Thessaloniki, Chania, Barcelona. He sparred with Neil, sizing him up. And he liked Nicky. Everyone liked Nicky. Nicky talked to Andrew about his work building the bypass: he was a carpenter's assistant, unloading hot sacks of cement fresh from the factory, putting together the wooden frames into which the mixed cement was poured. Andrew didn't even mind Baz; he held him in long conversation at our kitchen table once, when Baz came looking for Jude while she hid upstairs. Baz was twitchy from whatever he was taking that had cranked him up so high, he looked harmless and foolish beside Andrew's uncompromising bulk. All the time they were talking, Andrew was rolling up in his thick, deft fingers – sticking papers, dribbling a line of loose tobacco from his pouch, cooking the dope lump in his lighter flame, chipping into it with his thumbnail. The ritual absorbed Baz and calmed him. I was making supper at the stove and pretended to be taking no notice of them – I could see through the window that Lukie was safe, playing outside in the garden.

— How would you feel, Baz tried to explain (strained, focused on something deep inside which ate him up) — if she was your girl and they wouldn't let you see her? Wouldn't you worry? All I want is for her and me to talk. I need to talk to her.

— You've got the wrong end of the stick there, Andrew said almost jovially, sweeping up dropped shreds of tobacco into his palm. — The only person not wanting you to talk to Jude is Jude. I'm afraid she doesn't like you, my friend.

164

Baz was only hurting himself, Andrew suggested, by chasing after her. He might as well give up and go home, find someone else. (At the time, Baz almost seemed to take it from him.) But Andrew never put on that teasing expansiveness with women. When Jude thanked him for fending off Baz, he only batted away his smoke with his hand, warning that she should be more careful what company she kept. He told me later that he thought her embroideries were the cheapest kind of sensationalist trick. Sheila was tolerated, a comrade left over from the childhood he had abandoned. And he dismissed Daphne's organising energy, saying she made him think of a lady magistrate; he called her radical feminism 'politics for girls'. I thought that Andrew must despise me because I was so ignorant and I hadn't read anything. I never contributed to the kinds of conversation that he liked.

One evening while he was arguing with Neil, I went upstairs to check on Lukie, saying I thought I heard him cry out. Actually I was bored by their argument – about anarchy, which Neil was keen on and Andrew despised. Lukie was fast asleep, his face beautifully clear, emptied of the busy day, cheeks flushed, one arm thrown out across the pillow. I lingered out of reach of the raised voices, moving around in my bare feet between our empty rooms in the half-dark that was never complete because of the street lamps: the windows were all open, it was still summer. Outside it rained steadily and persuasively, drenching the gardens; the smells of wet grass, and rain steaming off the hot tar of the road, mingled

165

with the incense we burned in the house and the musty carpets.

Andrew must have followed me upstairs. I was suddenly aware of him blocking my way when I tried to pass him on the landing; he stopped me clumsily but peremptorily, as though I must know what he wanted. Confused, I wondered if he was angry with me for some reason. Then – buried in the completed blackness against his sour heavy clothes, nose and throat full of new intimacy with the unknown of his body – I was more mystified and gratified than anything. Or, I felt as if I was falling through the lit surface of things, out into a new realm of experience where everything was upside-down, and darker. As soon as I guessed that this darker world existed, I wanted to enter it and try what was there. Honestly, until that moment, I hadn't even liked him.

Of course, this way of telling the story – this stuff about the darkness – is also a romance, a dangerous romance. And looking back, I understand now that Andrew liked me because he made a mistake about me. Because I'd had a baby and hadn't gone to university, and because I was shy in those days and painted my eyes and could cook and was wary of joining in the arguments, he misinterpreted my character: which was fair enough, all the signs were pretty misleading. In his mythology women ought to be intuitive and enigmatic and wholesome – a safe place in which the lights of male striving and intellect could heal themselves. Whereas I was hoping: now he'll listen to what I think. To this man, I thought, I can tell the truth at last.

166

Each of us wanted the other to be the darkness, listening.

Nicky made drawings of the men he worked with on the bypass – I still have them. They are done in pencil in a notebook when they were taking a break, or whenever he wasn't busy and the foreman wasn't looking. He told me the men teased him for it but they gathered round to look at themselves: hunched against vibration, tamping the road surface with a rammer; or hunkered over the nub of a cigarette and a mug of tea, paging a thumbed-soft copy of some porn magazine; or craning, hands on levers, to see out of the cab of an excavator. Pages are torn out of the notebook where he gave sketches away. (These men also called him Blackie and gave him the dirtiest work to do, emptying the portable latrines.)

Nicky had lost his way at the art college; the teachers weren't interested in his drawings from real life. The paintings he did – his final show was a series of repeated marks in thick acrylic, built into rectangular blocks – were quite striking and seemed to impress people. He took them very seriously and they got him good marks. But I don't think he really knew why he was painting them or what they meant. He wasn't clever, not in that way. Although I never said so, I could always see through those paintings to an emptiness behind. I can't see through the little drawings in that notebook, or the ones in other notebooks which he did of me and Lukie and the others – so exact and sure and graceful. The surface of these drawings has its own interior which I can't penetrate, no matter how hard I stare. (And I don't stare, not all that often. All this happened long ago, it's history now.)

I stopped him drawing me in those last months, I couldn't bear it. (Pretending it was politics – 'I don't want to be your subject.') There's only one quickly scribbled sketch of me pregnant with Rowan. I'm in the bedroom, doing my hair in front of the mirror with my arms up, my mounded stomach a swelling line under the folds of a loose top. I'm probably wearing my jeans with the zip open, I went on wearing them long after I stopped being able to do them up. I'm not looking at Nicky. I probably didn't even know that he was drawing me. I'm only looking at myself.

I didn't know whose baby Rowan was until he was born and it was so obvious he was Nicky's (his eyes, hair, skin – though he was pale at first; and something fluent and musical, almost feminine, in their limbs). And then afterwards when Rowan grew up so angry with everything and so intransigent, although I knew rationally this wasn't possible, I couldn't help thinking that because I had also been making love to Andrew all during the time when I conceived him, and through the months of my pregnancy afterwards, some bitterness from Andrew's blood or sperm or spirit had got somehow into the mix that made Rowan up. (It's obvious there's a sounder explanation. The bitterness that got into him was me.)

And yet, during all that time when I was behaving so badly and no one knew, and when I was so guilty and full of foreboding, I was also often happy – happy in an unbalanced, ecstatic kind of way I've never experienced again in all my life. I was with Andrew once in the back garden out among the fruit trees and we weren't kissing because anyone might have been watching from a window, but the not-kissing was more heady than kissing and I hardly knew what I was doing. He advanced on me, talking about how British society was winding down to its own destruction because of the treachery of the intelligentsia, and I retreated ahead of him, ducking between trees drowning under their foam of white and pink blossom; my ears were full of bee-sound and we crushed a fumy mulch of last year's rotten plums and apples underfoot. The baby's mystifying bulk inside me came between us, connecting and separating us. He broke off a whole branch of wet, scented apple blossom and gave it to me. It was a criminal thing; bees were still dangling, desirous, around the flowers' stamen and stigma and their bulges of ovary which would now never grow into apples. The broken branch was an emblem of my too-much; it seemed more lordly not to refuse such bounty if it offered. What it was impossible to have without harm was also most to be desired. And after all, no one in the commune was supposed to own anyone else's body, or their feelings. Why, then, was it my first and deepest instinct to keep what was happening with Andrew to myself, as my secret?

If there was apple blossom then that must have been April; and Rowan was born in May. So that scene happened very late, not long before the end. There's

169

another scene in my memory, from when it was still winter: we're all bulky in our layers of warm clothes. Everyone's there, Andrew too. (Not Baz.) Daphne has come back from an afternoon modelling at the art college. Sheila has given up at the pie factory, a burden of sacrifice has fallen from her, she's buoyant and brittle (not much time left before she leaves Neil and goes off to South America). Jude and I have cooked and we're in aprons, ladling food out of a couple of big pans; the others are all sitting round the table. I remember all this because I have a photograph of it, a polaroid, its colours faded now to queasy green – there's some dark mess on the plates in front of us which we haven't begun to eat, we're all looking up expectantly at the photographer. I can't think who the photographer was. Some convenient outsider stepped into our story to record it.

What's striking about Andrew in the photograph is how thoroughly his looks now seem to belong to that period. His dun-coloured hair, parted centrally and grown down almost to his waist, makes his face seem too long; he looks young and pasty and his ears stick out. The appeal he once had for me has dated, I can't recover it. Whereas Nicky looks timeless and vividly alive, as if he could step so easily out of the photograph and across into the present. He has Lukie on his lap. Lukie isn't looking at the camera, he's twisting round to smile up at Nicky and touch his face. No wonder I don't look at this photograph very often. When we've finished eating we fall into shouting, drunken, earnest discussion of what knowledge is, and how it is that we know what we know. Sheila's been reading French philosophy and she says knowledge is only our struggle to have power over things and over each other. I am insisting that one form of knowledge is knowing what milk is like, say, as a baby knows, even before it has language. Andrew says that isn't real knowledge, it's only perception, which is different. Real knowledge is that water boils at 100 degrees. This shouting and arguing – all of us involved in it together – is a heady pleasure too, just like the loving in the garden.

And then I was a widow. I wasn't legally a widow, as Nicky and I were never married, but it's funny – especially under the complicated circumstances – how the word stuck to me right away in my own imagination. People were startled when I used it. I suppose I was formed by widows: my grandmother was one from before I was born, and my mother was supposed to be one until she married my stepfather. In the commune we believed we weren't going to do anything the way our parents did – we didn't want to conform to their types, we repudiated their categories. But when real trouble came those new hopes could look for a while like shallow scratches on a surface. I fell down, after Nicky died, into a very ancient hole. Widowhood didn't have any glamour for me, it wasn't a pose, I wasn't picturing myself poignant or mournful in a black veil or anything. I certainly didn't pity myself – not after what I'd done. But I recognised this stony place, this bedrock, as if I had been down here before. Somehow it was important to have a name for it, one of the old names.

His death broke up the commune. When I look back, I wonder if the rest of them didn't stick together for so many months just for my sake: looking out for me with poor little Lukie and my new baby (born on time, three weeks after it happened), doing their best to comfort us. Forensics delayed for a cruelly long time; when they finally allowed us to clean up the kitchen, Daphne invented a beautiful purification ceremony, covering the place with roses and blossom from the garden, burning incense and propping up some of Nicky's paintings against the wall, lighting candles in front of them. Each of us put something there in his memory, and spoke about him. Neil gave a full bottle of whisky, I remember; Jude gave one of her embroideries; Lukie made a card. Sheila brought the white-leather-covered testament she'd been given at her confirmation. Later we buried all these things in a hole in the garden, and then I had a horror of that place as if Nicky's body was buried there – even though I'd been to his actual, Catholic burial in Glasgow, where his mother broke down and screamed at us, blaming our way of life (hippies and dropouts) for what had happened. (When Rowan was two or three years old I sent his grandmother photographs and she wrote back; I took him to visit her every so often and for a while, when he was sixteen and we weren't getting on, he went to live with her.)

Daphne's ceremony seems a beautiful idea to me now, when I remember it. At the time I just thought it was a fake; I seemed to see through everything, to a grey fake. I can't even remember what I offered as my token. I think I chose perfunctorily – a bracelet or a pendant Nicky had given me which I hadn't even liked – because I didn't want to tempt fate by performing with too much conviction. I only began to cry after Rowan's birth and then I couldn't stop; but there was something fake about that too, this tap turned on full – spouting out its world-sorrows, soaking everything – which I couldn't turn off. Only breastfeeding helped (I was doing it for the first time – I hadn't even tried to breastfeed Lukie). For as long as the baby was sucking I could imagine myself connected almost impersonally into a great chain of life, one thing flowing into another. It wasn't a hopeful feeling, just a sensation of continuity, and necessity.

Sheila was the first to leave the commune, after a row with Neil which began when he announced he was going to give up his PhD and do a law conversion course. And then once I'd gone back with the children to live at Fred Harper's again, the others moved out quickly: that house must have been a dreadful place for all of them, we never got the stains out of the kitchen floorboards. I don't know how I ended up with the white stone; it's on my coffee table now, in a wide blue-glazed bowl by a cerami-cist whose work I like, kept among other stones collected on family holidays later. Perhaps Lukie brought it with him. It would have seemed a powerful totem to him after he'd watched us passing it from hand to hand, adults so solemnly absorbed in the game they were playing.

None of the others ever knew about my relationship with Andrew; Sheila may have guessed something but she's never asked me. About a year after Nicky died, Jude and I met up for a night out (she was renting a room from friends, Daphne had moved back temporarily to live with her parents). My mother had Luke and Rowan to stay: everyone was conspiring to cheer me up or take me out of myself. And somehow it happened that at the end of the evening Jude and I ended up in her bed together. We'd both had a lot to drink. It was the only time I ever made love to another woman. Jude hadn't been harbouring a secret passion for me, the thing just came about out of her kindness; she was consoling me – and consoling herself. She felt responsible, because of Baz. She lit a scented candle in her room and her clean bed linen was patterned with ferns; it was easy touching the cool skin of her body which I knew because it was like my own but not quite like. We didn't speak much but her light voice and northern vowels were caresses in themselves, inconsequent and soothing. In the dark under her duvet something was unblocked in me: a flood of responsive desiring, to begin with, which took me by surprise. I'd been quite numb and dry for a year, I'd thought sex could never touch me again.

And letting myself fall down into the slippery, brilliant whorls and corridors and intricacies of it, I got back my memories of Nicky too. I'd thought I'd lost these as my punishment – but they had been saved up all the time, in my body. Nicky had had a gift for sex, like his gift for drawing: attentive, inventive, easy, skilful. I think of him now like a shepherd boy in a poem, or a boy lover in a Watteau painting, with a lute. He had actually liked me – liked the clear, light, energetic person he saw in me. (I think over time I've become more like that person.) Sex with him hadn't been at all like conquest; Andrew was wrong, it didn't always have to do with submission and overwhelming. Actually Nicky was a better lover; or put it this way, he roused up more pleasure in my body than Andrew ever achieved. (But I have to reckon with the truth, too, that it was Andrew I had wanted more.)

I was packing to leave, to go and live with Andrew, when it happened. (Andrew had decided that living with me – and with Lukie and the coming baby – would save him from himself.) Lukie was at nursery. Nicky was hung-over, drinking coffee in the kitchen; he'd been out with his workmates the night before. I hadn't told him, but I was going to tell him as soon as he came upstairs. The words were ready in my mouth (I'm so sorry, sorry, sorry); resolved, I was listening out for his quick step, taking two stairs at a time as he always did. Afterwards I went over and over this in my thoughts until I was nearly mad (because he was dead, I couldn't help attributing omniscience to him): but really I don't think he knew that I was going, or about Andrew. He knew that something was wrong, but not what it was. If I'd decided to tell him half an hour earlier, he'd have died knowing. We were separated from that different story by a tissue-thin sliver of time, mere accident.

Waiting, I confused my dread with the heavy child inside me making it so difficult to move around, reach down, get out my suitcases from under the bed, empty my clothes out of the drawers. Outside the windows the day was stifling hot under grey cloud; sweat ran on the back of my neck and under my arms and between my breasts. Someone arrived at the front door and Neil opened it: I thought it might be Andrew already but it was Baz, I recognised his voice – always reasonable and temporising to begin with. We'd all thought he'd left Bristol, he hadn't bothered us for a while. Neil should have shut the door in his face. Baz pushed past him into the kitchen; Jude came running up into her bedroom. Hearing the raised voices from downstairs, and the remonstrating, made me more certain that I had to leave. I'd begun to take on some of Andrew's opinions on communal living: it was an indulgent bourgeois whim and I couldn't wait to get out of it, being mixed up in everybody else's craziness and stupidity. The atmosphere in the house had soured. It even smelled bad that day, in the heat; we had a cellar that flooded periodically, according to mysterious tides in a river that had apparently been taken underground when the area was developed. Sometimes when we opened the cellar door, foul grey water would be lapping at the bottom of the brick staircase and our buckets and rubber gloves and dustpan would all be afloat.

No one screamed but some alteration in their voices must have alerted me; I went downstairs. The door which opened out of the back of the hall into the kitchen was closed, but it was half glass – the original Victorian glass with a ruby-red border and a clear star at each corner – so

I saw most of what happened through that, unreal and stilted as if I was watching a peep show. Baz must have picked up our knife from where it was left on the draining board after washing up: it was only a vegetable knife, a Sabatier that Daphne had brought from home. He was threatening Neil with it, slashing it in the air ('I've seen that sneering look on your face, you fat pussy'), and I remember Neil was pirouetting fastidiously with a tea towel, like a matador with his cape, to get out of its way. In another life, with a different outcome, it would have been funny. Daphne was holding her hand out, calmly and sensibly telling Baz to give the knife to her, and I think he might have done it except that he seemed to hear something – did I rattle the doorknob, was I trying to open the door? Or was it Jude coming downstairs? So instead he spun round to where Nicky must have been coming from behind to try to disarm him, and he stuck the knife into Nicky, between his ribs, with all his weight behind it.

— You all think you're so bloody special, don't you?

And that was it. That's how disaster comes, without any fanfare – though none of us could take it quite seriously for a moment or two, even Nicky, who looked down at his jumper soaking with blood, more surprised than anything. Baz, still holding the knife, seemed as bewildered as the rest of us, and Daphne hit at his hand with the rolling pin which she'd snatched up from the draining board, kicking the knife away into a corner of the room before she and Neil tackled him to the floor. Sheila ran out to the phone box to call an ambulance

177

and the police. Then before the ambulance men could arrive, Andrew was suddenly at the door – and by that time I knew already that Nicky was dead, I'd been kneeling with his head on my lap, holding his hand, and I'd felt the life go out of him. I sent Andrew to pick up Lukie from nursery and look after him while I went to the hospital. And then when I got back from the hospital I saw Andrew just that once more, when I collected Lukie. They'd spent the afternoon together at the zoo. I told Andrew I could never see him again, ever. Never. I wouldn't listen when he tried to talk me out of it, I never responded when he phoned or wrote to me afterwards, not ever. And I never did see him again. I only had word of him from time to time, through Sheila.

Seven

One day when Fred came in from school, before he'd even put down his briefcase or taken off his coat, he said he thought he'd found God. It was part of his style to make these pronouncements, like a character in grand opera. Sometimes he would even sing snatches of opera to accompany them. And I used to think how if I'd been his lover or his wife these pronouncements delivered with such oracular solemnity would have got under my skin and made me impatient with him. (I'd have been annoyed by knowing that under the ironic play, sending seriousness up, he actually took himself so seriously.) As it was, I was tolerant of him, and didn't mind these games. The heavy black overcoat I'd found for him in a charity shop was too big, it swamped him like a cloak and added to the operatic effect, along with his big liquid eyes and drooping, doggy, olive-skinned long cheeks.

I was making a chicken pie, lifting the round of rolled-out pastry on to the dish full of pieces of chicken and ham in a creamy sauce flavoured with lemon.

— I didn't know God was lost, I said, concentrating on centring the pastry correctly, so that the hole I'd cut came down over the uplifted beak of the china blackbird meant to hold the pastry up. — Where did you find him?

— Don't mock, Stella. My life's burdened with sin, I need to change. It can't go on.

— You're not in love again, are you? With the new chaplain or something?

He groaned. — You see? How it's impossible to talk without joking about my spiritual life. I'm not blaming you.

My little boys, aged three years old and seven, were playing out in the garden. Fred's flat was in the basement of a tall, wide Edwardian house built of red stone; the kitchen door opened on to a paved yard where I hung out the washing and grew a few flowers in pots – not very successfully because the yard only got the sun for a couple of hours in the afternoon. Stone steps led up into the garden proper which was a wild place, crazily overgrown. It was supposed to be the responsibility of the old lady who had once owned the whole house and now lived in the first floor flat, but she had given up bothering with it; when we offered to help she said she didn't want us interfering. Judging by the state of her flat (her entrance was at the side of the house, up a metal staircase like a fire escape) she had given up bothering in there, too. Sometimes she was standing at her window and caught sight of the boys playing in the garden; then she rapped on the pane and shook her fist at them like a pantomime witch (Rowan showed me, screwing up his face and hunching his shoulders aggressively, growling).

The garden was surrounded with high walls built of the same red stone as the house; a portion at the end had been concreted over years ago to make a car park, which no one used because the gap where the drive ran between the side of the house and the wall was too narrow for the newer cars. The garden must have been handsome once. Massive boulders in the rockery were studded with fossils, roses still bloomed along a rusting arcade where ancient espalier apple trees had been trained. The roses and the apple trees sprouted in disorder, convolvulus smothered everything, brambles were invading over a wall, evergreen trees had grown too tall and cast long, blue shadows. The lawn and the flower beds were tangled with weeds and the drive was pitted with potholes; dock and buddleia sprouted through the asphalt. The boys had a den in the shrubbery. I knew that Luke sometimes climbed into a tree and sat on top of the wall, looking down into the ordered garden next door while Rowan waited obediently below, craning upwards to know what his brother saw. Luke led Rowan around everywhere by the hand, taking care he didn't step in anything or get stung by nettles. He knew his brother better than anyone did, including me – how best to cushion him against disappointment.

From time to time they made their way back to me down the stone steps (usually because one of them needed the lavatory: Luke would question Rowan sternly, in order to avoid accidents). I loved the sight of them bare-chested in the sunshine, dirty-faced, scruffy because I cut their hair myself, not very well. They wore clothes handed on to me by friends whose children had outgrown them: I patched the knees of the trousers when they wore through, and let down the hems or sewed strips of different fabric around the bottom as the boys grew taller. I gave them picnics to take along on their adventures, packed into Rowan's little red suitcase. I never spied on them but once when I was on my way to the dustbin I caught sight accidentally of them unwrapping the packets of biscuits in their den, sitting very seriously to eat them, side by side. Not wanting to break in on their secret, I crept away.

— I need a framework, Fred said, lifting the crust from the chicken pie with his knife and fork to sniff the steam. — I'm bewildered by too much freedom. That's why I'm thinking of converting. It isn't the chaplain – he's very unattractive. And he's a dreary Anglican, anyway.

— Do you have too much freedom? I said. — You're always complaining about how school takes every moment of your time.

— In my moral life, I mean.

— Oh, in your moral life! I didn't know you had one.

— What's a moral life? Luke asked.

Fred began to explain, wiping his mouth on his napkin. Drinking in new information, Luke watched his face intently. — It's the life you lead in the light of your conscience. Choosing whether to do right or wrong, trying to work out what right is.

— What's your conscience?

— Well, that depends on whether you believe in God, or Freud. The question is: how does your conscience *know* what's wrong?

Fred always answered the children's questions fully and with scrupulous seriousness. They loved this, and would follow him round the flat interrogating him ('Have you ever been in a war? Who invented writing?'), until he had to summon me to rescue him. I could imagine what kind of a teacher he was at the expensive private boys' school he pretended to hate: satirical, calculatedly eccentric, inspiring, sometimes arbitrary; disliked by the sporty boys, worshipped by a few clever ones, and with deadly enemies on the staff. By that time his persona at the school was probably larger and more dramatic than anything really going on in his private life. I teased him, but he was chastened and wary and as far as I knew kept his desires mostly to himself. Occasionally he disappeared to town in the evening and came back very late, always alone.

Rowan of course didn't like the chicken pie. I had to bargain with him. — Just four spoonfuls. Just three. Then you can leave the rest. I held up my three fingers so he could see I wasn't cheating. Really, I was saving my own face. The spoonfuls were very tiny, they were only tokens. (How could I force him to eat, when I'd been such a difficult eater myself?) After supper, when the boys were in the bath, I cleared up while Fred recited poetry to me: mostly, during that period when he was flirting with religion, Gerard Manley Hopkins ('earth her being has unbound, her dapple is at an end, astray or aswarm. . .'). I didn't mind this. If he tried to help wash the dishes or put the toys away everything took twice as long. Anyway, our arrangement was that we lived with him rent-free in return for housekeeping: scrupulously I fulfilled my part.

There were times when I didn't mind anything: the hazy yellow evening light, the midges swarming, the back door open into the yard where the boys' bikes and plastic racquets lay where they had dropped them, the thrush singing in a hornbeam in the garden, the intimately known round of drudgery, the sound of the boys' splashing in the bath and their absorbing games. And at the end of it lifting Rowan out of the bathwater gone too cold, his chattering teeth and wrinkled finger-ends, his snuggling close against me, seeping wet into the big bath towel, the fight between us quenched and dormant for an interval; while Luke pulled the plug and the water drained, leaving its flotsam and jetsam beached on the enamel: bath toys and garden grit. By the time I lay between them to read to them in my single bed (they slept in the same room as me, in bunks), I was so tired sometimes that I fell asleep mid-sentence. I half knew that I mumbled a few nonsense words before I lapsed. The boys would be lost in the story, incredulous and frustrated when it failed. Peering in my face and nudging me in the ribs (— Mum! Wake up!) they would try to keep me afloat for long enough at least to arrive at the end of the chapter.

Fred was always trying to persuade me to read

grown-up books. He said it would save me, and I said I didn't need saving, that was him, wasn't it? Wasn't he the one supposed to be wrestling with angels or whatever? I had been a reader once, when I was a girl. But these days, with two young children – I said to him – where would I find the time? While Fred did his marking or groaned aloud in pleasure over his philosophy books and religious books (sometimes he brought in passages to read to me), I sorted out the washing. I put the television on, I stood in front of it to iron the children's clothes and Fred's shirts and my own things (I was working in the mornings in a small art gallery so I had to look tidy). I did my bits of mending. I made lists of what I had to do the next day. I was all right.

And then every so often, as if a switch flicked between two versions of myself, I suddenly wasn't all right. That same night, the night of the chicken pie, I blundered up out of my bed when it was still dark. I couldn't stay between the stifling sheets; the carpet was greasy under my bare feet, I trod on sharp fragments of toy. The boys were sound asleep, flush-faced, limbs flung out heedlessly, duvets kicked down to the bottom of their beds. I couldn't recover my last night's life with its ordered calm, one thing after another; I wasn't that same person with her steady, sane perspectives. It seemed intolerable that in a few hours it would be Saturday and I'd be putting breakfast on the table once again, then eating it once again, then washing up after it, nagging the boys to get dressed, planning the shopping, putting clothes in the washing machine. These repetitions stood like a barrier I couldn't pass, blocking the time ahead.

I went into Fred's room and hunted in the dark for the car keys, feeling in the pockets of his jacket on its coat hanger. Confused, he reared up against the pillows and switched on the bedside light. The grandiose mahogany bed with its scrolled ends had belonged to his parents and had been his marital bed until his wife divorced him. Books were pressed open, spine up, one on top of another, on the floor beside the bed and on the bedside table – which was also crowded with cigarettes and full ashtray, empty whisky glass, bottles of tablets, alarm clock. He was incongruous in cream pyjamas – one of those men made to be fully dressed, his surface polished and finished.

— Please, let me have your keys, I said. — Don't be mad with me. I just want them for today. Or for a couple of days.

— What kind of time is it? Christ, it's the middle of the night, Stella. You might have been the secret police. You're lucky I didn't have a heart attack.

The car wasn't really the main issue. Fred scrabbled on his table for cigarettes and lighter, upsetting the pile of books. The hair on the back of his head was muzzy from his pillows: he slept obediently on his back like a child in a storybook.

— Are you taking the boys?

— You can take them round to my mother's. Is it all right? I'm sorry.

— But how will I take them, without the car?

— I don't know. Get a taxi? I'll pay you back.

I had found the keys spilt out from his pocket on to the dressing table along with a heap of change and some crumpled notes, nub ends of chalk; I gripped them so that they dug into my palm. It wasn't the first time I'd done this: 'done a runner', as my Auntie Jean cheerfully described it. (I was surprised when Jean confessed to runners of her own, when she was a young mother.) I didn't do it often – once or twice a year, perhaps. Fred knew me, he knew I wasn't putting it on. It was part of his character to support his friends without criticism in whatever adventures they got into. He told me I'd have to put petrol in the car if I was going any distance, and to take his cash, which would tide me over until the banks opened.

Fred really did mean it about the religious thing; he went through a course of instruction and was received into the Catholic Church. He began going to mass on Sundays and taking communion and confessing. It made him happy, I think. Intellectually and in his tastes in art and writing he was so sceptical, questing, doubting; nothing shocked him. And yet in himself, in his person, there was something resigned, he accepted convention as the frame of his life. The church suited him just as the rituals of the school day suited him, imposing their pattern on the succession of minutes.

My daily life was conforming and unexciting, I knew next to nothing about politics or society. And yet I felt this strength like a knife inside me, anarchic and

187

destructive, able to cut through whatever outward forms of authority I met – vicars or businessmen or headmasters in their grey suits, with their smooth arguments and dismissive irony, so confident in their unassailable rightness. I believed that I could see through them to their false core and their vanity. Some of the artists whose work was exhibited in the gallery were unassailable like this too, even if they didn't wear suits – they hardly noticed me perched on my trendy high stool, paid to answer the telephone and bank the cheques. I hated the school where Fred taught, for instance, and where I had once worked as a cleaner. Sometimes when I was going on about the hypocrisy of the school – its high-toned preaching about enlightened values while it taught its pupils to be competitive and arrogant, just because they had money – Fred would look as if he was quite afraid of me. I expect that sometimes I ranted and exaggerated. I don't really know, now, whether I was right.

The way out of Fred's flat was up a short flight of concrete steps where shrubs grew thickly on either side: a yellow-spotted poisonous laurel and some dark evergreen with spiky leaves. It must have rained earlier because these were wet when I pushed through them in the dark; I saw the sepulchral night-face of the street, moonlight on the slate roofs and the lawns. The little white 1970 Lotus Elan smelled of its vinyl seat covers; I had encouraged Fred to buy it, I loved its sleek sumptuousness and the dirty snarl of its engine. (His ex-wife Lizzie blamed me for the frivolity and expense. She and I had a rather tortured relationship.) The moment I was behind the wheel, I was calmer. I turned on the lights, heard the engine bark into life. Driving, it was as if a spring uncoiled in me. At first I was careful not to go too fast around the sleeping streets. I drove out to the motorway, under the suspension bridge strung against the grey first light, alongside the river snaking between banks of glinting mud. I filled up at a service station, paying with Fred's money. I drove north. Lights were still on in the windows of some factories; a white horse in a field seemed to race the car.

The traffic thickened. In the little Lotus I nipped in and out between the lorries, urgent as if I was forging on towards something. I hardly thought about the boys I'd left behind me, rousing in their beds and wondering where I was, Rowan stepping out of the parcel of his plastic pants and sodden ammoniac nappies, shaking Luke awake to play with him, Luke taking charge ('Let's go and tell Fred she's gone'). I didn't think about anything, I was transparent and alive, washed through with the present moment.

The first time I ran away, Rowan was only eighteen months old. I took the boys to my mother's and when she came to the front door she was dressed up to go out shopping in her coat and silk scarf and clip earrings, her face freshly made up.

I said I was stuck and needed her help.

I saw how she opened her mouth to make some remark about how I'd better get used to being stuck at home and bored. She couldn't help wanting to remind me that my difficulties were the consequence of the rash, headstrong life I had chosen, ignoring her warnings, mixing with the wrong kind of people.

— It's an emergency, I lied. — Madeleine's in some kind of trouble.

When she looked in my face she must have seen something that silenced her because resignedly she began unbuttoning her coat. Luke was already helping Rowan off with his shoes. Luke loved the ordered routines of his grandmother's house, the fitted carpets and big telly and central heating. He couldn't understand why I didn't want to live that way. I slipped away before Rowan could realise I was leaving. Madeleine was as good a destination as any other. I had her address, that was all, but no clear idea of how to find her. I hardly knew London. And this was in the days before the Lotus; I was in Fred's old Hillman Imp, which overheated if it had to wait in traffic. Madeleine might have moved house since I'd last heard from her (she had written a kind letter when Rowan was born which I hadn't replied to). Or she might be away on holiday, or have gone home to visit her mother in Bristol. I had a telephone number but when I called from the motorway service station there was no reply. None of this mattered, I thought. It wouldn't matter if I didn't find her. I could always sleep the night in the back of the car.

When I found my way at last to where she lived, behind Seven Sisters Road, I was frightened by the street with its boarded-up shops and gaudy off-licences and by the grim block of flats with its intimidating entry phone – I almost gave up because I didn't know how to use this. It seemed an improbable miracle when the real Madeleine was actually at home, both familiar and strange: the same yellow hair with its brassy glints, the same frank pink face, round baby-blue eyes staring.

— Stella! My God, how amazing! Is it really you?

— No, just someone else exactly like me, I said, as if I was picking up the tone of our old childhood friendship, where I was always one jump ahead.

Madeleine was wearing a vintage silky blouse and her hair was cut into a mop shape tied with a flowery ribbon; she looked glossy and competent and I was impressed and crushed. I imagined her belonging in a vivid round of parties and pubs and love affairs, all tinged with danger in the rough, dark city: this turned out to be more or less accurate and my envy never quite subsided during that whole visit. I stayed with Madeleine for two nights. I did telephone my mother to let her know where I was, and I telephoned the café where I was still working then, telling them that Rowan was ill and I couldn't come in. Mum was short with me, but then she was often short with me; and she said the boys were fine, and of course they were. They played up for a while when I went back, but they didn't sustain any lasting damage, of course they didn't. People leave their children with their grandparents or with friends all the time, there's no harm in it, it's a good thing. Once or twice I left the children by pre-arrangement with Mum or Fred, and went off for some visit I'd organised properly (I went back to Madeleine); nobody minded that, they encouraged me to do it. But my unplanned escapes seemed catastrophic at the time. Catastrophic and necessary. I always thought while I was running away that I might never go back again, that I might just disappear and move into a new life.

Madeleine and I sat up until late, that first visit, talking and drinking wine, cross-legged on her bed; she made up a mattress for me on the floor and we played LPs we'd bought together when we were teenagers. Her room was full of reminders of those old days – the same red bulb in the light socket, the same collection of soft toys, the same regiments of bottles of make-up and nail polish on her dressing table. She didn't give one hint that I'd inconvenienced her, turning up without warning; she seemed genuinely excited to see me. She still had her puppy-eagerness, slightly blank, adapting to whatever company she kept. We had to sit in the bedroom because she said her flatmate was 'insane, really' – apparently she was obsessive about cleanliness and Madeleine had to scrub all the surfaces she used with disinfectant. The girl complained if visitors smoked or were noisy or if their shoes left traces on the carpet. When we heard this flat-mate come in we turned the stereo off and began talking in whispers. I told funny stories about the trials of motherhood – which did even begin to seem funny, at this remote distance. Madeleine told me about her latest boyfriend, who worked with her in their company producing promotional pop videos; but there was some-thing going on as well with a man who worked in an office upstairs, though this was only at the stage of glances and snatches of conversation.

I didn't want to tell her that I didn't have a lover, that since Nicky died there hadn't been anyone else and I slept every night alone with my children. I made a big deal out of the drama of living with Fred, and told her about his reciting poetry and singing arias; about the huge pieces of mahogany furniture and the Turkish rugs that had belonged to his mother, about the difficulties with his children and my ongoing fight with Lizzie. I made the picture of our life in the flat deliberately Gothic and intellectual and adult so that hers seemed lightweight and everyday beside it. I even hinted that there was more between us than just friendship; when Madeleine said she'd always thought that Fred was queer, I reminded her that he'd been married and had two children. I was terribly ashamed about this silly story afterwards, though Madeleine never brought it up in conversation when I saw her again, so perhaps she hadn't believed it anyway. (And eventually there were other lovers for me to tell her about: real ones.)

Madeleine tried to talk to me about Nicky, too. When she asked how I was feeling she put her hand on mine but I pulled away, snagging one of my Indian silver rings in the wool of her coloured crocheted bedspread. If anyone asked about Nicky, in those days, I told them the whole story – carefully, lightly, in a tone of poignant regret. I couldn't tell them how I was feeling because I didn't know.

Another time when I ran away I got ill with some kind of virus – I suppose I was incubating it even before I left. At first as I drove I thought the illness was only my misery and desperation, so overwhelming that they were manifesting physically, thickening my throat and blurring my mind with headache. I made it as far as a B & B outside Ludlow, in a grim village strung along a busy road with no pub or shop, only a concreted farmyard, cows up to their flanks in shit and black mud. I was burning up with fever by then and knew I shouldn't go any further.

I hadn't stayed in any kind of guest house or hotel since I was a little girl and my mother was in charge; I was worried when I took the room that I'd misunderstood the price, or that there would be extras on my bill I couldn't afford. I couldn't follow the rules for using the bathroom (there were no en suites in those days), or where I was supposed to go in the morning for my breakfast. I felt ashamed of being ill, I hid it from the landlady and dreaded encountering any of the other guests. And yet when I was alone at last, and had pulled the orange-flowered curtains across to shut out a dour view (muddy, steep fields, sheep bleakly shorn, stone walls black with wet), I lay down between the strange sheets, scalding and shuddering, in a submission to my doom that was almost voluptuous. The wallpaper was orange too, with a pattern like gourds swelling and shrivelling in perpetual motion round the walls.

I had to confess to the landlady eventually, when she came knocking on my door next day (I hadn't made it down to breakfast), that I didn't think I could get out of bed, let alone eat egg and sausage. She wasn't enthusiastic about having a sick guest on her hands, but she did bring me cups of sweet tea and aspirins every few hours, which punctuated my delirium and seemed providential, life-saving. She offered to get me a doctor but I said I didn't need one. From time to time when the coast was clear I crept – hunched as if something had broken inside me – across the landing to visit the lavatory: the giant fronds in the pattern of the carpet seemed to move, coiling under my bare feet. For three whole days and nights I never even phoned home. I'd left the boys that time with my Auntie Jean. It was the longest I ever stayed away – but really I wasn't responsible, I hardly knew what I was doing. I don't think my mother believed me when I tried to explain, though Jean didn't seem to mind.

On the fourth day I woke up to the blessed sensation of convalescence – illness like a sweating devil had slipped out of me, leaving me weightless, weak, transparent as a shell. Relieved, the landlady brought me toast and corn-flakes. Drinking my tea propped up against the pillows, I was washed through with a delicate, passionate happiness. This had no apparent cause inside me, didn't seem to arise from the facts of my life or from my self – any more than the white sunlight did, burning in the rain-drops trickling down the windowpane. Washing at the tiny sink, resting between efforts, putting back on the cold jeans and shirt and jumper I had taken off three days ago, I tried to prolong this happiness, or find a code I could store it in, so that it meant something even when I wasn't feeling it. I imagined it as resembling the filmy skin of a bubble enclosing its sphere of ordinary air: impermanent yet also, for as long as it existed, flexible and resilient – real, a revelation.

When Fred tried to persuade me to read books and I told him I was too busy, it wasn't the truth. Actually, I was reading all that time – in bed, or while Rowan napped in the afternoons, or on the sofa in the sitting room in the evening if Fred went out. At the art gallery, where sometimes there were no customers for hours at a time, I always had a novel on the go. For some reason I wanted to keep my reading secret from Fred: perhaps I just felt that too much of my life was already open to his view and I needed to hold something back. Or perhaps I dreaded his triumph if he saw me absorbed in a book – and his tactful disappointment if it was the wrong one. I didn't want him to feel he'd won any argument. I didn't want him making recommendations or trying to form me by giving me a reading list, or opening up critical discussions.

I'd stopped reading abruptly when I got pregnant with Luke and had to leave school and the whole plan for my life changed track; or rather fell into abeyance, where there was no track at all. I think I felt cheated, as if the books I'd loved had held out a promise of strong, bright, meaningful happenings they couldn't deliver. If I'd read more carefully I'd have seen that falling off a track and nosing round and round unhappily in a tight circle was just what most books described. Yet for a long time, first when Luke was a baby and I worked at the school, and then when I lived in the commune and Rowan was born, my memory of the fiction I'd once read was tainted with a suspicion that it was written for somebody else, for someone initiated into a higher order of culture which shut me out. I'd once read Beckett and Burroughs – now I imagined these authors as my enemies because I thought they'd have despised the things I had no choice but to spend my life on: washing, cooking, shopping, cleaning.

Then not long after Nicky died and we moved back to Fred's, Rowan fell asleep in my arms one afternoon while I was breastfeeding him. I was sitting in the corner of an old chaise longue: its black leather worn away in places, it was sprouting horsehair and the empty time seemed unbearable. A marble clock on Fred's mantelpiece looked like a funerary monument and its tick in the silence was resonant, punishing. Fred was out teaching, Luke was at nursery. I reached over for a book, just so that I didn't have to think; deliberately I chose one that I'd never heard of – *The Cloister and the Hearth* – from the neglected bottom corner of Fred's shelves. Its thick pages were freckled with mould spots and smelled peppery with damp. I liked knowing that no one had opened it for a long time.

The Victorians saved me. Fred's mother had left him quite a collection, inherited I think from her own mother, or grandmother. I read *East Lynne*, *The Woman in White*, *The Water Babies*, *The Heir of Redclyffe*, *Lady Audley's Secret*, and much more. All those days of sickness in the B & B near Ludlow, I was wandering in my delirium in and out of *The Tenant of Wildfell Hall*. Of course I loved

Middlemarch and *Jane Eyre* too. But in that phase of my life the less good novels fascinated and absorbed me, the ones that were fairly dead and desiccated, embalmed in their lost world with its ideals of womanly sacrifice and goodness. I didn't read them with detached amusement; my imagination adapted to the alien forms and coloration of each book as I read like a life-saving camouflage. The very fact of these novels being so obliquely angled to my own life was part of the relief of my escape into them. And I didn't condemn the ideals of sacrifice, I could see how they would work as a way of getting through the day, dressing drudgery up as a poignant adventure, putting the whole burden of freedom on to the poor men. Some of those novels seemed like nothing less than an extended punishment of their men, who were drunk and heinous and craven in exact proportion to how far their women abased and subordinated themselves.

I made up my mind, every so often, that it was silly not to tell Fred what I was doing. I wanted to talk with someone about how strange these novels were. The whole pretence was ridiculous; I had to go to some lengths to hide my reading from him and from the boys, I was shoving my books out of sight down the side of my bed at night, against the wall. Then just when I was on the point of spilling over with my confession, I'd catch sight of Fred flicking through the pages of something – frowning or smiling knowingly as if he was communing with the author, scoring down the side of a text with his pencil to emphasise significance, scribbling notes. I was irritated in those days by these exhibitions of his pouncing cleverness, and his possession of what he read. (Now that he's gone I remember them with yearning.) So I shut my mouth and kept my secret.

The delicate first hour of morning hardened into prosaic day. I drove north. Traffic thickened, the Lotus got stuck, revving impatiently, in queues of people driving to work round Birmingham – as soon as I could I passed them, leaping on upstream, away from home, towards anywhere: even to Scotland, I thought in a mad moment. I was taking in the world spread out around me as I drove, less through my eyes, which had to be on the road, than through my whole awareness, through my skin, as if I'd emerged from a deep burrow underground. For long stretches where the conurbation was unbroken, there spread on either side of the motorway a dream landscape, smoke-blackened brick and corrugated iron, pastel-blank façades and rain-stained concrete, fat cooling towers, gasometers, the metal mesh of factory gates, tree trunks in a padlocked yard beside a scummy ditch. The land's fabric seemed dragged down and tearing under the sheer weight of the built environment, which never ended and could surely never be undone and wasn't even thriving: the monster machine was stalling, it had poisoned itself and now it had fallen into enemy hands (I was very political in those years): three million were unemployed, there was rioting in the cities. Because I was young, the ugliness didn't defeat me, it made my heart beat faster, it was my birthright. *Daniel Deronda* and *East Lynne* hadn't made me nostalgic. They made me know how we're wedged tight into the accident of our moment in history.

I stopped at a service station for a sandwich and a coffee and to fill up again with petrol; when I climbed out of the Lotus my legs trembled with the effort of driving so far without a break. Fred kept a road atlas in the pocket behind my seat and I studied it while I ate. Scotland was too far away for one day's journey – I chose Manchester instead, where I'd never been and knew no one. I drove on, following the signs, and made my way eventually into Manchester's city centre, where I looked around to find a place to leave the Lotus safely. By this time it was lunchtime, one o'clock. The city's exterior was more dour in those days than it is now; modern shops and billboards at street level looked perfunctory in the shadow of the old civic grandeur. Towering Victorian hotels and insurance offices were empty, with broken and boarded-up windows, as if a civilisation had fallen; and I suppose in some sense it had.

I was always frightened, all the time I was running away – not only by the big thing I had done, leaving home, but also by every small test of my inexperience. Even going into a strange branch of my bank, I quailed at having to speak to the cashier, handing my cheque over. I would never have dared go into a restaurant by myself – anyway, I'd hardly ever been to restaurants, I had no idea how to order or ask for a bill. (And a woman eating alone in a restaurant would have been conspicuous in those days.) I could just about manage a café, though

I walked around for a long time before deciding on the right one. I stumbled upon Manchester Art Gallery by chance and felt the relief of refuge inside its quiet rooms which I had almost to myself, hung with jewel-coloured paintings, companion pieces to the novels I was reading. The warmth and sleepy backwater-hush reminded me of the library I had loved when I was a teenager.

It wasn't robbery or violence I was afraid of – or certainly those weren't at the forefront of my mind. But I didn't want to make a fool of myself, I couldn't bear the idea of being exposed in my raw, unfinished ignorance. The expression on my face – frowning, spiky, defiant, I mostly think, in those days – was like a mask of closed competence which I wore and dreaded having torn away. I was twenty-five and it didn't occur to me to use my youth as power, I only felt it as weakness. At least at home I was able to tell myself I was a mother, wrap myself round in all the responsibility and importance of that – although the way women used that importance sometimes felt to me like cheating, an illegitimate short cut. (Also, I wasn't sure that I was good at mothering.)

If I was free, if I was just me, then what was I?

What could I do; what could I become?

It was dusk, and the gallery had closed, and I hadn't found anywhere to stay. I had wandered without meaning to away from the main drag; anyway, the shops had closed too and the cream and orange double-decker buses were packed with people going home. I found myself walking on a side road alongside a high wall overgrown with weeds; then where the wall ended a broad vista opened up across a stretch of wasteland overgrown with scrubby bushes and rugged with the flooring of vanished factories, the humped remains of brick outbuildings. Cranes stood up in the distance against a sky with a thin blue sheen like liquid metal, striated with pale cloud; puddles of water on the ground reflected the sky's light as silver. The beauty of it took me by surprise. Dark skeins of birds detached themselves, shrilling, from the bushes and ruined buildings while I stood watching. They twisted in long ribbons of movement, rising up against the blue light then subsiding, and as their mass configured and reconfigured I thought of Nicky who had existed warm and alive in one moment, and now in this moment didn't exist.

Ten minutes later I stood in the enclosed sour air of a phone box with my coins clutched in my fist, hearing my own breathing, dialling my mother's number, my fingers fumbling anxiously in the dial-holes.

Mum didn't like telephones. She answered warily and resentfully.

— Oh, it's you, she said.

I'm sure she was relieved to hear from me. My mother was a great support to me, really, in all those years after Nicky died. But she couldn't help herself trying to influence me and mould me; she wanted me to be disciplined in the collapse of my life as she had been in hers when I was a baby and her first marriage had failed.

— Are the boys all right?

She held back her reassurance as if I didn't deserve it; but I heard them in the background, laughing with my brother Philip, who was thirteen, just the right age to enchant and entertain them. (Philip was naughty at school but charming at home, witty and maturely considerate.)

— Where are you, anyway? she said.

— Don't worry, I said. — I'll be fine.

— Gerry and I were going out tonight, we've had to cancel. He's none too pleased.

— I'm sorry. I'll make it up to you, I promise. I'll iron his socks for you or something. (She really did iron socks and dusters.)

— It isn't funny, Stella.

My mother must have been afraid, every time I ran off, that I wouldn't come back. In the first hours of running, I was sometimes afraid of it too – holding on to the shape of myself that changed and struggled and almost got away. Someone tapped with a coin on the glass in the phone box door and I waved to them, signalling that I was nearly done. I told Mum I didn't know when I'd be home. —Soon, soon, I said: which could have meant days, or even weeks. I didn't want them to have me fixed in time or place.

Soon, soon. I drove through that night and arrived at my mother's house about one in the morning. (It wasn't my old home, they had moved since I lived with them.) The front of the house was dark, where my mother and stepfather slept; but at the back there was a light on in

Philip's bedroom. I got his attention by throwing gravel from the path up against the glass of his window; he came down to the kitchen door and let me in.

— What time d'you call this? he whispered with mock-severity. — Decent people are all in their beds.

— You're not.

— I know. We're so indecent. Where did our parents go wrong?

— I blame them for their moral turpitude, I said.

— So do I. Whatever it is, I blame them for it. Their moral turpentine.

Reprieved from his boredom in the sleeping house, he was comically eager to make tea for me. — Or have a whisky, he coaxed with a flourish. — Sherry, advocaat, Tia Maria. I'll join you.

— No you won't, daft oaf. I'm going straight to bed, I'm asleep on my feet here, I've been driving for hours. I'll get in with the boys.

— Driving *where*? Where've you been?

— Never you mind.

He shook his head sagely. — You're in trouble in the morning.

— Maybe, maybe not. He won't say anything.

— He's been saying plenty.

— Yes, but not to me.

In the close darkness of the spare room, the boys slept one in each twin bed. Mum had made blackout curtains for the windows so that the light didn't wake them in summer. Undressing down to my T-shirt and knickers, I climbed in beside Luke, trying to move him over without waking him. Heat, and the sweet-sour nutty smell of boy, rolled from his resisting limbs under the duvet; I could feel that he was in his old cotton pyjamas which buttoned down the front. Physical contact in the dark restored my vision of my sons – the intent, unguarded seriousness of their faces in sleep – as vividly as if I'd switched the light on. Their sleeping was always more urgent work than mere absence; they thrashed or snored or threw the duvet off with sudden purposeful violence. I felt relief, falling asleep at last. I wasn't free, I was fastened to my children. At some point in the night I woke to Luke's scrutiny, bent close over me. — Mum's back, he said to himself in mild surprise, as if he saw the funny side of the whole thing.

Eight

I fell in love with Mac Beresford, who came with his wife into the art gallery where I worked. He wasn't my type at all. To begin with, the painting they bought was sickly, in my opinion – a fantasy with blue horses and a sort of arc of roses in the air above a snow scene, sleds and snowballs and peasant children in mittens. The gallery wasn't cutting edge, it mostly sold the work of local artists to people who could afford original art but not the real thing. I liked working there because it was so easy after the café. Sometimes I could spend all morning reading my book while a few customers browsed.

Mac and his wife Barbara were tall and middle-aged. They both wore expensive long overcoats, his fawn and hers black with a big fake astrakhan collar; he was balding and stout, she had a big, sweet, pink face, made-up with pink powder and lipstick. She smelled sweet too, she was one of those women who moved in an aura of perfume and bath oils and hand cream. Her wavy blonde hair was fastened back in a black velvet clip and she was energetic, friendly, trusting. She had been into the gallery the day before; now she was bringing her husband to approve her choice before she paid for it.

— Doesn't it cheer you up?

— I'm cheerful, he said. — How much is it?

— No, look at it properly, Mac. We have to live with this staring down at us for years. Do we really like it?

— I don't know. Do we?

— Or are we just convincing ourselves we like it, and we'll regret it later?

— It's nice, we like it.

I guessed that they probably performed this double act often for the entertainment of their friends – his scepticism, her slightly scatty earnestness. I took them over a price list.

— My wife has to go a long way round sometimes, Mac explained to me, — talking herself into what she already knows she's going to buy.

I thought that I never wanted anyone to claim to know me in that way – fond, tolerant, exasperated.

— What about this other one? Barbara said. — The village is asleep, there are fish floating in the night sky. I suppose they're dreams. D'you like that better?

— I like them all, darling.

Waiting for her to make up her mind, he wandered over to the desk where I hadn't picked up my book again, in case I seemed too indifferent to the gallery's business. I was looking through the morning's mail (I was supposed to sort the serious from the not-so-serious for Nigel, the gallery owner) and because I was vaguely annoyed with his attitude I didn't look up. Mac told me afterwards that he guessed I was annoyed with him, and why, and that because of my not looking up he determined on the spot to make me change my mind and like him. He told me in fact that he had had a full-blown revelation, as he stood pretending to read the catalogue and really staring at the white skin of my neck under my ear, against my hair. (I was still dyeing my hair rusty henna-black, wearing it in a plait.) He said the sight of my neck washed him through with a physical pain which was his first ever panic at growing old; my disdain made him feel that life – savoury magnificent immoral life – was flowing away without his having had enough of it. He was imagining of course that I was an irresponsible girl; he had no idea I was the mother of two sons. By the time he found that out – he said – it was too late already, there was no going back.

I'm trying to remember all the things about Mac Beresford which were so overwhelming at the time, such a revelation. He had a degree in engineering from Salford and owned a successful business manufacturing precision instruments for surgery and medical research. He voted Liberal and read the *Financial Times*. He was opinionated, forceful, well-informed; inflexible sometimes, sentimental sometimes. He loved his wife, adored his two daughters and paid for them to go to private school, was an enthusiast for opera and W. B. Yeats and rugby union. He had inherited his eloquence and strong emotion from his dead father, an Anglican lay preacher – so all his stories seemed to have a hidden meaning, as if he was searching under their surface.

I looked up from the invoices and letters because Mac's mass, in his expensive coat hanging open (Barbara chose his clothes, but he wasn't indifferent to them), was blocking my light. His attention, fixed on me, was tangible and disconcerting. His head, I saw, was more interesting than I had realised when I only took him in as middle-aged – face broad and compressed, cheekbones not prominent, pale blue eyes protuberant, the skin tanned and tough and smooth, setting already in its firm folds at the neck. The last of his thinning hair was auburn, fox-coloured, light as down. I used to say, later, that he looked like a caricature of a plutocrat – he wasn't insulted, he enjoyed the good health and strength of his body without vanity (or, his vanity was in his confidence that his looks didn't matter). Barbara was still agonising between the paintings, and Mac was studying me so intently that when he asked which painting I liked best I had a feeling he saw past my prevarication (blandly, I said that it all depended on where it was going to hang) to the truth that I condemned all the paintings as trivial, which piqued and intrigued him. (— I guessed then that you were a little savage, a revolutionary, he teased me later. — Only waiting for your chance to tear down capitalism, and me with it.)

When the exhibition was over, it was Mac who came back to pick up the one they'd settled on. The gallery had been closed all day, its serene space disrupted by the chaos of dismantling. Nigel and I had been packing the

209

paintings for sending and collection; Nigel had taken some of them in his car for local delivery. It was dusk on the street outside and I was tired. It was close to Christmas; the last shoppers were hurrying home, there were fairy lights in the shop windows and wound through the bare branches of the trees, the jeweller's next door had been playing Christmas jingles all day until I'd stopped hearing them. I hadn't thought about Mac once since I last saw him, and yet when he rapped on the window, peering in at me, I felt caught out and exposed as if the bare gallery were a lit fish tank. With clumsy fingers I unbolted the door.

— Look, come outside on the pavement for a moment, he said. — I want to show you something.

I was obedient because I was dazed – it was stuffy inside, we'd had the Calor gas heater on all day, boosting the central heating. Mac put his arm round my shoulders, pointing up at the sky between the buildings. His wool coat and scarf smelled of lanolin and cold night air trapped in the fibres.

— See the moon: just like the one in our picture.

It was true. The real moon was quarter full just like the one I had despised as whimsical in the painting they'd bought; silver-blue, curled like a comma or a tiny embryo, snug in its blurry ring of frost like a moon in a cave. When we had looked at it for a minute or two, he led me purposefully inside and closed the door behind us, not letting go of where he gripped my arm.

— Now. Why don't you like our picture? he asked, frowning into my face in the bald indoor light, solemnly in earnest as if what I thought mattered. — You see it's true to life. What have you got against it?

— I don't mind it.

— Yes you do, don't fib. You think it's saccharine and mendacious. I've been working it out ever since we last met.

— Do you want to talk to Nigel? If you've changed your mind he may be able to come to some arrangement.

— I don't want to come to any arrangement. I don't care about the painting. I want to know what you think. I've been thinking about what you think, non-stop for two weeks. Won't you come out to dinner with me?

— I don't know, I said stupidly. What was I doing? Out of the two of them, I'd preferred his wife. — When?

— Tonight?

— I can't, tonight. I'd have to get a babysitter.

This was a blow; he reeled from it and let go my arm. — A babysitter?

— I've got two boys. Fred's picked them up from school because I knew I'd be working late. He's finished already, he's a teacher in a private school, they have shorter terms. Pay more, get less teaching.

— Fred? He's your husband?

I said Fred was just a friend, and that the boys' father had died. Mac looked baffled and unhappy. — Well actually, two separate fathers, except one just disappeared.

— Christ. You poor little kid.

— Oh, it's OK. It was years ago.

He asked me just how old I was, exactly, and I said twenty-seven.

Somehow Mac was tangled in the thickets of my life already and I was tangled in his. Ten minutes before this I had forgotten all about him. It must have been physical, I suppose. Underneath all the complicated negotiations we still had to get through, all the painful rash precipitations and withdrawals, we'd had a tiny taste already, out on the street, of how it would be to yield to each other, to sink down together into the deep safety of each other's flesh. No, that's not it. Mac didn't want to yield to me or anybody, he didn't want safety. He wanted what men want from spiky, wiry girls twenty years younger (almost) than they are. But I wanted to yield. In that moment it's what I wanted, anyway – to lean on his arm for ever, abandoning criticism, yearning up at the Christmas lights and the blurry moon.

We made love for the first time one afternoon in January at Fred's – actually in Fred's bed – while Fred was out teaching. It had to be Fred's bed, although I felt bad about it, not only because my own bed was a narrow single one and Mac was a big man, but also because my bed was tucked like an afterthought alongside the bunks of my sons, in the midst of all the evidence of them which Mac found so difficult, their scattered toys and treasures, their pyjamas dropped where they'd dressed in the morning, their drawings Blu-tacked on the wallpaper. Whereas the bed Fred had inherited from his mother was rhetorically perfect for the consummation of an adultery: mahogany, brooding, magnificent as a ship, with its scroll finial topping each of the four bedposts, creaking and swaying with us in tormented sympathy.

I know it's not meant to be all that good the first time, but actually I think that it was good, for both of us. I was cruel in my youth and my assurance, knowing how painfully Mac wanted me. I hadn't made love often in the years since Nicky died – once with Jude which didn't count, a couple of times awkwardly with boys from the crowd I had known in the commune. (Once – very passionately and extravagantly, so that I didn't know myself – with a stranger I met in a café when I'd done one of my runners away from home and the children; but he gave me something which shamed me and which I had to have treated at a clinic.) Mac, to my great surprise (I'd been attracted to the idea of him as a suavely experienced seducer), had never been unfaithful to Barbara before – he used that very word and I heard how the 'faith' in it was a substantial category for him. The first thing Mac said when we were finished was 'Dear God'; I lay pinned under the dead weight of his body collapsed on me and didn't know if he was actually praying, nor whether he meant remorse or thankfulness. I suspect now it was both at the same time. It seemed more momentous to me, making love to a much older man; not the act in itself but his presence in it, the heavy hinterland of his worldly experience driven in behind the fine point of the moment. I teased him that it felt like having sex with Winston Churchill or Bismarck. — I'm not that fat, he protested, but I think he was half flattered by the comparison, he didn't mind.

He came to me in his spare hours when he could get away from work. I used to fantasise that I could smell the factory on him – he'd told me they did injection moulding of plastics and had their own sheet metal and electroplating facilities. Of course I couldn't go there, I wasn't even sure in those days where it was (somewhere off the Bath road). All my experience had been with young men – boys, really – who came and went following their own lights. I liked how Mac had to draw his mind with an effort round to me, from all the burden of his real life – not that he ever complained about the burden: he enjoyed it, it was what he was alive for. All that time during our affair (which lasted something less than a year) he was deciding whether to expand the medical-surgical business into precision defence equipment (which he did, eventually). When I accused him of wanting to kill innocent civilians for profit, and said he would have blood on his hands, he laughed at me, stroking back my hair under his broad hot palms, pulling it tight against my scalp – he liked to look into my face that way, as if he was stripping it naked to read something fundamental in it. What he wanted to develop, he reassured me, were explosive-detection and disposal devices; for saving lives, not harming them. There was a strong market for this because of the terrorist threat.

In the time after our affair, when I'd stopped seeing him, Mac grew in my imagination almost into a kind of beast, I repudiated him so ferociously. I told myself I'd had a lucky escape, made a terrible error of judgement – he was so fixed in his place in the world, so insensible to any counter-narrative. Where would the defence contracts end, once they had begun? How could I have allowed him to contaminate me, touching me? I had introduced him to Fred once, because I longed for someone else I knew to know Mac, as if that would anchor him in my real life. I thought fondly that they would like each other – weren't they both knowledgeable, voluble, religious? But it was a disaster. I arranged an evening when the boys were at my mother's and I cooked something special to impress Mac – boeuf bourguignon with julienne potatoes, followed by chocolate chestnut cream; though I didn't have much idea of what he liked (we'd only eaten together a few times at the beginning, when we went for dinner in restaurants). Mac had told Barbara that he was dining out with clients. He ate with his shoulders hunched and his head bent over the plate, oblivious to the food, which offended Fred on my behalf; afterwards Mac felt in his pockets for his indigestion medicine. Fred held forth at high pitch – about literature, school, boys – as if the conversation was a lost cause; Mac was monosyllabic in response, though I was used to him eloquently ruminative in bed. I tried introducing the subject of Yeats but they both clammed up, not wanting any blundering into sacred territory.

The whole set-up, I think, made Mac miserable: the lying to his wife like a cheating husband in a farce, the idea that he was being paraded for the approval of my friends – he wasn't ever really interested in my friends. Anyway, he was one of those men only expansive on his own spacious ground – displaced on to alien territory he was diminished. After Mac had gone, Fred wouldn't talk to me about him; I had looked forward to a gossipy dissection over the washing-up, Fred not drying anything much but waving the tea towel about to accompany his probing into how we met, and what was going to happen with us next. (I'd imagined myself saying stoically that I didn't know what would happen next, and I didn't care.) I'd hoped that Fred would see what I saw – the rarity of Mac, his compressed power like a burnished glow, something wholehearted in how he gave himself. Because he wasn't my type, I had fallen for him too fast and too deep, with no markers to signal any way back. I melted when his heavy eyelids drooped in pleasure or humour, his careless authority dazzled and enveloped me.

— It's your business, was all Fred said. — If you think he's a good thing. He's not what I expected. Isn't he very square?

— He's grown-up, I said, bristling. — If that's what you mean. He's a man with responsibilities in the real world.

— Oh, the *real* world. I see.

— He makes real things that help sick people. Do you disapprove?

— You know why he didn't like me, don't you? Because he doesn't like queers.

Blushing and furious, I said Mac wasn't like that, he was open-minded, and it was just Fred's own prejudice because Mac was a businessman. But actually I wasn't

216

sure, when I thought about it. Mac had asked once whether Fred brought his boyfriends back to the bed where we were so happy together; when I said 'not to my knowledge' Mac seemed relieved, not having to imagine it. He was never vindictive towards what didn't fit his moral compass; he wiped it out, rather, as if it didn't exist. I'd never told Fred that we used his bed, and of course I always changed the sheets afterwards, but I suppose he'd guessed at it (he must have noticed all those clean sheets). Once Fred and Mac had actually met and disliked each other, our beautiful bed was impossible for us and we had nowhere else to go. Mac said that on my narrow mattress in the boys' room he felt as if he was suffocating.

We went to a hotel in the city centre but it made us both miserable; I knew how out of place I looked at reception in my black jeans, with my scrap of chiffon tied in my hair and my cheap silver earrings. Mac said it was the only time he worried that people would think I was his daughter, and when I asked him what he'd be doing taking his daughter to a hotel room in the afternoon, he didn't find it funny. Showing off, I paraded around naked on the thick carpets, behind stiff brocade drapes five flights up, with a view through nylon curtains over the misty city blown with rain. I insisted he get in the shower with me and soap me, though this wasn't his kind of thing – nor mine really, though I did love the endless hot water and the thick towels (there was no shower in Fred's flat, only a bath and a quirky gas geyser). I performed like the tart Mac might have picked up in a bar at lunchtime if he'd been different. But he wasn't different, and there was something fake and self-conscious that afternoon in our love-making.

And then I met Barbara out shopping – she smiled as if she recognised me but couldn't remember where she'd seen me. I was on my way home from my morning shift at the gallery, with an hour to spare before I picked up Rowan (Luke had started at secondary school; he came home on his own on the bus). Winter had come round again and she was wearing the same black coat, with the astrakhan collar turned up; her wide pleasant face was rosy and roughened with cold and hard lines showed up in her cheeks; her nose was red. She was only a few years younger than my mother. I followed her to the delicatessen then stood outside and pretended to be looking at the packets of sponge fingers and tins of cooked chestnuts and pimientos in the window. Inside, the shop assistant sliced and cut according to Barbara's orders, I saw them laughing and chatting; she put out her gloved hand for packets of ham and salami and cheese, stowing them in the basket on her arm. I realised that I'd fallen into the wrong kind of love with Mac, a daylit, sensible love inappropriate to our circumstances. I felt shame, as keen as the scream of the meat slicer. Mac wouldn't talk to me much about his family but I knew their house was big and Victorian, outside the city at Sea Mills, with fifteen acres of land where his daughters kept their horses. I knew that Barbara volunteered for the Citizens' Advice Bureau.

I crossed the road to the supermarket and by the time I came out again Barbara had gone. I went into the delicatessen and bought expensive chocolate although I couldn't afford it; at home I ate it piece by piece until I felt sick, standing at the kitchen table without even taking my coat off. Then I hurried out to wait among the other mothers in the school playground; nausea made a sweat break out on my forehead. Rowan was one of the last to appear, bad-tempered, struggling with his coat hanging off his shoulder, sugar-paper pictures unrolling under his arm, dragging his gym daps by the laces. I crouched on the asphalt to help him put on his coat – my hands were shaking too much at first to join the zip at the bottom. — What's the matter with you? he asked suspiciously. — You look funny.

— It's all right. I ate too much chocolate.

After school Rowan was always angry and empty, with pale smudges under his eyes against his brown skin; he wouldn't ever eat his packed lunch, only the crisps. He was popular at school and he did well, but it took a great effort because he was naturally guarded and sceptical. Fumbling with his zip, leaning close into his restlessness and boy-smell, I was desolate suddenly because I would never pick up his brother from school again. From now on Luke would always arrive home under his own steam, jaunty and faintly feverish with the import of what he'd seen and couldn't any longer tell me. I had hardly registered the momentous change, I had let it slide past on the surface of my life as a mere practicality, because my selfish dream of Mac had suffused me from hour to hour. Next it would be Rowan's turn to go. My eyes filled with stupid tears and I was drenched in regret. (— What are you doing? Rowan protested, shifting aside indignantly from my kisses.) I recognised the whole sequence of my reactions to meeting Mac's wife as a stock guilt that could have come out of one of my Victorian novels. But what if the novels were right? What if sentimentality was closer to the truth of life and cynicism was the evasion?

That evening I telephoned Mac at home (I looked the number up in the directory), and when Barbara answered I asked to speak to Mr Beresford. She said he was watching the rugby. I heard her rather musical voice, wholly unsuspicious, calling for him through the house I couldn't see and couldn't enter. (— Mac! It's for you!) All I had to go on was the painting with the blue horses. I imagined golden lamplight pooled on the walls, fitted carpets, fat-stuffed comfortable fringed sofas and armchairs, the teenage daughters attending with religious seriousness to their split ends (Mac had never shown me a photograph, but I guessed they both had long hair). Perhaps I could hear a far-off television. Long before Mac picked up the receiver, I seemed to sense his approach through the invisible rooms – a dissenting male shadow cast against their brightness. He barked his name into the phone. I told him I'd seen Barbara at the shops, I said I thought we should stop doing what we were doing, it was too awful. — I'll have a think about it and talk to you tomorrow, Mac responded, calmly but with suppressed distaste, as if I'd bothered him at home with a query about office paper clips. Of course he had to sound calm, because his wife was listening. (He told her I'd rung because there were some new paintings in the gallery I'd thought they'd like. I couldn't believe that she'd believed this. — They must be desperate for trade, apparently she'd said.) When he spoke to me from his office the next day, at least I couldn't hear the distaste.

Those calls didn't end our affair immediately, but they were the beginning of the end. Mac sent me a letter where he copied out a Yeats poem about love's impossibility: 'Until the axle break/ That keeps the stars in their round . . ./Your breast will not lie by the breast/ Of your beloved in sleep'. He added a PS at the bottom of the page, pointing out that Yeats had had some pretty crazy millenarian ideas and probably believed all this might actually happen in real time, the axle breaking and the girdle of light being unbound and so on. So it wasn't such a despairing poem as it first seemed.

I was on holiday in Somerset with the boys and Madeleine. We were climbing up a steep incline where there had once been a railway line transporting iron ore eight hundred feet down from the Brendon Hills to the valley bottom below: the weight of the ore going down had hauled up the empty trucks. Luke found a rusted iron bolt but most of the evidence of the railway was long gone, apart from the winding house at the top and the incline itself, descending through thick woods, cut in places into the red sandstone. Rowan had been dragging his feet ever since we left the rented cottage, complaining that he was bored, tired, thirsty; now he was revived by the tough scramble and out in front, bare-chested and lithe, pulling himself up by hanging on to the saplings that colonised the stony slope. Luke was climbing more slowly behind him, scanning the ground for trophies.

I was talking to Madeleine intently, whenever I could catch my breath and the boys were out of earshot, about my affair with Mac, which had been over for months. I knew that I sounded fanatical and was boring even Madeleine, who was an absorbent listener, questioning and commenting dutifully. My fixation was unworthy of the fresh summer sky and the tranquil wood, where we hadn't encountered any other walkers – but I was shut out from loveliness, my grievance twisted and turned in its small space. Madeleine was the only one of my friends apart from Fred who knew about Mac; she'd met him once when I went with her to the theatre in London, on a day I'd arranged to coincide with Mac having dinner there with clients. After his dinner he had come to meet us in a pub near the theatre. (That had been the only other time he and I went to a hotel, and the only time we spent a whole night together.)

Picking over Mac's character and behaviour, I was full of scorn. I claimed I couldn't see now why I'd ever succumbed to him. He wasn't even good-looking, he was middle-aged; for goodness' sake, he read the *Financial Times*! He had contracts with the Ministry of Defence! I pretended to analyse dispassionately the flaws in both of us, which had made a fatal combination – had I fallen for a father figure because I'd never had a father of my own? My neediness, I said, was worse because I hadn't been prepared for it, because I'd thought that as a feminist I'd seen through all that mechanism of power in attraction. There was some truth in all of this. But it was also true that I couldn't help returning compulsively to talk about Mac, shucking off every other subject with a shudder of impatience or a few perfunctory words. Even my contempt, licking around his edges, connected me to him, gave me the illusion that an electric current went sparking and surging between us. At night in the holiday cottage, in my damp bed with its sagging middle, I wrote him passionate letters on a pad of lined file paper which by the end of the week was also damp – indicting him or imploring him, it didn't matter which, page after page. I tore the letters up in the morning.

— But I liked him, Madeleine said. — He was nice.

We had paused to rest halfway up the slope, while the boys forged ahead. Tendrils of Madeleine's wiry yellow hair, darkened with sweat, were stuck to her forehead. We were both in cut-off jeans and sleeveless vests; she was rounded everywhere I was angular.

— *Nice*, really? I doubted.

She shrugged. — He seemed nice to me. There was something about him . . . She searched for the word, uneasy under my scrutiny but determined. — When he came into the pub that time, I thought he was – nice. Because I wasn't expecting him to be, from your description; even though you liked him then. I was thinking I'd better hurry off as soon as he arrived, and leave you two alone together, but – do you remember? He persuaded me to sit down again and bought me a glass of wine. He made them open a new bottle, of something better. I mean, when he might have had (she put on a mocking voice here, fooling in her embarrassment) 'eyes only for you'.

— I don't remember.

— I got the impression he was kind. I could imagine you two together.

I lay back, thinking of the old railway with its inferno of noise and dirt, trucks wheezing up and clanking down, miners suffering underground, the earth ripped open, effort and ingenuity on a scale that seemed so disproportionate to its ends – the iron ore? the money? Now the tree trunks rose in peace, like pillars, into their leafy tops blotched against a sky mildly blue. There was shrill birdsong: goldcrest, Madeleine surprisingly knew. She told me they liked the tops of the Douglas firs in mixed woodland. I floated above my loss of Mac for the first time, as if it was poignantly sad but it was finished, as if there were other possibilities. A spring burbled and trickled among ferns nearby, into a pool lined with pebbles the clear colours of humbugs, bedded in red silt. Fred said that people threw coins into water for luck because in primitive religions water sources were believed to be openings between the upper and lower worlds. I had no money on me, so I threw a satisfactory small stone – black, shaped like a fat nub of charcoal. When the pool dimpled glassily and swallowed it, I made a wish: the choice presented itself as if it had been lying in wait all along. Men, or books?

With relief, I chose books.

I let something go and I felt very empty without it, and very clear.

I enrolled in evening classes in September and did my A levels (English Literature, History, French) in a year. I got As in all of them and also grade ones at S level, which was a supplementary exam in the same subjects, for good candidates. With these good grades I applied to the university, and although this was in the days before the big rush of mature students, I got in to study English Literature. I was thirty at the beginning of my first year, the oldest in my cohort. This age difference didn't matter, in fact it was a kind of convenience, because it set me apart from the other students' chaos of self-discovery, their hungry interest in one another. Compared to them, I felt my motivations purely: for all the three years of my degree, I seemed to see myself clearly as if from a distance, through a thick lens. It was such a relief to be clever at last. For years I had had to keep my cleverness cramped and concealed – not because it was dangerous or forbidden, but because it had no useful function in my daily life. In the wrong contexts, cleverness is just an inhibiting clumsiness.

At first I didn't try to make friends with the other students. I was shy as well as aloof. I took against the girls and boys with glossy hair and loudly assured voices who'd been to private school; I despised their pretence of slumming it for the three years of their degree. I sat pointedly alone in the high-ceilinged, white-painted classrooms; the faculty was housed in spacious red-brick Victorian houses along a tree-lined street. My hair was dyed orange or rusty black and screwed up in a studiedly careless knot, my eyes were thickly painted with black kohl; I retreated behind the mask of my difference. I didn't have the money some of those girls spent on their clothes, but I didn't want their kind of clothes anyway; I wore tight jeans and men's shirts and suit waistcoats bought from the junk stalls in St Nicholas Market. When they found out that I was a mother too, that made a gulf between us; they didn't know how to talk to me about the children so they didn't talk to me at all. Meanwhile I was scathing, at least inwardly, when they didn't bother to read the books in preparation for classes – what else did they have to do with their long hours of leisure? I had plenty to do (apart from home and the children, I was still working three mornings a week in the gallery, for the extra cash), but I was zealous – my ignorance ached in me and spurred me on, I made the time somehow to read everything.

All this was at first. As time passed I relaxed, and they got used to me; I made some friends among them. But I wasn't there for the other students. I was there to find my way into another, higher order of meaning, behind the obvious one that lay around me every day. I worshipped my lecturers because they seemed to move at ease in this other world of light – when one of the younger ones made a pass at me in my second year I was startled and disappointed; I only wanted him to see my disembodied intelligence. I spent every hour I could, when the boys were at school, in the university library with its ordered monkish hush. The long desks were sectioned off into individual cells, each with its own light and leather inlay; arranging my books, I felt myself chosen, dedicated. If the weather outside the high windows was grey and indistinct, so much the better for my rich inward journey. Sometimes when I was looking into a page of text it seemed transparent, all its meaning and ironies and metaphorical thickness and musical arrangement showing themselves to me easily. What I wrote about the texts in my essays seemed almost obvious, it was just *there* – except that not everyone saw it. Excitedly, and with a new competitive zest, I took in that some of the critics who'd published books didn't see it as clearly as I did. Nor did some of my lecturers.

When I lifted my head from my absorption – roused to a pitch of excitement, breathless and dizzy, because I'd been reading *Oedipus the King* or *Adonais* or Donne's Holy Sonnets – I couldn't believe that everything was going on unchanged around me in that quiet library, so muted and still that I could hear the pages turning and biros scribbling. In winter the daylight would even have drained away behind the windows without my noticing, and then I felt a niggling unease as if I'd missed some-thing – although all I could have missed was my ordinary life with its prosaic clock-time, trundling from hour to hour.

There was upheaval during my second year because we had to move out of Fred's flat. He and his wife Lizzie were trying to make a go of it again: he was moving back into the family home.

— Of course there won't be any sex, Lizzie said to me. — But I mean, who cares? Who still wants boring old sex after they've been married to the same person for twenty years? I'd rather read a book in bed any day. Or just fall asleep, even better. (Fred had a French name for their arrangement, a *mariage blanc*, making it sound sophisticated.)

Lizzie was one of those miniature women who go on looking like a child well into middle age: pretty, with brown eyes and russet colouring and an injured expression. She and I hadn't always got on well, there had been some awful scenes in the past. The first time I moved in with Fred she thought I was his mistress and brought her disgruntled children round once in the middle of the night in their pyjamas, flaunting them to me like a tableau of wronged virtue. And later, when I moved back into the flat after Nicky died – even though she'd got the hang of Fred's sexuality by that time, she was convinced I was after Fred's money or his property. She insisted he make a will listing all the antiques he'd inherited from his mother, and she couldn't bear it that I didn't pay him rent. If the children were allowed to visit Fred they came with supplies of her home-made wholemeal bread because she believed shop bread was poison, along with crisps and sweets. She didn't want their minds contaminated by watching television or reading comics. When I talked about them to my friends, I called them the Holy Family. She nagged in her regretful sing-song voice, explaining how much better it was for the children to be outdoors, learning the names of plants and birds. Piers and Frances exchanged looks; they seemed to communicate in coded ironies. They were sullen and secretive even when they were small, ungainly beside their tiny mother; they looked more like Fred, with big, pale, definite faces.

As her children grew into teenagers, Lizzie underwent a kind of conversion – funnily enough, just around the same time Fred was converting to Catholicism – and started to talk very boldly and debunkingly about the facts of life. She took to drinking, too; not too much, but enough to unbind her and make her garrulous. Often she came to confide in me at Fred's kitchen table. There were a couple of boyfriends, neither of whom came up to scratch. (One of them was a vicar; the other one, much nicer, she met when he came to fix her central heating boiler.) — I really didn't want twelve red roses on my birthday, she complained. — Is that awful of me? I mean, he's so *nice*. And when I'm in bed with him I can sort of *see me*, coldly, in the middle of all the excitement, as if I was looking down from the ceiling. Like a pink shrimp thing on the seabed.

Lizzie asked Fred to go back when she discovered that Piers was smoking 'pot', as she called it. I reassured her that I'd smoked it, off and on, since I was fifteen. Her brown eyes fixed me in stern scrutiny. — Oh really, Stella? But you seem perfectly normal. When Piers took it he was a nightmare. His eyes were sort of rolled up in his head and he was hideously pleased with himself. Then afterwards puked up.

I asked her if she would mind if Fred went off with men every so often.

— Cripes, no. As long as they're not actually doing it under my nose.

I thought Fred ought to go back: I told him so. He really was better at dealing with Piers than Lizzie was. And he was very attached to Lizzie; he had a fixed belief, in spite of everything, in the sanctity of marriage. Fred wanted a family, he liked family life and couldn't bear coming home after work to an empty flat. Luke and Rowan and I had been his family for a long time but this had changed, the ease had gone out of it – which had something to do with Mac and more to do with my new-found purpose in life, my academic work. It wasn't Fred's fault – he was delighted that I was studying, he had encouraged me more than anyone. It was my fault. He wanted to talk to me about the books on my courses and read my essays and advise me – and just because we had been intimate and he knew me so well I couldn't bear the idea of his charging around familiarly among the things that were new and raw and fragile in my mind. I think I found it discouraging too that Fred was always so irreducibly himself – not transfigured by reading and thought as I was expecting to be transfigured. All this was ungenerous of me; and it did produce a mild sort of estrangement between us. After we parted and left the flat behind, I felt remote from him for a while. (In his fifties Fred got ill with cancer and we grew very close again through the years he lived with that. I grew close to Lizzie then as well.)

Fred gave up the flat and I moved with the boys to live with Daphne and Jude. Jude had made a lot of money selling her embroidered pictures (prices way out of reach of Nigel's gallery, and the embroideries too unsettling anyway for his kind of clients); with the proceeds she bought a tall handsome Georgian house in a state of disrepair, hanging on to the side of a hill overlooking the docks and the steep wooded cliffs running down to the river. A skinny staircase, with a polished wood handrail and gaps where the banister rods were missing, wound up through four floors. On each draughty landing a long arched window was vivid with changeable sky and vertiginous cityscapes. Jude said we could live in the attic for nothing because we would stop it getting damp, but I insisted on paying a small rent. I wanted to do things properly this time. There was only one bathroom in the house but we had a toilet to ourselves on the top floor, and one of our four rooms was a quirky kitchen with gas rings and white-painted shelves for plates and mugs and a big Belfast sink and a rope fire escape with a sling (the house had at one point been a residence for girl students). There were gas fires in each room to keep us warm. We didn't have much furniture but I was so happy to be up in the light, I felt myself weightless and free, sitting alone among the birds flying round outside the windows, losing myself in the airy delirium of my reading. It reminded me of the attic where I lay dreaming once with Valentine.

I did very well at university. I got first-class marks for my essays and in exams almost from the beginning. My imagination grew bolder every day, I was buoyed up by praise and success and the sensation of my own newly unfolding power: sometimes I was drunk and ecstatic with the delight of it. I had no doubt that I had found a new direction for my life. At the end of my three years I would get a first-class degree (and indeed I did). Then I would apply for funding for research and I would work on a PhD. I didn't look beyond that, not having much idea how an academic career was likely to proceed; but I suppose I vaguely imagined publication, an academic post. I carried my future around like a talisman inside me, warming me with its promise. We had had compulsory Anglo-Saxon in the first year and because I loved the words I learned the Lord's Prayer off by heart, saying bits of it over to myself in the most unlikely places, cleaning the toilet or shopping in the supermarket. 'Fæder ure þu þe eart on heofonum, Si þin nama gehalgod . . . Forgyf us ure gyltas . . .' The boys would nudge me. — You're muttering that thing, they said. — It's embarrassing.

My lecturers were kind, encouraging my ambitions. I think I was exotic for them; they cherished me just because I wasn't the usual kind of student who went on to graduate studies. I was a single parent, I'd worked for a living, I pinned political badges – Greenham Common, Solidarność, anti-apartheid – to the military jacket with brass buttons which I'd found in a memorabilia shop. I'm embarrassed now, remembering the badges. Not because I didn't believe in all those things, but because the truth was that at that time I was absorbed in my inner life: novels and drama and poetry, the past. I went to a few demonstrations with Daphne and Jude, that's all – and a day trip once to Greenham. In my third year I came across the French feminist critics, and then the American ones, and I suppose that counts as a kind of politics, though I was bored by Kristeva.

For those three years at university, I felt a steely satisfaction in my singleness, as though I was sealed up and made self-sufficient by my work. My mother was very doubtful about my taking up my studies so late in the day – what was the point? But she hoped that at university at least I might meet someone responsible and hard-working (naturally, she knew nothing about Mac). I explained to her that they were all ten years younger than I was, and that I was the responsible and hard-working one. And it was true, I was hard-working. I was often exhausted, I wasn't ecstatic all the time. I kept myself awake late into the night with caffeine tablets, to write my essays. My friends all helped generously. Fred didn't want to lose touch with Luke and Rowan; they were often at his place. Daphne had a job as a social worker with youth offenders, she was good with kids and took the boys out at weekends; Jude let them loose in her studio, where she was sewing the life-size dolls that were her new project (Luke told me afterwards that he dreamed about those dolls for years). On fine summer evenings the boys went to play football after supper, in a scruffy park ten minutes' walk away. I would wash the dishes then sit reading or writing at my desk beside the open window. When they came home at dusk with a gang of their friends, I could hear them before they turned the corner into our street – their voices echoing off the tall house fronts, Luke bouncing the football ahead of him along the pavement. Amazed at being out when it was almost dark, keyed up with the glamour of their headlong game, they lingered outside, calling poignant goodbyes to one another. Sometimes their voices were portentous with drama, some quarrel or injury. I didn't worry while they were away, but as soon as I knew they were safely home I felt myself completed. They weighed down my life on the side of blood and warmth, where otherwise it might have floated too free.

It's important to get what happened next in the right order.

First, I changed my mind about carrying on my academic work. That was all quite fixed and settled before any of the changes in my private life. There wasn't any violent moment of disillusionment but imperceptibly, over the months leading up to my finals, two things – which had seemed for a while to be one thing – separated out in my imagination. On the one hand there was the great world of literature and thought, and on the other the smaller world of the university and academic life. I began to be bored with the sound of my own tinny authority in essays. I didn't like the idea of choosing a narrow specialism – I wanted to read everything. I was grateful to the university, it had made all the difference to me and been the gateway into my new intellectual life; but now I chafed inside its frame. Sometimes when I looked up from my books I was overwhelmed by the real moment in the air around me, its nothingness richly pregnant. My studies were still a path into mysteries; but I saw that the path could take you underground, if you weren't vigilant. It could lead into substitute satisfactions, ersatz and second hand.

From time to time we had postcards from Sheila, who was travelling in South America. The cards were laconic, with minimal information – 'I am here', or 'I saw this', or 'it wasn't really like this'. The pictures on the front were in brilliant kitsch colours, Mayan ruins or bougainvillea or smiling Guatemalan peasants in costume. We had no address for writing back to her. Daphne disapproved, she said that the whole backpacking thing was only another twist in the whole history of Western voyeurism and exploitation. I pinned the cards above my desk because Sheila's adventures felt like a counterpoint to the adventures inside my head – as fantastical as anything I read about, yet in a real life, plotted on the earth's solid surface.

I decided I didn't want to embark on an academic career and for a while I had no idea what to do instead. Then my brother Philip had an accident on his motorbike, breaking both legs, and an occupational therapist came to my mother's house to measure the steps and examine the bathroom to see if he could manage at home on his crutches. I was casting about in my mind for the shape of my future life and something about that work appealed to me: its mix of imagination and practicality.

I liked the fact that each case was something new, with a unique set of problems – material ones jumbled together with psychological ones, like in a story or a novel. I hoped that the work would take me out of myself and plunge me in the world, making me bolder and more generous; until I was tested, I didn't know if I was capable of these qualities. Even before I'd taken my Literature finals, I applied to an Occupational Therapy Diploma course, and got a place. And OT was a good choice, it suited me; I have worked more or less in this field ever since. Of course there was a lot of idealism in my reasons for choosing it – the reality was bound to be more complex, less heroic.

All this happened before Mac ever got back in touch. Sometimes he tells the story – not apologetically, but proudly – as though he interrupted my brilliant academic career, stormed into my life and carried me off when I was on my way to being a Professor of Anglo-Saxon or something. But it wasn't so. At the time when I was making these plans for my future, I had put Mac entirely out of my mind – love had healed over behind him, like water swallowing that black stone I'd thrown into the pool. The first time I had any news of him was one afternoon in the summer, after I'd finished my last exam and before I started my Diploma. Lizzie came round and I made her tea; we sat drinking it with all the casement windows in the attic open to the falling rain, because the air was so hot and heavy. A horse chestnut which grew across the road was as tall as the tall houses; my room looked into its top branches and I could hear the intimate settling noises the rain made, soaking through the tree's layers. Lizzie talked on to me about her children in that burrowing, persistent way she had – everything was Frances now, who played the cello; Piers was written off as rather a disaster. I wasn't bored, exactly, but I wasn't concentrating; the weather made me restless, as if I was expecting something to happen – or perhaps I only filled that in afterwards, after something did. When Lizzie was at the point of going, she remembered she had a message for me.

— A man came looking for you, she said. — A peculiar man, Stella! Something about him – head down in his shoulders, like a bull charging; said he didn't know where you lived, but that he'd found out where Fred had moved to, from the school. Very persistent. I told him I'd only known you vaguely, had no idea where you were now. I thought he might be a debt collector.

And she gave me Mac's card, with something written on the back in pencil, in his big, wobbling, separated letters, with the hollow full stops. Mac had terrible handwriting – not scrawled or hasty so much as naively deliberate, as if, at school, in his impatience to be grown up, he had bypassed ever acquiring a cursive style. He was always angry writing anything by hand, preferred stabbing at a typewriter or a keyboard with one finger. I couldn't read his message while Lizzie was there in the room with me. I pretended I had no idea who he was and kept tight hold of the card, its corners digging into my palm, while I went all the way downstairs with her and watched her put her umbrella up, crossing the street,

237

rain fizzing on the taut red nylon and my heart straining painfully, impatiently.

— Call me, Mac wrote peremptorily. — I have news.

He'd given 'news' a capital N, and drawn a ring round his printed telephone number, his work number, in the same thick pencil. I hid the card in a pocket of my handbag and didn't do anything. Sometimes I thought I could hardly remember Mac. He belonged to the past, when I was abject and dependent and hadn't achieved anything.

Then he and I bumped into one another, quite by accident, only a few weeks after I got his card – at the Royal Infirmary, of all places. We had never met up accidentally before, in all those four years we were apart. I was at the hospital with Rowan, who had problems with persistent ear infections and needed grommets to equalise the pressure. Taking Rowan to his appointments was always fraught; he dreaded the examinations and reacted badly to the tedium of the waiting – although he was stoical when the doctors probed painfully in his ear (I knew how much it hurt because of how he stared ahead into nothing with a set face, and gripped my hand which he wouldn't hold at any other time).

Mac had never seen either of my sons except in the photographs I'd had around in the flat. When we three were suddenly confronted in a corridor (I was lost and in the wrong place, Rowan was berating me), the encounter felt momentous. Luckily the corridor wasn't busy. Mac seized me by the elbows, almost accusing me

('Where have you been?'), and I was aware of Rowan transferring his resentment on to the stranger. I think Mac was surprised by Rowan in the flesh; I don't think he'd taken in from the photographs how dark-skinned he was, or how striking. I loved seeing other people respond to his beauty – the skinny lithe length of him, the spatter of freckles of darker pigment across his nose, long hollow cheeks, lashes clotted as densely black as paint. He didn't look like my child. I explained about our appointment and that we were lost; Mac said he was just visiting. He and Rowan stared at each other, calculating. I could hardly take Mac in, bulky in a beige raincoat with rain splashes on the shoulders, preoccupied and out of place. I had always expected that if I ever bumped into him I would be shocked by how old he was – but actually he seemed unchanged, utterly familiar: his vigour and willpower, the taut thick skin of his forehead and neck. I saw that his round head did sit on his shoulders like a bull's. He was holding a greengrocer's paper bag and I guessed he was bringing grapes for someone ill.

I thought all of a sudden that it must be Barbara who was ill, she must be dying. Perhaps that was why he'd come looking for me at Fred's, why he was holding my arms now so tightly, as if I might try to escape. But Barbara was fine, Mac said. He realised his grip was embarrassing me and let go. At least, she was fine as far as he knew. He was visiting a nice chap who worked for him and had had an operation on a duodenal ulcer.

— What d'you mean, I said, — as far as you know?

239

— Come *on*, Mum, Rowan insisted.

Mac explained that Barbara had left him. She had found out about certain things – here he glanced severely at Rowan, cutting him out – and when she confronted him and he told her the whole truth, she'd gone. (She'd found, he told me later, a forgotten leaflet from the gallery at the bottom of his sock drawer, with my name written on it. — Something was funny, she'd said. — Because you've never liked that painting.) Mac had tried to reason with her – she'd been adamant. (Apparently Barbara had asked him whether he still felt anything for me, and when he had reflected, he'd said that he did, he loved me.) This had all happened a few months ago, and he'd been looking for me ever since.

— The axle has broken that keeps the stars, he said. — And all that.

But I had forgotten the Yeats poem and didn't know at first what he was talking about. Anyway, now he'd found me, he wasn't going to let me go again without a struggle – unless I told him where I lived, that is. Though probably he was too late, I'd made arrangements with someone else, hadn't I, by now? I said I hadn't. I asked about his daughters and he said one was married, the other at the Royal College of Music. We stood smiling at each other then (and he reached out to hold me by the elbow again) in the blandly lit pastel-painted corridor with its signs pointing to rheumatology and cardiology and the renal unit, its sickly suspect smell of antisepsis and hospital food; we moved aside for a nurse pushing a trolley of drugs. Rowan was tugging at my arm, dragging me away. I scrabbled in my pocket for a pen, I wrote down my telephone number on Mac's paper bag. Our luck – it was luck, wasn't it? we scarcely knew what to call it yet – seemed a vivid improbable hopeful flare against this background of subdued suffering, shut away behind the hospital walls.

Nine

Of course I regretted it, marrying Mac Beresford. Often I regretted it. Oh, the violence of those early years! I don't mean physical violence. (Mac would never, ever hit me – and I've only hit him a few times, not all that hard – though once I threw a hardback book which grazed his temple and drew blood.) I can remember cleaning my teeth in the en suite bathroom of the house he took me to when we first lived together – the same house where he'd lived with Barbara, at Sea Mills with fifteen acres (it's not where we live now) – and spitting into the sink and saying to myself over and over between spits that I cursed the day I met him. Cursed the day! For that moment it was quite true. What was I doing there in that bathroom – which was not to my taste at all, with its pastel luxury, concealed strip lighting, seashells stencilled on the walls, fish-shaped stone soap dishes, painted seaweed climbing up the shower tiles? This was Barbara's taste, we were haunted by Barbara. (What pangs of longing, for my plain old attic at Jude's.) I couldn't meet my own eyes in the mirror over the sink, for rage at myself, at what I'd let myself in for. How could we two, Mac and I – with our infinite complexities, and our so-divergent experiences, which had hardened into our natures – be forced to fit inside this shared circle of a marriage, curled up as tightly together as yin and yang? That's what marriage is like, I think – this squeezing of two natures into one space which doesn't fit either of them. At least, that's how mine was for a long time – now, it's settled down into tranquillity (which brings its own complications).

One night I ran away from Mac in my nightdress. This was only a few months after I'd moved in with him – before he was even divorced, before we were married in the Registry Office. Usually we quarrelled about the boys, but they were away: Luke was staying with friends (he was sixteen), Rowan was at my mother's. For Mac's sake, I tried to set up these occasions when he had me to himself. Our quarrel that night wasn't about any subject in particular; it was about the way Mac talked at me. I'd cooked something special and we'd been drinking Mac's good wine (he knows his wine). Mac loved to tell me about his ideas. All day long at the factory, in the intervals between all the practical things he had to plan and decide, he was working out his theories of everything. He said, for instance, that he needed to believe that our experiences weren't lost in time but were all held somewhere, coexisting simultaneously – in God's mind, or in an alternative dimension where time was a kind of perpetual present. But if that were so, he puzzled, then everything terrible must also be held for ever as it happened: suffering would have no end, there'd be no relief in oblivion.

I knew he'd never talked about these things to anyone before. He had chosen me as the necessary listener, the one person on earth to whom he wanted – needed – to explain himself. He thought that no one else understood him as I could. (Barbara hadn't ever wanted him to talk like this to her, she'd feared it. She had believed superstitiously, Mac said to me once, that talking about suffering could bring it on.) But when I tried to answer him and put in my part of the argument, it seemed to me that he waited kindly for me to finish then carried on regardless, uncoiling the tight-wound spool of his own thoughts. It might have been like this, I thought, if I'd been the wife of a great philosopher or a poet in the past; I would have sat at his feet and written down his ideas devotedly, then consoled him for them in the dark. Only Mac wasn't a great philosopher, he was a factory owner, and it was me who had a humanities degree; I had read as much philosophy as he had (though he did remember more of what he read than I did, and was better at logical argument). Yet if I stopped speaking altogether – sat with my expression closed to him, rage in my heart – he didn't even notice. (Perhaps it was a small thing to get mad about. Nowadays, when I love him steadily, I don't want him to know my inmost thoughts.) Undressing in the bedroom that evening I felt I was smothering, because of the central heating and the fitted carpets everywhere. We didn't bother to close the curtains in that room because the windows only looked towards the Portway and the river gorge, over the scrubland in front of the house where the horses grazed (these belonged to Lauren and Toni, Mac's daughters). The windows were black and cold with night; I could see our lamps and our room reflected in the glass as if I was looking in from outside, and I saw myself moving around, putting away my clothes. Of course Mac wanted to end the evening with love-making.

— Don't touch me! I snapped, pushing him away. I complained that he wasn't interested in my opinions, he never asked me what I thought and only wanted me as his audience.

— It isn't small talk, you know, Mac said, hurt, his forehead wrinkled and reddening with feeling. When I hated him I saw how his head was round and dense like a cannonball or a hard nut. — I'm telling you what's really in my heart, things I've never shared with anyone. I'm talking to you freely: I thought you appreciated what that was worth. Would you rather I was polite, and paid you compliments and asked after your knitting?

I couldn't believe he'd said that about knitting: martyred, exulting, I said I'd got a first-class mark for an essay on Bergson and T. S. Eliot. — Why would I want to talk about knitting? I can't even knit! You don't even know that about me.

Mac said I must be drunk (and probably I was – we often finished two bottles between us, sometimes we started on a third). He got into the shower and I ran downstairs, escaping outside. On my way out I picked up the keys to the little Peugeot he'd bought me for work and for running around in. I might have driven off, just as I was, barefoot in my 1940s vintage nightdress – and if I had, who knows whether I'd ever have come back again. But I saw in the light from the windows that the horses had come up to stand against the fence, and I went across to talk to them. Because I was cold, though the adrenalin from our fight was still surging in me, I nuzzled into their peppery smell and greasy, dusty heat – a secret life, rich with its own purposes, out there in the dark which had looked empty from inside the house. Misty was Lauren's jaunty chestnut mare and my favourite; she jabbed at me with her nose, snorting and hoping for treats. (I cherished those horses partly as my way of making up to Lauren and Toni, who wouldn't have anything to do with me at first.) Mac came out of the house behind me, calling my name, his towelling bathrobe tied over his pyjamas. He didn't like the horses; he was afraid of them.

I climbed up over the gate and on to Misty, clinging to the tufts of her mane with both hands; then I set off riding across the field bareback. It was stupidly dangerous, I probably was drunker than I knew. (And on the way I lost the keys to the Peugeot, the only set: Mac was out early the next morning, eyes down, hunting for them everywhere. We never found them, and had to buy replacements.)

— Follow me, I yelled back over my shoulder. — If you want to keep me, follow me.

— You're an idiot, Stella.

— I don't care what you think. Follow me.

And he did follow – though not just obediently trotting after the horse, as I'd rather pictured it. (Misty shucked me off anyway, halfway across the field, not too roughly.) Mac went back inside first for a torch and wellingtons, and put one of the old picnic blankets over his shoulders, then set out to where I was waiting for him under the beeches. By the time he arrived all the anger had drained out of me. It was marvellous out there under the huge old trees soughing and groaning in the wind, dragging at their roots in the dark. Mac turned off his torch and on the blanket I clung to him passionately.

— We could be in our comfortable bed, he said, bemused.

(I told him later that I believed there was a solution to the problem of time and suffering he'd proposed. It was only intractable if you came at it head on, wanting a single story; instead, you could try imagining that two time dimensions coexisted. In one, still moments were all held objectively for ever; in the other, time as experienced subjectively was always a flow, bringing the relief of endings. Nothing was added, in that model, to anyone's suffering; on the other hand suffering – like happiness – wasn't obliterated in the total sum of things, which it shouldn't be if the sum of things is justice. I thought my idea was something like Bergson's *durée*, but a proper philosopher explained to me years afterwards that I'd got this wrong.)

Mac was made to be the father of daughters. There's a photograph of him holding Toni minutes after she was born: he looks astonished as a bear with a princess in a fairy tale, afraid of his own strength, dreading already the boyfriends she'll bring home. The girls brought out a patriarchal, sentimental streak in him and in return he fostered in them an inward-turning femininity. Self-important with their father's adoration, they were bruised and scandalised by his betrayal. Toni, rounded and blonde like her mother, was a teacher in a primary school, and married by the time Mac and I moved in together (though she'd had a wilder phase, and before I knew him Mac had fought off a succession of unsuitable boys). Lauren was moody, a talented clarinet player, a change-ling who didn't look like either parent – very white-skinned, tiny, gamine with black hair and glasses and a sharp little muzzle like a fox. Mac and Barbara had worried together – and out of all proportion, I thought – through the various phases of Lauren's gifted-ness and restless dissatisfaction. Later, when Toni got pregnant (by which time the sisters were more or less reconciled to the idea of me) I was ready to be supportive through the difficulty of her young maternity – only she didn't find it difficult, she loved it uncomplicatedly.

It seemed to me that I worked hard at building rela-tions with Mac's family, while he hardly tried with mine. This was our longest-lasting and worst fight. (Then in his mid-sixties he capitulated all at once, genially making friends with everyone.) Mac said that it was different because the boys were living with us and of course that was true; but he couldn't see that there was an imbal-ance in the settled hostility between him and them – he was an adult, so ought to hold back the whole force of his scowling intolerance of their mess and mistakes and ignorance. He claimed he was protecting me from how they took advantage of me. It was obvious, though, that he was jealous of how I loved them, and I told him so – in front of the boys, which wasn't a good idea. But I think Mac would have fought with his own sons too, if he'd had any. His was that touchy, growling kind of masculinity which can't resist tussling with other males and testing them. (Yet he was tenderly solicitous towards the craftsmen who worked for him at the factory.)

So we had some awful confrontations. Mac had never had to deal with anything like Rowan's scenes before; Lauren had only ever slammed doors and sulked. He thought each row with Rowan was terminal – which was what Rowan thought too; in his tantrums he was desperate with self-destruction, provoking you to say the worst thing possible to hurt him, reaching as a simplification for the last unforgivable gesture which would pull down the whole edifice of his life. I can remember Mac holding Rowan at arm's length by the shoulders, bellowing ('How dare you speak to me like that?'), while Rowan kicked at Mac's knees and Luke tried to intervene physically between them; or Rowan punching through a door panel; or Mac locking Rowan outside one night and Rowan appearing ghoul-like at the downstairs windows with his face flattened against the glass, smearing the panes with tears and snot. It all seems fairly absurd, in retrospect. What I can't recover is what the rows were actually about, what small seeds of daily cause gave rise to those hurricane effects.

Mac managed to pick quarrels with Luke too – for smoking weed, for sleeping late, for missing school – though he was such an easy teenager and only ever did these things in moderation. Mac went berserk when he found that Luke had taken the Mercedes out one night while we were away (without a licence or insurance or driving lessons: like me, Luke was a natural driver). I had the dream-sensation sometimes that I was closeted again with the stepfather I'd spent my life getting away from. ('Do you think the world owes you a living?') When Rowan and Luke developed a comic parody of Mac's outrage, I didn't know if I was relieved or disappointed: was he ridiculous? Perhaps that was the mistake I'd made, I'd married a fool: not the more interesting one, of marrying a monster. I knew Mac blamed Rowan's behaviour on the way I'd brought him up. And no doubt it partly was because of the way I'd brought him up, but I wasn't going to concede that. The trouble was that Mac took him on as an equal, refusing to see the suffering child with his white face and inchoate despair. (Though in the long run it may be that Mac's refusal was better for Rowan than my sympathetic penetration. When Rowan came home at seventeen after living for a year with his grandmother in Glasgow, he and Mac were suddenly close, conspiring in glum distaste against my interrogations: 'How are you feeling now? Are you happy?')

I used to console myself, when things were at their

worst, by spending Mac's money. He didn't mind me doing this, in fact he liked it; I suppose he thought my shopping expeditions were a sign that I acquiesced in the outward conditions of our life together. But I came closest to leaving him when I was using my credit card; I defied his logic, that his money was a power over me. I'd never had money in my life before. All through my twenties and early thirties I'd bought my jeans and shirts from charity shops and vintage stalls; it was strange to be in a position to choose whatever I liked – it was almost inhibiting, I didn't know where to start. Mac joked that although some of the clothes I bought cost a fortune, they looked as if I might have picked them up at a jumble sale after all: silky slinky scraps, faded prints, torn bits of net and lace with velvet trimmings. That waif look was fashionable and it suited me – I even adapted it for work with plain black cashmere jumpers and flat shoes. I had my hair cut off short and spiky at Vidal Sassoon's; I was still very thin. (Some of the women I worked with in my first job as an occupational therapist, attached to the adolescent unit in a psychiatric hospital, couldn't forgive me for the cashmere and the thinness. But they didn't like me anyway, they thought I was arrogant and aloof because I didn't join in their gossip. I was out of my depth all the time I was at that unit – and I identified too sympathetically with the teenagers who were our patients.)

I think what I felt about my appearance at that time in my mid-thirties was elegiac. It seems comical, looking back from the age I am now: but I believed then that I was at the end of my youth, on the brink of leaving certain experiences behind, losing my old freedoms inside the substantial middle-aged categories of a career and marriage. The clothes and the hair and the way I still painted my eyes, that whole look with its sexy bitter twist – I entered into it as though it was a last flare of possibility, before youth vanished for ever.

In the early nineties, when Mac and I had been living together for about four years – and before Rowan went to Glasgow – I had a visit from my old friend, Sheila. I hadn't seen her since the break-up of our commune; the last I'd heard of her was that she was settled in Brazil and teaching English. She arrived one Bank Holiday weekend when we were all at home. Everyone who called at our Sea Mills house came to the side door into the kitchen, but she turned up in a taxi without warning at the front and used the heavy knocker – which seemed significant when I thought about it later, because her entry into the house brought a momentous change. I struggled to drag back the bolts in the dusty porch, which depressed me because it was heaped with cast-off coats and boots (I wasn't tidy like Barbara), and by the time I got the door open the taxi was just driving off. For a moment I didn't recognise who was standing there. When she was twenty-four, Sheila had looked like a saint in a medieval painting: austerely stately, pale with long auburn hair which was wiry and burnished like threads in an old embroidery. Now, her hair was cut short and bleached dry by the sun, her skin was tanned and roughened: she looked rakish and unsettled, challenging. She was wearing some kind of long bedraggled print skirt, and hoop earrings. In those first moments I hardly took in that she had a baby slung in a tie-dyed vermilion cloth against her breast – a little girl, asleep, with a tiny closed perfect face and thick black hair.

— Is it *yours*? I exclaimed.

— Of course it's mine. Did you think I'd borrowed it?

We were awkward together at first – or perhaps it was just that she'd always been angular and abrupt. She seemed to find it funny that our house from outside looked like a child's drawing: rectangular and red-brick with a chimney at each end, planted bang in the middle of its flat garden which was really just the same scrubby field as outside the garden walls (Barbara had grown things but I'd neglected them). Mac wandered across the hall, pretending to be preoccupied, taking flight from introductions behind his air of being a hundred years older than any of my friends. Inside the house, Sheila went around touching everything, exclaiming that she couldn't believe I owned all this. I thought she was criticising me – because of the world of poverty she'd come from, or out of the returned traveller's disdain for everything they'd left behind and forgotten – and I felt weighed down by the settled, responsible life I'd taken on. It was mid-autumn and a gloomy light, muddled with damp from the river, seemed to have got every-where indoors; we had all our lamps switched on in the middle of the day, and the wind was tugging round the house, teasing it.

In the kitchen, Sheila wouldn't take off her coat; she really wasn't dressed for the English climate. She snuggled with a groan of relief close to the Aga, unwrapping the sleeping baby on her lap. I bent over to make a fuss of it: it was the most satisfying, perfect creature, clear-skinned, the eyelids closed in straight black lines, the brows tiny upward brush strokes, purplish lips pressed shut as if in repudiation. Her name was Ester, Sheila said, pronouncing it the Brazilian way, as Esh-tair. She was three months old, born in Recife. Sheila talked about motherhood with a stiffly comical air, avoiding my eyes. No one had told her that you couldn't send the baby back if you weren't enjoying it. The Indian women seemed to have a completely different kind of baby; they slept all day, you could take them to work in the fields. She'd wanted one of those. I suggested that Ester looked like an Indian baby anyway, but Sheila wouldn't give anything away about the father. She explained that she had six months' unpaid leave from the language school where she worked, and that she'd come home to show the baby to her family, then after a week couldn't bear being at home – she was hoping I would let her stay for a few days. When Ester began to stir on her lap, she seemed immediately strained and anxious. There was a bottle of formula mixed up in her bag; would I warm it up in a pan of water?— I suppose you think it's awful that I'm not breastfeeding, she said accusingly.

I reassured her and asked if I could give Ester her bottle. Sheila watched her feed with a curiosity that was half appalled. — It's sort of terrible to think one was ever like that, she said. — I mean, with one's own mother. Because I don't like my mother much. I don't like to think of myself so desperately attached to the teat of her provision (whether it was the real teat or the rubber one – and I'd rather not know). So keen on survival, at all costs. It seems better form, once one's adult, not to want anything that badly.

When I'd lived with Sheila in the commune, I'd been in awe of her education. She seemed to have read everything; her contralto voice and her slow, debunking, considered speech had appealed to me as an ideal of an intellectual woman. Now that I'd done my own degree and felt more like her equal, I was eager to talk to her about books – but she only wanted to talk about babies. I saw that she'd come looking for me because she needed help and remembered me as a young mother from the commune; whereas I'd finished with that phase of my life and wasn't interested any longer. She exclaimed in despair when I managed to keep the baby from crying, winding her and then jigging her in my arms, walking up and down and singing to her.

— You see? She won't ever stop for me. What am I doing wrong?

I said that everyone felt like this at first. After a while it would come naturally.

Sheila stayed at Sea Mills with us for six weeks. She was alone with the baby all day while Mac and I were out at work and Rowan was at school (Luke was in his gap year with a place at Exeter to do history and politics; in the meantime he was working for my brother, restoring classic cars). Sheila said she walked around the rooms of the house for hours with Ester in the sling, because it was the only way she could get her to sleep. Also, she could just about read the newspaper while she was walking round, though it did make her seasick and sometimes she was so tired that the words swam in front of her eyes like a hallucination. If she tried to read while she was giving Ester her bottle, Ester pulled away from the teat indignantly. — But what if, Sheila asked, — when this is over, I've forgotten how to think? And anyway, when will it be over?

I said that now Ester was getting older, she was bound to be awake more during the day; Sheila said that when she was awake she didn't know what to do with her. — Am I supposed to play? I was never any good at playing.

— Give her to the boys. They'll look after her.

Sheila was relieved and guilty when Luke and Rowan carried Ester off into another room. (— But do they know what to do?) They unwrapped her from her shawls and teased her irreverently, throwing her in the air, flapping her blanket at her to make her screw up her face comically, blowing raspberries on her stomach, laughing at her miniature dictator's outrage and stolid frown. (They were experienced in all this from playing with Toni's babies, Mac's granddaughters – she had two by this time.) Of course Ester loved it, and gave her first wet smiles for them. Sheila had been so sure that Ester's not smiling meant she was unhappy, judging against the life where she found herself. The smiles gave away another Ester: more foolish and less punishing.

I borrowed a carrycot from Toni and made Sheila put Ester down in it while we all ate supper round the long table in the kitchen. Sheila stared at the food on her plate as if she'd last eaten in another life. She was bone-thin under all the layers of her jumpers and cardigans and scarves: despite her determination to leave everything English behind, she was beginning to be one of those sinewy, sun-toughened Englishwomen of a certain class, angularly elegant, expertly informed. Mac grew to like her when they discussed Brazil and South American politics, and he deferred to her insider's insight (— the only continent in the world, she said, — where communism is still romantic). If Ester cried while we were eating then Mac picked her up and would walk round with her, crooning to her, kissing her little fists and her head with its night-black shock of hair. We were all as tender with Sheila as if she was convalescent. Mac was the assured paterfamilias presiding over his extended household. He was inspired in this role: even the boys were charmed and he courted them, including them in the generous circle of his affections. He was never handsome, exactly – bald and overweight, with that distinctive round face like the face in the moon – but he gave off a heat of life and force, his fox-colouring was a russet glow.

Sometimes there would be ten or eleven of us for supper if Luke's girlfriend was there, and Toni with her family – they lived nearby. Lauren honoured us from time to time, visiting from London (where she was a great success, playing in the orchestra at the ENO). If we were too many then we had to decamp into the grander dining room, which I didn't like because it still seemed like Barbara's space – yellow-striped wallpaper, electric wall candelabra, antique table and chairs. I confided to Sheila how trapped I sometimes felt in that big comfortable house, decorated in Barbara's taste – conventional, expensive, *gemütlich* – overlaid now with what Mac called my 'hippie style'. I told her about the faithful cleaner who loved Barbara and couldn't forgive me (secretly I called her Mrs Danvers). Sheila asked why we didn't move and I explained that Lauren and Toni – who'd grown up in this house – wouldn't let Mac sell it, not yet.

— Then couldn't their mother live here instead?

— She can't, because of what happened.

— But what about you? Don't you get to have a say?

I let her know about the difficulties between me and Mac. When she asked whether Barbara was awful, I tried to convey how she was really the nicest person, impulsive and imaginative and kind: which made everything worse.

— It was a sort of quixotic thing, when she left Mac. She had an ideal that she shouldn't keep him if he loved someone else – even though we hadn't seen each other for several years. And Mac believes that too. He believes passion is a life force you have to submit to. I don't know what I think. It's a force for a while and then you can step past it. (I was thinking of Sheila's brother Andrew. She had told me he was married with children, and had given up drinking, and was writing a book.)

258

Sheila thought that passion was a story people dreamed up to save themselves from boredom. — I'd lived all along as if I was acting out some turbulent drama; then I woke up one day and found I'd stopped believing in the play. Since then my life is saner and more manageable, but it's thinner – as if this whole colourful noisy troupe alive inside my head had upped and left. I am quite empty sometimes.

— You've had a baby. That's dramatic.

Right now, having a baby seemed more like the end of the story, she said. I asked her again then who Ester's father was, but Sheila claimed he didn't matter, she said she couldn't even remember his name. It had all been a misunderstanding, she said, entirely her own fault; and he didn't even know Ester existed. Anyway, a baby was not the end, I promised her. I could see that she was studying us, to see how to make a family; she had plenty of friends in Brazil but she had lived alone, and liked it. When she laughed about Mac with friendly scepticism, I felt a defensive pang as if I betrayed him. — He's like a busy engine, isn't he? Sheila said. — With you lot all yoked on behind, his caravanserai. Determinedly on his way somewhere: so there's a lot of heat and dust. Still, it's better than just turning round in the same space, as I do.

Sheila hadn't seen Rowan since he was a few days old; as a teenager, he looked startlingly like his dead father Nicky, whom he'd never known. How could it be, she and I wondered together, that these characteristics had been stored in Nicky's DNA, waiting to unfold inside his son's separate life: the impatient way Rowan turned a tap full on, then gasped through a hasty glass of water, spilling half of it, with the tap still running; or his careless swaggering walk; or dragging at his school tie as if he needed air? I thought Sheila was almost afraid of Rowan at first, because of how he brought Nicky back and yet didn't. But she was good at talking to the boys, they liked her. Rowan sang and played his guitar for her. (— Oh, he's good, he's really good, she said.) Luke claimed to remember her from the commune, though he was only four when it broke up: and he did have an extraordinary memory, which was part of his personality – open, accepting of everything he found, storing it away. He remembered visiting the zoo, on the day Nicky was killed. His frank gaze was full of irony mixed with tolerance: his hair was still childishly blond, though darkening, cut short in a thick pelt I loved to push my fingers through. Rowan was taller than Luke was already (and they were both taller than me); Luke was stocky, popular, good at rugby, clowning for his friends with a quick humour, not cruel. He'd been through several girlfriends already, though he'd been protectively uxorious in turn towards each one (and I didn't think any of them good enough).

Luke brought Sheila the white quartz stone I'd always kept, which we had used in our discussions in the commune, passing it round between the speakers. Sheila hesitated to take it from his hand. — I'm afraid to touch it, she said.

— Why? he asked with interest. — Because it all ended badly?

— It wasn't our fault, I insisted. It felt so important, that they didn't carry the wrong story forward. — You do know that, boys? Nicky's death was just the most terrible accident. The man who killed him was ill.

— It's not that, Sheila said. — It's because I hate the idea of my youth. I was so wrong about everything, and so sure I was right. I'm frightened when I remember myself. I worked in a factory making meat pies, out of solidarity with the working classes.

— What's wrong with meat pies? Luke protested.

— That was quite honourable, I said. — I liked you for it.

— It wasn't honourable, it was insufferable. How dared I, play-acting other people's real lives? And of course the women who had no choice about working there hated me, and I didn't know how to talk to them. It was such a sham.

Rowan remarked that his father had worked building a road.

— That was different. Nicky was different, everything he did was graceful and the right thing. Anyway, he wasn't doing it out of politics, he just needed the money. I needed the money too; but I could have earned it doing something less ostentatious, something I was actually good at. I was so hopeless, with the pies. I made such a mess of it, I was always dropping them.

We had to go to a family party one Sunday lunchtime: my Auntie Andy's silver wedding anniversary. Mac complained ungraciously. He thought he was reasonable,

261

and didn't see any point in submitting to an occasion so utterly against his nature. Wouldn't it be awful? Weren't Phil and Andy boring? Couldn't we just send a cheque? I explained how these obligations weren't optional, they were the ritual that bound my family together. We weren't connected because we found one another interesting. Offence was taken even if you forgot to send a birthday card or write a thank-you letter, and my mother and stepfather were always too ready anyway to be offended by Mac; they didn't really like him, he frightened them. Mum put on an arch, unnatural voice when she was talking to him, as if she was flirting; Gerry was hollowly hearty, hot inside the neck of his shirt. Gerry wasn't much older than Mac, and yet with his strained good manners and fading handsomeness (inky smudged features, thick head of iron grey hair) he seemed to belong to a different era. He and Mac couldn't even discuss sport, because Gerry liked football and Mac was a rugby man. The complication was that my parents would expect to be superior themselves, at Phil and Andy's party. They thought of themselves as having moved into a quite different social tranche – golf, the Masons, even dinner parties; whereas Andy had worked on the production line at the chocolate factory until she retired. Mac blundered across the subtlety of all this, not even noticing he was condescending.

The party was in a function room in a hotel in town, a stuffy low-ceilinged basement with florid carpets and gold drapes arranged across blank walls. Before we arrived Mac was already martyred, because we'd had to drive around for twenty minutes before he found anywhere to park. The boys were chafing to be free of our tension. I threw myself into the occasion and drank a couple of glasses of wine quickly. (Mac took one look at the wine and stuck to beer.) Circulating round the family I hugged and chattered, probably overdoing it.

— Why are you talking like that? Mac asked me at one point.

— Like what?

— Putting on that Bristol accent.

— This is my accent, I said. — It's the other one I'm putting on.

I was wearing a mauve top over black jeans, with green silk tied in my hair: my mother said the top reminded her of a bedspread she once had. These days, she said with a jollying air to make it seem as if she was joking, couldn't I have afforded something smarter? (Her attitude to Mac's money was peculiar: partly complacent on my behalf, partly affronted, as if it was an offence to moderation. If I'd told her how much my top cost she'd have been horrified.)

I made a fuss of Auntie Andy, whom I'd always liked: she was small and fat and cheerful, with her hair dyed orange and a short dress patterned with enormous roses. Clumsily tender, she tucked my arm into hers and introduced me to her friends from work, telling them I'd been close to her little boy who died (which wasn't strictly true). These women were formidable, raucous, enormous; their talk was very blue, and already their table was in a fug of cigarette smoke. Now Andrea was retired,

she lamented, she missed the comradeship of the factory.
— Stella, I don't know what to do with myself all day.
Phil does all the housework, because he knows how I
hate it. (Queenly, she took for granted the devotions of
her stooping, spindly, hypochondriac husband.) Her
friends had better suggestions for how Phil could save
her from boredom; Andy wagged a finger at them, telling
them to be on best behaviour.

— We 'an't got started yet, they said.

— They're good girls, Andy confided tipsily in my
ear. — Only a bit rough around the edges.

Although there was a buffet, there were place names
at every table, written out in Phil's anxious copperplate:
he must have fretted for weeks over the nuances of family
feuds and precedence. He panicked now when Andrea
insisted on sitting just anywhere among her guests,
waving away his remonstrations with her cigarette and
gin glass. I was relieved that Mac and I were separated;
I sat next to my cousin Richard, Auntie Jean's oldest
son, the one who'd lent me his bedroom when I first
left home: he still had a motorbike and he made money
as a builder, buying old houses and doing them up to
sell, putting back all the original features people had
taken out in the 1960s. Skinny and attractive, Richard
always flirted with me: husky from all the weed he
smoked, with a ponytail, a dreamy, narrow face and grey
eyes. (My brother Philip was supplying the weed at the
anniversary party; I noticed my sons disappearing outside
with him at regular intervals.) Richard's girlfriend had
been segregated at another table. I knew he and I were

bending too intimately towards each other, conferring too exclusively, but I'd drunk enough not to care. Jean complained that we hardly touched our food: — No wonder you're a pair of scarecrows! Richard told me about his dream of going to live in Spain, when he'd made enough money from the houses: not among the expats and English pubs, but somewhere unspoiled in the mountains, with land and a well in the courtyard. You could pick up a medieval farmhouse there, he assured me, for next to nothing.

— How about it, Stella?

— I'd love that, I said. — I've never lived anywhere except this city. I'd like to live on a mountain top. I'd like to drink water from a well.

— Come with me. Seriously. I'd like that.

Of course it wasn't serious, it was just a joke, it was a game: I knew that when I lifted my head and looked around me. I had two sons and a job and a husband, I was not free; probably Richard was not really free either. (Although, later, he did go and live on a mountain top in Spain.) When everyone had finished eating, the disco started up: pounding, and with flashing lights. Mac wouldn't be able to stand the noise for long. The women from the factory danced in a line together, they knew a set of moves for all the songs. Richard and I slow-danced to 'Killing Me Softly', though he wasn't much of a dancer; he touched me on the waist to steer me and I saved his touches up to remember later. Luke and Rowan were showing off, learning dance moves from the factory girls. I was aware of Richard's girlfriend, and of Mac looming, bored and restless, on the periphery of the party. I couldn't forgive him in that moment for not being able to belong inside this world – though I had spent so much of my own life trying to escape from it. He came to claim me, frowning at his watch, saying he had paperwork to do at home. Philip suggested that the boys could stay behind and sleep over at his place; I arranged to drop Rowan's school things off on my way to work.

It was raining when we got outside. I pretended to be drunker than I was, leaning against the ticket machine in the car park and humming the music I'd been dancing to, while Mac hunted in his pockets for money. He said I was in no fit state to drive, when I offered. The excitement of the party dropped; stark recognitions blew round inside my emptiness in the cold car park. I thought that Mac and I were strangers joined by meaningless accident, unfathomable to one another and I caught sight of him, freshly with surprised dislike – middle-aged and preoccupied, with a thick wrinkled neck. Our intimacy had only ever been a delusion, monologues passing and missing in darkness – which was all that was possible anyway, with anyone. All this seemed open to the naked eye, as if I saw through everything. In the car Mac started up the heater and I hugged my apartness to the rhythm of the wipers clearing fan-shapes on the windscreen, watching the smudged wet grey-green suburban streets as they passed. At least Mac wasn't nursing grudges; he didn't care about me drinking or flirting, was only relieved to be on his way home. He asked cheerfully whether I knew that in the eighteenth century whalers had gone out from Sea Mills Dock for a few years, and blubber had been boiled there; I said I hadn't known it. I tried to imagine all that scurrying filthy effort and activity, all the endeavour, the great distances and risks of danger, but I couldn't believe in it. Everything seemed too far off and too tiny.

The rain was heavy, Mac had to put on the wipers at top speed. As we turned into the yard at home we saw that Sheila was standing outside in it: rain was streaming down her face and her clothes were sodden, clinging to her. She looked like a medieval saint again: tormented, and rigid as if she was carved in wood.

— I can't do it, she announced to us over the noise of the rain as the car engine died.

— Do what?

— I give up.

She was deliberately flat and calm.

— What's happened, Sheila?

Ester apparently had woken up and begun crying almost as soon as we left for the party (which was at about eleven; it was now almost five). Sheila had no idea what the matter was. Ester wouldn't take her bottle, she screamed all the way through a nappy change. She wouldn't be cajoled by Sheila putting her in the sling and walking round with her, which had always worked before. Sheila had tried everything she'd seen me try: the singing, the jogging up and down, the distracting her by carrying her in and out of different rooms; even the blowing on her tummy. But Ester only redoubled her

267

paroxysms: she was swollen and purple with rage, throwing herself backwards in the sling, shuddering and howling. Sheila said she'd tried for a long time, and then she'd thought that the baby and her simply weren't doing each other any good, she wasn't making anything any better. So she might as well just walk away from her. She'd put her down in the carrycot, in the bedroom.

— It's all right, Mac said, putting his arm round Sheila in all her soaking clothes. — You did the right thing.

— It's so hard, I sympathised, — when you're on your own.

— In fact I thought, if I stay in there with her, listening to her, I'm going to do something dreadful. So I came outside. And I've been out here ever since.

How long had she been outside, for goodness' sake?

— Two hours? Three? Or perhaps that's melodramatic. I don't have my watch on. It's felt like three hours. Actually it's felt pretty much like an eternity. I've walked around some of the time. But mostly I've stood here because the rain splashing over from the gutter meant I couldn't hear her crying. There didn't seem any point in hearing it, as I wasn't going to do anything about it. It's all very exaggerated, isn't it? I never knew anyone had that much crying in them.

— That bloody gutter, Mac said. — I keep meaning to clean it out.

— Shall I go and have a look? I said.

— I want you to keep her, said Sheila. — You two. Adopt her. Please, won't you?

Mac was coaxing Sheila towards the back door, saying

she needed to get into some dry clothes, to have a cup of tea or a stiff drink. When I went inside I couldn't hear Ester at first. Sheila hadn't switched the lights on; the rooms were almost dark because of the rain at the windows, and the white tiles in the chequerboard hall floor seemed to float in the gloom. I picked up the full bottle of formula abandoned on the hall table, and as I climbed the stairs I caught the tail end of a thread of noise, a thin remnant of exhausted sobbing. Sheila was staying in a spare room on the first floor at the back, papered in pale Chinese-green with a pattern of bamboo stems and white flowers. Coming into it in the dim light felt like stepping underwater – and the air in the room was heavy with baby-smell, animal and close. Everything was quiet. The carrycot was on the floor beside the bed; I slipped out of my shoes so as not to wake Ester if she'd fallen asleep at last, though when I tiptoed across to peer into the cot I was sure that she was awake, listening out for me, reciprocating my prickling consciousness of her. Sure enough, when I leaned over the cot her gaze was ready for me, wide-open eyes glassy in the shadows. Her silence seemed full of an awakened intelligence beyond her age. For a long moment of mutual exchange, before she resumed her crying, we stared and seemed to hover between possibilities: I might remain a convenient stranger, she might remain someone else's baby, sweet but tedious. Or something different might come about.

Mac came into the room to get towels and a bathrobe for Sheila, while I was giving Ester her bottle. She was hungry, she had snatched eagerly at the teat as soon as I offered it. Now as she sucked she was gazing up at me in moist reproach, her breath still catching and snuffling in the aftermath of the long-drawn-out adventure of her sorrows. When Mac leaned over us she tugged away from her sucking, twisting her head to take him in; I thought she might begin to cry again but she only gave him the same slow, measuring look that she had given me, then slid back on to the teat luxuriantly.

— It's a crazy idea, I said to Mac. — Sheila doesn't mean it.

— We could do it, he said. — If she did mean it.

— You must be mad, I said.

But I had a vision in that moment of the three of us together in that room, remote as if seen from a very far off place – like the vision of Mac's whaling ships. And I thought that the substantial outward things that happened to people were more mysterious really than all the invisible turmoil of the inner life, which we set such store by. The highest test was not in what you chose, but in how you lived out what befell you.

And so we got our daughter. (Though we always told Ester that she was Sheila's daughter; we were her foster parents.) I left my job at the adolescent unit to look after her. I'd been unhappy there anyway, I'd hated it when the nurses gave the girls their sedative injections and the girls fought against it, and then the nurses wrote down in their records that they 'displayed paranoid symptoms'. I stopped working altogether for six months, staying at

270

home with Ester. And after that I got a part-time job at the Gatehouse, a network of accommodation and services for adults with mental health problems, where I was much happier. The boys loved Ester; Rowan believed that he and she had an extra kinship through their Brazilian connection. Toni and Lauren made more fuss, but they came round to her in the end. Sheila returned to her teaching job, and after a year she came back and was still sure it was what she wanted, so we did all the necessary bureaucratic stuff, and were checked by social services, and became Ester's legal guardians. (The bureaucracy wasn't straightforward, it was horribly complicated, but Mac was good at fighting his way through all of that.) Without making any deliberate decision, we slipped into pronouncing her name the English way, Es-ter: it was easier, anyway, when the time for school came round. She keeps her other name, Esh-tair, as if it's a clue to a different life running parallel to the one she's actually had. Everything Sheila sends her from Brazil she keeps in a box under her bed, segregated from her ordinary possessions. When Sheila visits, they are mutually guarded and interested and polite; Ester treats Sheila like an eccentric aunt whose favour is flattering but faintly ridiculous and risky.

Ester seemed to settle things between Mac and me. I know that usually it doesn't work, having a baby to bring a couple together; but perhaps just because she came to us in a roundabout way, she seemed to set a seal on our marriage. Mac was lordly in his confidence that we were doing the right thing; I never caught him out in any petty

271

panic, and I admired him for it almost dispassionately, as if I were admiring a stranger – though dispassionate isn't the right word, because at that time the passion between us was running rather strongly again. (This was during the same period, too, as he steered through a crisis at work: when they were advised to diversify into calibration systems for long-range weaponry Mac decided against it on moral grounds. Some of the team thought the company would go under, but it didn't.) The funny thing is how Ester's grown to be so much like Mac – more like him than either of his actual daughters. Not that she looks anything like him, or like either of us – or like Sheila, for that matter (she's vividly pretty; people think she's Malaysian with her dead-straight black hair and neat shallow eyelids and clear brown skin – her skin is like Rowan's). But Ester is stubborn, diligent, even-tempered, clever at sciences and with machinery. She steadies me when I'm restless or dissatisfied; she cools my heat and saves me from myself.

Ten

I wake up first, while Mac is still asleep. This waking up early is new, it has something to do with my age (I'm fifty, with everything that brings). There's a thin grey light in the room and the night is over, but that isn't encouraging. Night suits me, with its depths like infinite rooms sprawling underground. The daylight is exposing, prosaic, bleak – although I don't know why I'm afraid of its exposure, nothing's the matter, there's nothing to be afraid of. But something sour and dreadful seems to have collected, while I was sleeping, in the hollow under my breastbone: it's both a physical sensation and a mental anguish at once and I have to sit suddenly upright so as not to succumb to it. Then I discover that I need to pee. Was that all it was, after all: the poison and the anguish? So I mutter something to Mac, and potter in bare feet in my pyjamas to the bathroom, trying to keep my mind shuttered against the light which presses into it. I don't pull up the blind in the bathroom, I try to hold off the day which I can hear gathering its force outside the window: the breezes stirring in the garden, the birdsong in its slippery purity, the whole urgent, ordinary machinery of the present resuming its forward movement.

But I can't hold it off. I prefer to wake up gradually, lingering half inside my dreams; but sometimes waking is as abrupt as falling over an edge of sleep, the doors to conscious awareness fly open involuntarily between one second and the next. I have a vision of despairing clarity then, as if my life were a featureless bland landscape stretching behind and ahead of me: all surface, all banal anxiety and difficulty, unredeemed nowadays by any promise or hidden content. It's in these early mornings, if I were an Anglican like Mac, that I'd pray.

Then that passes over. I go downstairs in the quiet of the sleeping house. Usually Mac gets up first but this morning I don't want to go back to bed, I know I'll only lie there in the grip of this wakefulness. On the landing halfway down the staircase (this is the house which Mac and I bought together when we moved from Sea Mills), there's a tall arched window, much taller than a person, with a narrow seat like a shelf across the bottom. I pause there as I always do, because I like the way the garden and the oak tree and the church tower beyond the trees all look mythic through the distorting old glass, like something in a film or a dream. Then my bare feet are cold on the stone-flagged kitchen floor, so I go into the boiler room where I keep a pair of old slippers, worn comfortably to shiny black hollows in the shapes of my heels and toes.

274

I fill the kettle under the tap and put it on to boil. I open the back door and carry the teapot across the wet grass, soaking my slippers; I empty last night's cold tea leaves into the bedraggled dahlias. Since Mac retired and sold the factory, he's thrown himself into gardening with the same zeal he once put into business. It's autumn, these dahlias are a velvety dark orange-red, smouldering in the cobwebby light. Silky floss is tangled amongst the seed heads in the herbaceous border, the plant stems are beginning to blacken and I can smell the frost: frowsty like rotten apples. Back in the kitchen I open the bread crock and get out the bread for toast. Mac makes all our bread, and our marmalade as well. I pour out glasses of orange juice. I go through the motions bringing in the morning, one ordinary thing after another.

Mac would like me to give up work and settle down with him here in the country, but I'm not ready yet. So we keep on our flat in the city, I stay there two or three nights a week when I'm working (I'm still at the Gatehouse). But Ester's at school down here, Mac drives her back and forth every day and on the way he tests her on her homework – French and poetry and maths and science. I worry that this puts too much pressure on her but she loves it, she nags him to ask her questions; she seems to learn easily, picking things up as a pure pleasure. She learns poems by Herbert and Marvell and Yeats off by heart ('Love bade me Welcome', 'The Song of Wandering Aengus'), and she and Mac recite them in unison. I thought Mac would be bored at home but I understand now that he addresses himself to whatever room of his life he happens to be in with the same kind of serious absorption that doesn't fail him.

When I've taken his breakfast upstairs I sit reading my book at the kitchen table with my legs tucked under me, refilling my mug with tea from the pot keeping warm in its cosy. The book is about the idea of Nature as it was imagined in classical philosophy and then as it developed under the Romantics; I'm reading a section on the Eleusinian mysteries. The last time I was in the British Museum, I saw a Greek red-figure vase which depicts an element of Eleusinian ritual: the demigod Triptolemos sits in his winged chariot with a sheaf of corn in his hand, preparing to descend and bestow it upon mankind. I'm searching all the time, in books and films and paintings, for signs of transcendent meaning like this that I can puzzle over. They excite me and elude me, escape ahead of me as I try to grasp them. And all the time that I'm reading, I'm watching the clock – at quarter past seven I'll get Ester up and Mac can make her breakfast and then I'll drive to the station to catch the ten to eight train. It's unusual to have this interval of reading and abstract thought on a work day. Perhaps I'll pay for it later and be tired: but for now my mind is racing, leaping from sentence to sentence. Everything's momentous as if I'm looking through a magnifying lens in my mind, seeing through the words to the whole, to their core; sometimes I'm actually breathless and my heart is racing, in pursuit of the meaning emerging so close within my reach.

I needn't go to work, we don't need the money, I

could stay here and read and think all day, every day. This house is the first home I've ever actually chosen for myself: a Georgian frontage, all light and air, tacked on to a much older farmhouse behind, with walls two foot thick and squint-eyed windows to keep the weather out. For a year after we bought it I devoted myself to doing the house up and buying furniture for it, trying to fulfil the soul I felt it had: subtle with its shadowy corners, poignantly haunted by its past. And then when the house was finished I couldn't quite bear it: I felt as if I'd made it for someone else to live in and not me. Or it seemed like a bargain I'd made with middle age and the bargain sickened me; I was ashamed of all the money I'd spent, contriving an effect of spontaneity and accidental charm as if the place had been in my family for a hundred years. I thought that I'd bargained my youth away with this house, giving it away in return for a shell, the sordid trick of material things. (But of course youth was over anyway, whether I bargained or not.)

That was a silly fuss, it didn't last. I'm very happy here now, I know how lucky I am. Though I'm not quite ready yet, to move in finally. I'm holding that day off. When I jump on the train at the last minute on work mornings, I still feel sometimes as if I'm running away, escaping from something coming up behind me.

In the evening after work I have dinner in the city with Madeleine: she's home from London visiting her mother. We meet in a lively place I like which was the old river police station when the harbour was still for commerce and not just for leisure; the restaurant is all glass on the river side so that you can watch the boats and the swans passing, the water in its metamorphosis (through gold, mercury, steel) as the light goes. Madeleine is there first and finds a good place by the window; when I arrive and don't see her for a moment she half stands up, tottering on high heels, calling and waving to me eagerly: blonde hair pinned up untidily, protuberant blue eyes, plump chest rounded as a pigeon's, hot colour of tiny broken capillaries in her cheeks. She's wearing a tight skirt and big earrings and she's ordered cocktails already. Madeleine and I don't meet often, but whenever we do we fall easily into our old companionableness. I talk to her more intimately than I ever talk to Mac, I can tell her anything and she tells me everything too, we spill over to each other eagerly. It's better without the men (though she likes Mac and I like Donald, her partner). Madeleine doesn't read and she doesn't think about abstract things, but she takes in what she sees, without defensive judgement.

She's Ester's godmother (Mac insisted that Ester was christened, though the boys aren't). She doesn't have children but Donald has teenagers who live with them at weekends and she likes them and is kind to them and comically doleful about her relations with them. (— I think you have to be broken in first by babies, she says. — The teenage craziness comes as too much of a shock otherwise – just as you've settled down yourself, into being sensible.) Her job these days is something deep inside the intangibles of management: in public

278

relations, for a company selling software to other companies for managing their systems – she's not even conducting the public relations, just overseeing the process through which they're conducted. When I ask her what fills up her day she says it's too boring to talk about, but I don't believe she hates it, I suspect she's happy enough in keeping her fragment of the machinery turning over effectively. I think that I couldn't bear to do something so null, but then I'm sorry for thinking it: what right have I to criticise? And in its different way that's what my job is too, just making tiny adjustments to individual lives swept along in the flow. I don't have all the ambitious ideas about OT I used to have, believing it was a lever for changing things. Mostly it's just organising badminton or art classes for the service users, or trips to Butlin's or the ice rink (we did go to Paris once). Madeleine loves my story of the young man in one of our Gatehouse flats who is autistic spectrum and not coping with venturing out anywhere; I've taken photographs of his bedroom, bathroom, hallway and kitchen, and laminated them for him, because he feels safer if he can look at them while he's away from them.

— Oh, those are what I need, she says. — On a bad day, I could stare at the furniture in our spare room and take comfort from it.

— It's not exactly building a new world, though, is it? Bedroom, bathroom, hallway, kitchen . . .

— Who wants a new world?

Night falls while we are eating and the darkness outside

presses greedily against the glass; an autumn moon swims up over the water, dowager-stately, trailing clouds like scarves, looming over its own reflection. The restaurant by this time is crowded and noisy. Somehow we get on to talking about coincidence: Madeleine believes in premonitions and synchronicity and ghosts and we quarrel about this amiably enough, not for the first time. She gives me examples of things that have happened to her which can't have been accidental and I insist that this perception is only confirmation bias. She says there are patterns of energy we can tap into, if we allow ourselves to read the signs. We're neither of us going to change our minds. I tell her how I've dreamed often about Fred since he died, but I don't think that's because he's visiting me or sending me messages, it's just because I miss him and feel sad about him. (One of these dreams was so horrible that I can't recount it to Madeleine or to anyone, it's safer if I keep it to myself. In this dream Fred came to stay with us and was just the same funny, exuberant, glum self that he had been when he was alive, except that he brought his dead body with him as if that was a normal thing to do, and kept leaving it carelessly lying about the place; this body was a disgusting thing, half opened up like a body in an autopsy. I was terrified all the time that the boys or Ester would come across it and be traumatised – often in my dreams the boys aren't the grown men they are in real life, they're still children and I'm still responsible for them.)

I'm happy in the restaurant with Madeleine. We're genuinely hungry and everything tastes good and I like the way the night beyond the glass closes us in with the crowd of strangers also enjoying themselves. There's a kind of freedom too, no doubt about it, in our being fifty. It's painful and terrible that youth is over, and with it that whole game of looking and longing and vying for attention, hoping for something, for some absolute trans-formation of everything. But it's also a reprieve to be let off that hook and know that you're simply in your own hands at last. Although Madeleine insists at one point that some man or other is eyeing me up; I don't really think he is, and I don't fancy him in any case. Anyway, I say, I'm old enough to be his mother. Madeleine says that as I was a child bride I could be anybody's mother, and I remind her that the one thing I wasn't as a child was anyone's bride. And then she breaks off and gives me an odd kind of glance as if that's reminded her of something she ought to tell me, but doesn't want to. It takes a bit of coaxing to get it out of her, but she's hope-less at dissimulating and explains to me eventually that she's heard news from her mother (who still lives in the house where Madeleine grew up, next door to me) that Valentine has come home.

Valentine! No! I'm surprised by how the news disturbs me, after all this time.

— Do you mean home from the States?

— I mean home to his old house, where he lived when we knew him. His mother's still there; he's staying with her, apparently. He's been there for months. Mum says he's ill. Or he's been ill and he's come home to get better, I'm not sure which. His mother must be a hundred and ten by now. She was ancient when we were teenagers. His father died, you knew that.

For as long as he's been in America it's as if Valentine stopped changing when I stopped seeing him – I've gone on imagining him as a boy of seventeen. He ages now all at once with a rush: Valentine's the same age as we are – no, he's a year older. And then I think that I can't really remember him at all. I'm interested in the news of his return, of course, but I don't know what it means: perhaps nothing. He's been at home for months and hasn't looked for me. The past is closed up inside its own depressing little museum of faded styles and codes and anticipations; you can't re-enter it. Actually I feel angry with him for returning. Of course Madeleine wants to ask me about Luke, whether Luke knows anything about his father. And I reply firmly, as if it's not up for discussion, that he knows his biological father went away, that's all. He knows that his father never knew anything about him. Mac is his father now and he loves Mac, Mac loves him. Nothing else matters.

Really Valentine's return doesn't seem to matter much. I reassure Madeleine that it's most unlikely his path will ever cross with mine. As far as I'm concerned, I tell her, his being a thousand miles away or three makes no difference at all. We progress to talking about other things instead: she's staying over at her mum's for a week so we arrange to go shopping one afternoon, and to take both our mothers out to lunch together at the weekend. All this gives me a good excuse for staying on in town beyond the days when I'm actually at the

Gatehouse. I confess to Madeleine that I find myself seeking out excuses so as not to spend too much time in our country house, though there's nothing wrong between Mac and me.

— But I'm just not ready to settle down to country life, and he is.

— I don't blame you. All those green wellies and Tories and garden fetes. Perfect for holidays, but you wouldn't want to *live* there.

The country is more complicated than Madeleine thinks (she's such a Londoner these days and can't believe there's real life anywhere else). Our country friends aren't really Tories, they're just not very interested in politics, they're interested in other things. Our nearest neighbour, for instance, is an ecologist and expert in early music; the woman who helps Mac with the heavy work in the garden used to be in West End musicals. And I love my view of the church tower – its rooks rising like specks against the clouds – through the arched window on the staircase. Only I have the idea that moving down there permanently would be like passing through the quiver in the old glass to the other side, leaving something unfinished behind.

I do really, mostly, meanwhile, forget about Valentine; only every so often, underneath the surface of my conversation with Madeleine and then in the days that follow, at work and in the flat, I come upon the new knowledge of his nearness in the city – like knocking up against some disconcerting piece of loose flotsam. Funnily enough, if there had been even the remotest chance of some kind of romantic renewal between us, I think the idea of him would be less interesting. There's something infantilising and shaming in those Friends Reunited stories of childhood sweethearts getting back together. But I'm not succumbing to any secret hope that Valentine will have changed his sexuality while he's been away. Quite the contrary, in fact: it's the absence of the sexual motive which makes the idea of him intriguing for me. I realise that I'm starting to exaggerate him in my mind, imagining him like the demigod on the Greek vase, set apart from mortals, initiated into mysteries, bestowing gifts. Bestowing them on me: gifts of wisdom, or some kind of absolution. How absurd. He did use to look a bit like a demigod, when he was seventeen. He had that swaggering air of careless luck and a blissful uncomplicated beauty, as if his face and body were drawn in a few clean lines.

But now he'll be middle-aged, I tell myself.

He'll probably be dissipated, raddled, awful.

I don't know how much it matters, knowing your biological father. I've never known mine. A few years ago my mother suddenly became very agitated and conspiratorial: it turned out that, of all things, my real father had got in touch with her. He had got hold of my Uncle Ray through the internet (Ray's a computer enthusiast) and sent a message to him: the whole process was alien to Mum, who won't have a computer in the house – though Luke has tried patiently to persuade her.

Anyway, he'd not only found out Mum's whereabouts

but was asking what had become of me, his daughter. After all this time, nearly half a century! I think Mum had even persuaded herself that he was dead, just through sticking to that story for so long, no matter how I pressed her for the truth (with other people, as far as I know, she never even discussed him). She fell out dreadfully over the whole business with Uncle Ray, who in the first flush of excitement had responded to the stranger, giving him Mum's new married name and her telephone number. She and Ray didn't speak for months, until my stepfather and Ray's wife engineered a reconciliation.

I begged Mum to tell me what exactly my father had said to her: I was more interested in this fact of my parents' contact than in any implications it had for me.

— Oh, I don't know, Stella. We only spoke for a few minutes. The usual.

— What d'you mean, the usual? It can't have been usual!

— I mean, just the usual sort of things that people say.

— How did he sound? Did you recognise his voice right away?

— Of course I did, I'm not senile. He wanted to know what you were doing and I told him. He's going to ask Ray to pass his email whatsit on to you, so you can be in touch with him if you really want to.

I longed to have overheard how she reacted when she realised it was him: raw perhaps, for once, and startled, implicated. After all, she hadn't put the phone down on him. Was she alone in the house when he called? She

285

was. Had she asked him about his life, what it had been? That was none of her business, she said.

— But what was it like? How did you *feel*, when you knew it was him?

— I was trying to think of a way to get rid of him.

In the end I took my cue from Mum: I decided I wasn't eager to see my father. And of course I might have met him anyway, when I had driving lessons so long ago from a man with the same name. I still remembered how we had liked each other and how proud he had been of my driving. I was wary of spoiling it now: either finding out my instructor wasn't my father after all, or, if he was, then muddling the decent clarity of our old contact with new overlays of guilt and effort. Ray gave me the email address, but I never did anything about getting in touch.

In the wake of the little drama of my father's turning up, my mother was peculiar: cross and flattening, impatient with my stepfather if he was slow or forgot things. I felt sorry for Gerry, flinching under her brisk regime where everything personal and emotional had to be tidied out of sight – just when he might have liked to open up more expansively. He was still physically fit and energetic in his seventies and he was allowing himself new luxuries of feeling: listening to classical music, cooking, growing passionate over the birds visiting his garden. It felt for a while as if he and I were allied together against Mum and her lack of imagination, or her refusal of it. I made a point then of often taking Ester round to see them, because she and Gerry got on so well; he could occupy himself with her for hours, involving himself seriously in her games. He found something painfully poignant, I think, in her sweet looks and contained, fastidious manners: she was his bossy princess, he was her dedicated retainer. He asked me once, while we were watching her on the swing that he'd put up for her, how Sheila could bear to see her when she came visiting from Brazil.

— I'd have thought it would have been better for her to make a clean break, he said. — Never to set eyes on the child.

Defensive, I assumed that he was criticising our whole arrangement (my mother had predicted disaster when we first took Ester on). I was ready to be brash: no, why should she mind, so long as Ester was happy? When I realised he was genuinely interested, I told him what Sheila had said when we talked about it once: that she was surprised how far she was able to choose not to feel regretful. — Obviously she's sad sometimes, for a while. But it surprises her, how most of the time it is all right. She says she's come to the conclusion that the biology – the blood and genes and stuff – only means as much as you choose it to. You either confer that power, emotionally, on the genetic connection, or you don't. Likewise, you could confer the power on someone who isn't genetically related to you.

Then Gerry and I realised that we could be talking about ourselves, and my relation to him, so we were both uncomfortable and changed the subject.

It is fun and sinful, shopping with Madeleine. It's supposed to be Christmas shopping even though it's only late October; we have congratulated ourselves on our resourceful forward thinking. But the truth is that at least half of what we spend is on ourselves, on clothes and shoes and bits of jewellery. I don't often shop so impulsively these days, spending so much at once: it feels like being drunk (actually we probably are slightly drunk, having shared a bottle of wine at lunch), caught up in heady anticipations, believing we can renew ourselves and be different by changing our clothes. All day I am greedily interested in owning things. I'm paying cash but Madeleine's putting all her purchases on her credit card; I'm anxious about debt because of those long years when I had no money to spare, but she reassures me that she can pay it all off later. And after all it's only a technicality, where the spending comes from: owning the money doesn't make it more or less virtuous. The power of the bright flood of things in the shops is overwhelming, dazzling – and a triumph of taste, because there's much more nice stuff to go around now than there used to be. It's as if some ancient knot of material difficulty has come unfastened all at once, old puritan certainties have slipped away; but a residue of that grit makes me uncomfortable. (And Mac doesn't like credit cards. He's always on the side of manufacturing: he says we should be making things to sell, not buying things with money we don't have.)

Madeleine is using her mother's car and gives me a lift back to the flat afterwards. Alone there, surrounded by my carrier bags, I embark on an anxious session of trying the clothes I've bought, pulling them on with abandon, discarding them crumpled and inside out on the bed. When it's over I feel guilty and cheated and I have to run a bath because I'm sticky with sweat. I'm not sure now whether anything I've bought really suits me; I'm afraid in case I've lost my good judgement, or don't know any longer how I want to appear. Last summer when I was looking through clothes on a rail in a shop I saw a young girl's glance slide over me, embarrassed by my mistake in thinking those fashions could be meant for anyone my age. I'm relieved that I've arranged to go round to Luke and Janine's for supper; I don't want to stay in the flat alone with my purchases. I put on one of the new blouses, gauzy and flowery, over new leggings, then I take these off again and put on my old jeans and a white shirt. I've bought presents for Luke and Janine – a jumper for him and a bag for her – and I decide not to keep them for Christmas but to give them away now, like an expiation.

Luke and Janine are both junior-school teachers. They're buying a tiny terraced house on a steep street in Totterdown, which was where I brought Luke to live with my Auntie Jean when he was a new baby. Jean and Frank are still around the corner; Jean probably sees Luke as often as I do. It was a working-class district then; now it's alternative middle-class as well, with lots of young families, some of the houses painted in bright colours as if it was the Mediterranean. Luke and Janine grow vegetables in the back garden and Luke wants to install solar panels on the roof; he's good at all those practical kinds of things. They are pleased but bemused by my presents. Janine says that she has a bag already, but that she will save the new one until she needs it. I don't explain to her that if you're like Madeleine you don't have just one handbag at a time but a whole cupboard full of different ones to choose from, to go with different outfits.

We eat vegetarian lasagne for supper; Janine's a vegetarian so Luke's become one too. She doesn't put any salt in her food and I would like to add some to my plateful but I don't, because it might seem like a criticism of her cooking; I don't think Janine would mind but Luke might, he's very protective of her. I notice him explaining me to her now and then, mediating what I say as if he's afraid I may be too overbearing. They are gentle and conscientious and acutely attuned to one another. I wonder sometimes whether Luke has toned himself down too far to be in tune with Janine; when he gets together with his brother he's more like his old self, scathing and funny. But perhaps this gentleness is what he's always really wanted. When I first met Janine I was afraid that I was bound to offend her somehow; she's mournful-eyed and graceful like a girl in a Burne-Jones painting. But she's observant and clever too, and it turned out that she and I like each other, we're tolerant of each other's differences. I expect she has her own opinions about the kind of childhood that Luke had, and some of the chaos in it – but she keeps them to herself. Luke disappears upstairs after supper to the computer, and she and I wash up together.

We discuss Rowan and his music, the success he's

having and our worries about the new pressures on him: he's been supporting headline acts at the big festivals this summer. Songs pour out of him. I have them on my iPod and I listen to them on the train and round the house: they are a miracle, they come from a place in my son that's unknown to me. Janine has entered wholeheartedly into Luke's attitude towards his brother, at once sceptical and protective. Rowan still picks fights with me when he comes home; he recounts episodes from the past to illustrate how I neglected him or carelessly put him in danger – sometimes in a calmly forgiving voice, as if he appreciates I was too ignorant to know what I was doing. What possessed me, for instance, allowing him to go off to live with his grandmother in Glasgow for a year? Did I have any idea of the kind of place I'd sent him to, how violent it was and how racist? I lie awake at night and go over and over these narratives, asking myself whether he's right and I was wrong. I don't remember allowing Rowan to go anywhere, exactly: he presented his move to Glasgow pretty much as a fait accompli at the time and I don't think I could have stopped him – but perhaps I should have tried harder. I lose my confidence in my version of what happened. Luke is impatient if I try to talk these anxieties over with him, he says I ought to know better than to take Rowan's complaints too seriously. He says Rowan talks nonsense about how bad it was in Glasgow; Nicky's mother adored him and made a big fuss of him, the area they were in was perfectly friendly, Rowan was fine.

I think while I'm washing up with Janine that I might

mention what Madeleine told me: that Valentine has come home. I could see what she thinks about my telling Luke. But in the end the words won't form in my mouth; her steady competence makes me ashamed to raise this issue of my ancient mistakes, like dragging up some dirty mess out of the washing-up water. Janine has such an attractive way of doing everything: the rubber gloves are turned inside out and dried and hung by a peg on the draining board; then she makes us lotus blossom tea bought from a Vietnamese company online and we drink it out of the bone china teacups she found in a charity shop. Perhaps it's best to leave all those old stories in the dark. Luke has always known that his father's first name is Valentine and that he was in America: that's just about all he knows. I also told him long ago, when he was a little boy and asked me, that his father was very good-looking and very intelligent. (— I loved him desperately, I said. — But he didn't love me, not in that way. Though we were very good friends.) Nowadays Luke avoids the subject as if it embarrasses him. He calls Mac Dad (Rowan never does), even though he was a teenager by the time we all moved in together.

And then on my last day in town, I go to find Valentine. Of course I do. How could I know that he was in town – my long-lost twin, the secret father of my child – and not want to set eyes on him even just once after all this time? I dress carefully in new wool trousers I've bought – midnight blue – and a cream silk shirt and Paul Smith jacket. I want to show him that I've done all right, that

I'm powerful, I'm not nothing. In front of my mirror I'm full of trepidation, wishing I was taller. I could have taken a taxi out to Valentine's old house but instead I catch the bus, which has a different number now but follows the same route as the one he and Madeleine and I used to get back from school together. I look over-dressed for the bus, as if I was going to a business meeting; I regret my effort with the clothes now, and realise how provincial I will probably look anyway to Valentine, fresh from New York. As the bus penetrates deeper into the suburbs, it's extraordinary how unchanged it all seems – the old stage-set bourgeois innocence, the heavy quiet in the empty streets, house-fronts bristling with tactful paint, autumn gardens tied and tidied, a few late roses blown and tangled in the bushes. Perhaps there are more parked cars than I remember and they make the roads seem narrower. I never liked it here, this peace was always my enemy. And the deep familiarity disorientates me, as if after all what separates me from the past is tissue thin.

Valentine's house is detached, and different to most of the development around: older and gloomier and bigger, built in ugly blocks of red stone with a rough-hewn finish. The garden gate is off its hinges, propped inside the wall, and I wonder for a moment if the place isn't abandoned: the paint on the woodwork is faded and flaking off, evergreen shrubs in the front garden have grown high up against the front windows, flyers advertising pizza take-aways, dropped in the porch, are sodden with rain. But there are reassuring expensive lined curtains at the windows, even if the lining's ragged, and after I've pressed the bell I hear slow footsteps in the hall. Then Valentine's mother opens the door to me. I'm surprised how easily I recognise her, though Hilda was in her fifties when we last met and now she's an old lady; in her mid-eighties at least. Her shoulders are humped with arthritis and her heavy brown hair has turned iron-grey – but it is pinned in the same old French pleat, she wears the same dangling earrings. She is still daunting, elegant, ravaged; even fumbling with the latch her impatience has its old savagery, as if she'd like to break something. She doesn't recognise me, naturally enough, because we haven't met since I was seventeen. I tell her that I'm Stella, that I'm an old friend of Valentine's; for a moment while she peers unfocusedly I think she's forgotten me, and I'm relieved. She is disappointed because she thought I was the supermarket delivery.

– Who did you say you were?

And then when I tell her again, she does remember.

– Oh, Stella. You used to live on the new estate.

I don't know what she might have guessed, when she heard about my having to leave school because I was pregnant all those years ago, in the months after Valentine ran away to America. No doubt she heard about it, everybody did. Probably she just thought I was the kind of girl who was bound to get into trouble sooner or later, with some boy or another. She may have believed I was partly responsible for Val's going; or she may have understood all along the mistake I'd made, imagining I could

294

have him for my lover. Now I see calculation in her face behind the old frigid politeness.

— Your parents moved away. How are they?

I tell her that they're well; then I enquire whether Val's at home. Hilda is looking behind me all this time for the supermarket van. I can see she's irritated that I've arrived because it's distracting her from this delivery which has been at the centre of her day. — Val does the orders on the internet, she explains crossly. — They give you a two-hour time slot but they're awfully unreliable, and this one's late already. Though sometimes he thinks he's put an order in, and then it turns out he's forgotten to press the final button or something. He gets mixed up. Perhaps he just pretends he got mixed up, when actually he couldn't be bothered.

Then she says that he's usually in, he doesn't go out much.

She shrugs when I ask if I can come in; I say that I'd love to see him, though it will be very strange after such a long time. — You may as well go up, she says. — He hasn't been in touch with his old friends. I suppose that most of them have moved away.

The hall is more or less as I remember it – spacious and shabby with a cold cellar-breath. It's dark because of the feeble light bulb and the overgrown shrubs against the window; a gigantic sideboard carved in black wood takes up too much space – one of the things they brought with them from Malaya. Hilda explains that Valentine doesn't live in the attic any longer, he's moved down into his father's room because the attic's full of junk.

Then she seizes my hand in an awkward grip, heavy as iron, her knuckles swollen and freckled with age. — You know he hasn't been well?

And I think in that moment that it is AIDS, which would fit in with Valentine's timing perfectly. She asks if I have sons and I say I have two, both grown up now; I dread – because of her bowed head and the drooping, tragic face – that she is going to say something significant and terrible, about her love for her son and the pain of losing Valentine, because he's going to die. Stupid tears force their way into my eyes in readiness; she must see them. But after all she only talks on in her deprecating way about her various grandchildren (none of them Valentine's, of course) who seem all to be in expensive private schools, or at Oxford or Cambridge. I'm not quite sure what message this is supposed to have for me. Perhaps she is reminding me that I was never really quite good enough for their family. Or perhaps she's just rambling round familiar territory because she's an old lady and she's distracted, she's forgotten what she meant to say.

She doesn't come upstairs with me, she wants to keep looking out for the van; and I hesitate on the landing because I've no idea which room was Valentine's father's. I call out, but there's no response so I try one of the doors, which opens into a bedroom that must be Hilda's, at the front of the house: there's a ghost in the air in here of her cosmetics and scent, a high bed with a pink candlewick cover, and a cheval mirror (carved in the same black wood as the sideboard) that seems to stand in for

Hilda's presence, pulled stiffly upright. I try another door. In this second room it's dark because thick curtains are pulled across the windows, and there's an Anglepoise light switched on above a desk where an old man with a shock of white hair is sitting with his back to me, writing. I think for a startled moment that Madeleine made a mistake, Valentine's father isn't dead after all. Then the old man turns round and I see that it's Valentine.

He isn't really an old man. It's the white hair which is so disconcerting: and yet it's that pure white which is quite beautiful in itself, silky and light as floss, seeming charged with static because it floats like a translucence round his head. And Val's got a lot of it, he's not balding, it's just receding in a distinguished way at the temples. He doesn't really look so very old, more like someone who's been seriously sick and is just coming back to life. He's gaunt, his skin is papery-dry, his eyes seem huge and the folds of flesh under them are puffy. (It isn't AIDS – Val insists on that at some point in our conversation, as if he knows what people guess. I don't know what happened to him, exactly – some kind of breakdown, physical and mental, a consequence I suppose of all the drink and the drugs, and the lifestyle. It could so easily have been AIDS, going to America and to the gay scene and sleeping around just when he did; but if he'd got it then he'd probably have been dead by now. So he was lucky in his own way, charmed.)

The old faun-face is still there, behind the mask of age and illness. After the first moment's shock of non-recognition I find it: the heart-shape and defiant jaunty chin, the curious deeply curved eye sockets, a sardonic twist to the long mouth. He is still handsome; and his looks are more densely male and less androgynous after thirty years – their style that was poised and provisional is etched now deep into the flesh. The bruise-black eyes are suffering and eloquent against that white hair. He's wearing an old shirt which I guess was his father's, half buttoned and without cufflinks, so that the sleeves dangle off his forearms. I feel ashamed of my smart outfit. There's a stillness and steadiness in him which is new. He used to be too restless to sit at a desk for very long; but now as I look around I get the feeling that he doesn't venture much out of this room. It smells stale in here; the bed is unmade, clothes are lying on the floor where he has dropped them. The walls are pinned all over with pictures, postcards, things cut out of the newspapers, scraps of paper scribbled with writing. There's a Mac laptop open on the bed, though at the desk he was writing by hand. Books – not novels but heavy reference books, numbered on the spine as if they're borrowed from a library – are piled up on the floor and the chairs. I'm sure when he stands up from his desk, turning enquiringly towards me, that he's sorry he's been interrupted.

I know right away that Val has no idea who I am.

It's not only that he's stalled for a moment, as I was with him, by how I've aged and changed. Even when I've told him my name and explained who I am and how we were friends before he went away, his expression

doesn't register anything except a vaguely polite hopeful-
ness. — I'm so sorry, he says. — It's part of my illness.
Or rather, it's part of the drugs they gave me to cure the
illness. I've lost whole chunks of my past, you'll have to
forgive me.

His accent is faintly transatlantic; but his voice is the
same, I'd know it anywhere: not deep, a tenor voice
with something cracked and teasing in it, creaky and
smoky. It's because of the old known voice speaking
out of him that I don't just back off and make my
excuses and leave right away. I feel at home with him,
I know him, even if he doesn't know me. — Tell me
about yourself, he says. — Perhaps some of it will
come back to me. Stella. Maybe I do remember a
Stella. Come in. Shut the door behind you. I'd ask my
mother to make you coffee only she's driving me insane,
I can't bring myself to speak to her. Did she let you in?
Did she pounce, the black widow?

He's smiling but it's not quite his old tautly mocking
smile; I wonder if illness has wiped some of his irony.
When he lights a cigarette (he's kept Hilda's lighter, after
all this time) his hands shake. He goes around the room
tidying up, pulling the sheets straight on the bed, lifting
some books off a chair so that I can sit in it – and then
he's at a loss because he can't find anywhere to put them
down. Opening the curtains, he lets in a grey daylight
which shows up the thick dust. Valentine was always
indifferent to his surroundings but the mess seems more
of a risk now that he's older, and ill. When you are young
and strong you can be sure of springing free of your

299

material envelope through your own vitality; later, any dinginess or fustiness may seep back into you.

— Do you remember Fred? I say encouragingly. The chair that Valentine cleared for me to sit in is an ugly heavy thing, elaborately carved and high-backed like a throne; he's sitting on the side of the bed, opposite me.

— He was your teacher, he loved you.

— Yes, something. I'm getting something. Fred. A nice guy. Little guy, dark hair, liked poetry.

— You studied poetry with him at school.

— Did I know you at that time?

I tell him about Fred. Then I try to explain to him how it was when he and I went everywhere together, spent all our time together, read the same books, even dressed in the same clothes. I tell him how I worshipped him, though I leave this worshipping ambiguous, because I don't want to embarrass him by bringing up the subject of sex: there's something in his fragile body and his demeanour that forbids me even joking about it – as if he was a monk or a saint. He's touched and interested, listening to my stories. Some of it does come back to him as I talk: mostly places, and some people. He remembers that he had to leave in a hurry because someone was looking for him; he says he often used to get into that kind of trouble. Before his illness, he says, his life was a mess and his perceptions were clouded and obscure. He has wasted so much time. I want to insist that he hasn't wasted it, nothing's wasted; but then I shut up because it surely is wasted if you've forgotten it, if it's just gone. Anyway, Valentine isn't really listening to me now, he's holding forth with a new urgency as if he's found his way on to a well-worn track which interests him more than a past he scarcely recognises.

— You've got to use your time, he says. — That's what I've learned. I think of my illness as a gateway into a new more authentic life. More disciplined. Not 'use' time: that's not the right word – as if time could be digested through the machinery of production and consumption. That's the mistake we make. You've got to inhabit time fully, dwell inside it, every minute of every hour – which mostly we dissipate in false consciousness. If you learn to dwell in every minute then the spirit will make itself at home in you, you're opened up to knowledge of the truth.

I'm not thinking that he's completely crazy as he comes out with this. Partly this is because while he's saying it I seem to be in the presence of the old Valentine, excitable and convinced. But partly his words seem like the answer to an intimation which I have sometimes too. Visiting old churches in the country with Mac, a horrible urge comes over me to fall on my knees and pray: though I'd never really do it while Mac was with me. Instead I tease him with my sceptical remarks and he instructs me on the history and architectural features of the place. Mac's not the kind of religious person who gives way to transports, though he climbs up into the pulpit to check whether they're using his beloved King James Bible. But I'm half wishing all the time that I was alone and could yield to this heaviness dragging me down, this longing to fall on my knees and supplicate something, I don't know what. It feels for a time as if the something is the only real thing and all the rest is fake.

— So, is that what you do in here? I say to Valentine. — Inhabit time?

He thinks, he says. Sometimes he sits and thinks for hours. He reads, he writes. When I ask if he gets any exercise, he says he walks for hours at night across the Downs and through the city. — I don't sleep much. It's probably another consequence of the drugs. So I walk instead.

— I wish I'd had your solitude.

It's true that sometimes I've imagined a life lived for contemplation and inward striving with ideas. I explain that I haven't had time for these, even if I'd wanted them, because I've been wrapped up in caring for my children and family, and I've always gone out to work. I'm over-stating somewhat; because I did have that time when I studied for my degree, and gave myself over to literature for three whole years. And the truth is that I'm only working part-time now, and I could leave my job if I wanted to. Mac cooks most of our meals, we have a cleaner. If I stayed at home I could have as much time to contemplate things as I liked.

— The exterior life is just a shell, Valentine says. — It's a distraction.

— Well, you're lucky. You're lucky you don't have to go out every day to a distracting workplace.

For a long time this blocked him, he admits, this perception that reflection and solitude were privileges reserved for a few. Eventually he realised that the block was inside himself, he was using it to excuse himself from the effort of change. The gracious thing to do was to accept the beauty of the opportunity if it was given. I ask him what it is that he's writing, whether it's poetry, and he says it's sometimes poetry, but that he's also working on a book which brings together ideas from the Platonic tradition with aspects of Hindu and Sufi thinking, about an unseen reality behind the surface of things. That's extraordinary, I tell him, because I've been reading about those mysteries, too. And I explain about Triptolemos and the sheaf of corn. Valentine gets quite excited, he knows a lot about the cult at Eleusis, the latest thinking about its rites, the initiates conducted in search through the darkness, culminating in Demeter's reconciliation with Persephone. I joke that this is proof that we are twins after all, even if he has forgotten all about me. Separated for thirty years, we're still thinking in tandem. I don't enquire whether he's got any plans for publishing his book. Something tells me that it's not that kind of project, with a fixed end in sight and a plan for its promotion in the outside world.

— You never wrote to me, I say. — You didn't even tell me you were going. I waited to hear from you. For months I expected to get a letter.

What he does then is to take my two hands in his and hold them, looking into my face intently, searching me. The touch of his hands is the same as it was when we were young, it brings back the past and at first all the old electricity seems to flow out of him and into me, and the tears that pricked into my eyes downstairs when

I thought he might be dying come flooding back. And then the next moment there's a flood of resentment too, because he hasn't asked me any questions about myself, or what's become of me: how many children I've got, who my husband is, what I do for a living. Isn't he even in the least interested? Why must the world of real things always be relegated to second place, as if it was a lesser order, as if everything abstract was higher and more meaningful? I'm seized by the impulse to force Valentine into relation with my real life. I'm on the brink of telling him my children's names and their dates of birth, to see whether he notices anything. But just then we're interrupted by the commotion of the supermarket delivery arriving downstairs and Hilda's voice raised imperiously, directing operations.

— Oh, it's spider-woman, Valentine says, dropping my hands. — Here she goes.

— I think she was worried they might not turn up.

— You don't know what she's like. She's aiming to stop me finishing the book. She blocks it. Her spirit blocks it. She crouches down there in the shape of a black spider. I sometimes imagine that she isn't really my mother, she's been taken over by a demonic force. I can't write if I have to think about her.

I'm frightened now. I calm down because I'm frightened.

I think I ought to go.

I don't know if he's being funny or not. Perhaps he's just exaggerating his paranoia, sending his craziness up for my benefit in the same deadpan way he used to do when we were teenagers. But in any case I stand up and make excuses, pretending I have an appointment to get to. Valentine doesn't protest, and when I say something stupid and false about how we ought to keep in touch, he just smiles the funny remote smile he used to use against my parents, as if he could hardly hear them when they spoke to him. I don't kiss him in farewell, I don't touch him again; something in the way he stands apart from me forbids it.

Downstairs in the hall the front door is wide open and there are plastic trays of groceries on the floor, milk and fruit and sliced bread, lots of ready-meals. I can hear Hilda in the kitchen, but I don't stop to say goodbye to her. And I don't wait for the bus, I walk into town, all the way across the Downs. I'm so relieved, on my way back, that I didn't get carried away and tell Valentine about Luke. I won't say anything to anyone about this visit, I decide, not even to Madeleine. Valentine is a crazy irrelevance, he's pitiable and ridiculous. (I know that's what Mac would think if he ever met him.) I try to conceive of him with detached kindness and sympathy, as if he were one of the service users at the Gatehouse. But my connection with him feels like a liability, it feels loose inside me, a door swinging open on to danger.

On the train going home, I can't concentrate on my book. The carriage is crowded and my legs ache after my walk across the Downs, the glare of the low sun is in my eyes. I wish I'd upgraded to first class as Mac is always telling me to do (but if I spend my money on

305

that, it seems to turn my time at the Gatehouse into playtime, a self-indulgence). I see Mac standing on the platform at Taunton station when the train draws in: he has Ester with him and one of Ester's friends. I'm filled with a rush of gratitude for his waiting there so faithfully and reliably; I'm moved by the idea of his kindness and solidity, my dear companion. I thought I'd calmed down but in fact all the emotion left over from my reunion with Valentine is still washing round inside me, I'm brimming with feeling. They don't see me at first when I get down, they're looking in the wrong direction (towards first class). The girls are in the green-striped dresses which are their school uniform. (Mac insisted on all this, the private school, the violin lessons, the tennis coaching. He's talking already about Oxbridge. We quarrelled over it to begin with – I wanted Ester to go to the local state school, I hate the pushy privilege of the private places. And then I decided I didn't care where she went as long as she was happy.)

The girls come running towards me as soon as they see me – of course her friend is only running because Ester is; when Ester wraps her arms round me she stands waiting awkwardly. I'm glad the friend is there because her cool, appraising stranger's glance steadies me, so that I don't spill over with my tenderness. My children prefer me to be dry with them, slightly withheld. Ester's showing off, she's full of some story which she's garbling deliberately, about how she and Amy are doing their science project together and how they nagged at Daddy until he agreed Amy could come and stay the night so they could work on it. Ester drapes herself round Amy's neck, Amy looks self-conscious. In the company of her friends, Ester overdoes it as if she's studied carefully how to be a gushing schoolgirl; alone with us she's quite different, astute and watchful, almost prim in her reserve.

Mac's putting on weight, I think: I notice because I've been away from him for a few days. He could easily be mistaken for Ester's grandfather. On the whole, though, he's not ageing too badly: he has that tough good skin which doesn't collapse, there's something appraising and sensual still in the heavy-lidded eyes, and he stands so perfectly upright that people think he must have been in the military. Picking up my bags he tells me about the science project and about the ice-cream the girls have wheedled him into buying. He loves this role as the doting, bemused father. I can't enter into his wholeheart-edness, I think. I'm not wholehearted. He makes some comment about having me back from doing my good works, and then I'm irritated even though it's only a few minutes since I got down from the train overflowing with love for him.

The train leaves and the spacious red-brick station resumes its air of being under-used and sleepy. Carrying my bags to the car, Mac asks me how it's been in Bristol and I'm disconcerted for a moment, thinking he must know somehow about Val; then I realise that he means the weather. Mac loves to talk about the weather, updating me frequently: not as the small change of conversation, but with deep interest in an unfolding story, as if it's eternally surprising. He follows the forecasts on television with the same responsible seriousness as he follows the news; although he's retired he hasn't given up his old pattern of attending to the world as if real things depended on his being accurately informed.

— Dull here, he says. — A lot of cloud over the estuary. Rained a couple of times, but nothing much. They're saying it may brighten up tomorrow.

I can't believe he never notices my lack of enthusiasm for these reports.

— I've no idea, I lie. — I was indoors all day. (Actually I put my face up into a bitter squall of rain, on my way home across the Downs.)

— Give me the car keys, I say. — Let me drive.

Mac doesn't like driving through the country roads at twilight, but I feel better as soon as I'm behind the steering wheel. We get out of the town and I take the back route, though there's always a risk of getting stuck behind farm vehicles: the road winds through apple orchards to begin with, then up between the hills. Under a low ceiling of blue-grey cloud a strip of paler light is stretched along the horizon like a ribbon of creamy satin. Birds seem to start up, as I squeeze round the narrow corners between the hedgerows, from under the very wheels of the car. I imagine Valentine reading absorbedly in his room, like a dedicated St Jerome in his cell in a medieval painting. Mac is giving me a detailed report, as he always does, on all the things he's achieved while I've been away – he's bought straw to put on the shrubs in case it's a hard winter, he's cleaned out the shower head, he's made his special bolognese sauce with chicken livers, to go with the pasta tonight. (I wonder whether Amy will like chicken livers.) The girls are chattering in the back seat: Ester is courting Amy, fussing over her excitedly, holding on to Amy's hand in her lap.

— I want to show you everything, Ester says. – You can hold the guinea pigs, I'll show you my secret den. You can read my diary if you want to. You can find out all about me.

Amy is not ready to commit herself.

I know Mac is listening and smiling in the seat beside me, tense with protective love for Ester, fearing in case she gives herself away too easily. Some dark shape – a cat, or a fox – flows across the road for an instant ahead of us, then disappears into the hedge. I switch on the headlights and the car seems to leap forward into the night.

Acknowledgements

With thanks to Dan Franklin and Jennifer Barth, Caroline Dawnay and Joy Harris. Thanks to Deborah Treisman (versions of two chapters in *Clever Girl* first appeared as short stories in the *New Yorker*). Thanks to Shelagh Weeks and Stephen Gregg, for inspirations.